Telma Rocha

THE

ANGOLAN
GIRL

A True-Life Novel

Word Tree Publishing

WordTree Publishing

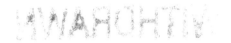

Some names, identifying details of characters, and settings in this book have been altered. All dialogue comes from the author's creative imagination.

DEDICATION

To my Avó.

For showing me courage, strength, and love.

To the memory of my Avô, and my uncle, Armando.

You will always be alive in my memory.

CONTENTS

PART ONE
1975

CHAPTER 1

Lobito, Angola
October 1, 1975
Present Day

A S I STARE out the dusty window across the angry Atlantic Ocean, I ponder what has brought me to this point where I am trapped in my home, fearing for the lives of my whole family. There comes a time in most people's lives when one must decide if they should stay or if they should go. This could be in relation to: a relationship you are unhappy in, a job that is no longer satisfying, or a friendship that brings much pain. For me, this decision is about leaving my home, my country, and all I have known and loved for forty-six years.

Angola is at war. It has been since 1961 when the War of Independence from Portugal first started. Angola is an African coastal colony, the Atlantic Ocean to the west and The Democratic Republic of Congo to the east.

We moved into this house less than one year ago. Eleuterio Carvalho, Leo we call him, is my love, my companion, and my husband. He wanted to provide a better environment for our family. He felt this neighbourhood was safer than the last one we lived in. We do not own this current house, we rent it. We have a house we own, the one we left behind, and it sits on the top of a hill overlooking the bay. Leo built that house with his own hands, and we now rent it out to another family. The income from the rental property helps cover this rental. I thought the house on the hill would be our forever home, until one day it was not. Now, instead of rolling hills and a faraway view of the bay, we live on the Atlantic Ocean and our backyard faces the unpredictable sea. It is a different landscape than what we had for many years.

This neighbourhood is more prestigious and luxurious, but prestige and luxury do not matter when you are in the middle of a war zone. War affects everyone, every nationality, every race.

My biggest concern now is for my family. Telma, my granddaughter, celebrated her first birthday only one month ago on July 29th. She is one year old, but still is, and forever will be, my baby. My oldest daughter, Anabella, Telma's mother, has a good, high paying job, but is often away working for a custom's broker. And so Telma is my responsibility, and I would not have it any other way. She clings to me as if I am her mother, and I am all right with this arrangement.

My youngest daughter, Natércia, is only thirteen years of age. I wonder if she will be haunted for life, or if she will one day forget this memory of war. My other children are older. Carlos, the oldest of my children is now twenty-four years old, and still lives at home. He has a good job and helps us out plenty during times of need. He put me through my paces with his mischievous ways when he was little, and there are many stories I could tell you. João is twenty, and he is the most like Carlos; they are both adventurous. And there is Armando, my youngest boy, who is eighteen. He is quiet, shy, does not make eye contact, and often does not like company much. And so, you can see, it is a full house with many mouths to feed during a war.

Leo and I have been together for twenty-six years, and it was he who picked me up from despair and brought me back to life. My wonderful husband is warm, caring, and forgiving, but he is also spontaneous and has a habit of starting many things but not finishing them. He is a dreamer, always hoping for the best.

But today is a different type of day. Today he takes no chances with his family. As he comes charging through our front door, he is out of breath from running up the driveway, and his eyes are wide open. I know right away something is wrong.

"Rosa, darling, where is everyone?" he asks as he searches each room.

"Quiet, you will wake the baby." I place my finger to my lips to indicate silence before checking the baby's bassinet to make sure she is still asleep, and she is.

"Where are the others?" Leo asks me.

"Bella and Carlos are at work, the others are most likely at the beach."

They love the beach, we all do, and it is a family tradition to spend each Sunday there during the summer months. Even now in August, during our coolest month, it is common for the beach to be full, but rather than swimming, most people would instead be walking, reading, and enjoying the breeze. The kids have always spent a great deal of time walking along the beach, looking for sticks and shells. They have always gone on their own, off on their own adventures, whenever given freedom.

"Why, has something happened?"

"Yes, the town is under open fire not too far from here. There are bullets flying everywhere. We need to get everyone back to the house; it is a war zone out there. Draw the curtains, lock the doors, and stay away from the windows just in case."

Leo begins to do what he instructed me to do.

Only days before this horrific day, I had been listening to our radio and heard of rebel troops moving west toward our town, but there had not been warning signs otherwise. Certainly not anything alluding to what Leo describes now.

"Rosa, get away from the window, it is not safe," says Leo.

Hearing his voice brings me back to reality. It takes me a few minutes to comprehend the severity of a problem and then a minute or so to formulate a solution, or at least a plan. So, it takes me a long time to get over the shock of hearing Leo's words. A ringing in my ears makes me dizzy and I stumble, losing my hearing for a minute. I then back away from the dusty window. Once I get over the initial shock that our city is under attack, I move Telma's bassinet away from the window for safety, before running out the back door.

The beach connects to our backyard, and it is here I search for Natércia, João, and Armando, my three youngest children. I am hoping to find them soon, here on the beach. I remember Leo had said he was going out to get Bella and Carlos from work. Because I was in shock at the time, his voice had sounded muffled, so now I question if, in fact, it's what he said. I search the beach areas I know the kids frequent, but I cannot see them.

The beach that is almost always full is deserted today, which seems strange. Perhaps others heard of the troubles in town and evacuated long before. Why am I not more prepared, more on top of this? I criticize myself. I am a planner, and I am almost always organized, but I am not so organized and in control today. I shake the thought away and focus on looking down the long, sandy beach for my children. Suddenly I remember Telma. If Leo left to get the older children from work, and I am out here, then oh God, oh God, Telma is alone. The thought stops me mid-stride, and I run back, tripping over a log on my way. When I return to the house, the others are already here. I say a silent prayer upon seeing their faces.

"Mother, where were you?" says João. "We came home and found Telma alone."

"I was out searching for the three of you. Your father was here earlier because there is trouble in town. We need to stay inside."

"Yes, we know, we heard people running along the beach telling everyone to get inside, so we came straight home," says Natércia.

With all the commotion and loud voices, Telma wakes up from her peaceful and innocent nap. I pick her up and hold her close to me while the five of us wait for Leo to get home. We huddle together in the middle of the room, and I wish we had a safer place to hide, but we do not. So we remain, waiting, and Leo returns within the hour. Both Bella's and Carlos' places of employment are not too far, so Leo manages the task fast. I now have my entire family here with me, safe. For now.

The radio broadcasts are keeping us informed of what is happening, and soon we receive confirmation of what everyone fears. Two of the main nationalist movement parties fighting for control of Angola are at battle with one another, right here in our own city.

Most of the fighting has happened further east, mainly in the mountains and jungle. This is the closest we have come to the war. Natércia, who is the youngest of the children, other than the baby, of course, is asking many questions. She talks a lot when she is nervous and bites her nails. We are all nervous, but at the young age of thirteen comes an innocence that clouds reality, making it difficult for her to comprehend what is happening. The older two boys, Carlos and João, are trying to appear tough, but I know my sons and I understand they, too, are scared and nervous inside. Anyone would be frightened in this situation, no matter how tough and strong you are, especially if you can hear guns firing in the distance as we can.

The hair on my arms stands tall, and fear crawls deep beneath my skin. I need to go to the bathroom so bad, but I hold it and do not dare go. I am afraid to move for fear I might bring attention from the enemy. I know this is ridiculous, but fear is overpowering my rational thoughts. What to do, oh dear God, I pray and pray today like no other. I have a strong faith and a close relationship with God and so I pray for peace that is long overdue, and I pray for safety. God has been good to me over the years. He has answered many prayers of mine from time to time. He has given me strength and courage to survive many ordeals throughout my lifetime, and I only ask today for the courage and strength to survive one more tragedy.

CHAPTER 2

Present Day

W E REMAIN LOCKED up inside, still listening to horrifying updates coming from the radio. It is now Day Two of hiding. I try to sneak a peek out the window to check if I can see anything, but I cannot see a thing, not from where our house sits. Out the back of the house, the beach is empty, and out front many palm trees block our view for any real distance. "This is probably a good thing," I say, out loud to no one in particular.

Leo does not want me anywhere near the windows, and he reminds me of this. "Rosa, get away from there at once, it is not safe."

Upon hearing his warning, I rush back to the area we designated as our safe zone. We push the furniture into the middle of the front room; this is the room with fewer windows. Since the back part of the house is most exposed, we avoid that area. We barricaded the front window as best as possible with furniture for additional protection, creating a small cave-like space for ourselves.

The second day of hiding in our own home is the most difficult, as the shock has worn off and reality sets in. I fear the unknown, and I also fear the news on the radio. I cannot decide if I am better off knowing or remaining in the dark about the evils brewing outside.

Everyone is antsy and wants to move around. Leo puts an end to this by reminding us of the dangers. On the third day, we try to convince ourselves this is not real, this is a false alarm, and the gunshots are practice runs held by the activists. But this is no practice drill or false alarm; this is real, and more real than we could ever imagine it to be.

To try to help pass the time, we play cards as a family. This is Leo's idea. He says it helps to soothe the nerves and gives us something else to think about other than the fighting outside. I join in some of the card games, but sometimes I excuse myself from the game to read instead, it is my reprieve. I love a good romance book, and reading now provides an escape from this dreadful situation into a new world with no war. An escape is something I desperately need now, even for just a few short minutes.

After the third day we get low on food, and I wonder how much longer this battle will last. I need to get to the market to replenish my stock, and I try to take a mental inventory of what remains in the pantry. In my mind I count the cans as I imagine them on the shelves. I am used to going to the market often to buy fresh vegetables, meat, and milk. Preserving food for a day like today is something I have always done. But as of late, some days even the markets lack food. We wait for hours in long queues only to discover there is no food left. This is an effect of the war. I tiptoe across the room and make my way to the kitchen, to our pantry to get more canned food for us to eat tonight. Everyone is hungry.

On the fourth day of hiding, the radio broadcast announces a story that brings a rush of tears to my eyes. It is about a young woman in her early twenties who had apparently gone out to the balcony of her apartment building to see what was happening, most likely due to curiosity. We are all curious at times, and sometimes we do things without thinking of the repercussions. This woman must not have been thinking straight going outside during a battle in the middle of a conflict. We listen to the radio announcer say the young woman was caught in the crossfire while standing on the balcony of her apartment building. It is a small building, with only five stories. This woman lived on the fifth floor. It is assumed that she was looking out over her steel balcony because she was found bent over the railing. The lower half of her body hangs on the inside of the balcony, and her upper body is slung forward, hanging on the outside. The railing itself is not too high, reaching below her chest. Red blotches stain the light-coloured dress she wore. As I listen, I place my hands over Natércia's ears to try and shield her from the story, from the pain it will cause; because as they announce this dead woman's name, I realize we know her. She is an acquaintance from town, and I often run into her when we are at the market. My attempt to shield Natércia from this news is too late because she has already heard. She looks at me with her big dark eyes, silently asking me if this is happening. She does not speak, but I know her unspoken words. I think back to the time, just a couple of days ago, when I too, due to curiosity, stared out the windows. Shivers run across my dark skin. That woman could have been me. That woman could still be any member of my family.

The Portuguese arrived in Angola in the early 1500s, and its new rulers set about establishing cities, towns, and transport routes, as well as imposing their Western European culture on a country steeped in ancient Angolan traditions. Over the ensuing years, there were also around one million slaves exported from its shores to places like Brazil and North America.

When the Portuguese discovered petroleum in Angola in the 1950s, this once poor country developed rapidly, both economically, and socially. Because of this rapid development, new movement parties became interested in the colony with three of them eventually fighting for control. On April 25, 1974 the Portuguese government granted

Angola independence in what we call the Carnation Revolution. Although Angola gained independence from Portugal, a Declaration of Independence was not declared, and so a new internal fight began. Angola was not yet decolonized, but that day, April 25, marked the start of a deadly war, a struggle for power resulting in the battle we face today.

⁓

Leo is now pacing. He does this when he is deep in thought. I remind him to stay away from the windows, as he reminded me. He remains quiet, not saying anything for a long while, before finally speaking. "We need to leave the country."

He found his voice once again.

I do not say a word back, but I look at him and then at the children as we sit in silence on the rug on the floor of our living room, in the little haven we created for ourselves. The only noise now is Natércia's anguished scream.

There is smoke outside our house, and I stare through the crack between the couches and window, watching the smoke rise, taking in the environment around me. This is where I live. This is where my children and my granddaughter live. How did I end up here, in this place, at this moment, in this situation? Has my life always been this unstable? I begin to think back over my life, and I start to remember how I got here.

The last thing I hear before my memories take hold of me is Leo's shaky voice, once again repeating those six words into my ear.

"Precisamos sair do país." *We need to leave the country.*

PART TWO

1935 - 1940

CHAPTER 3

Luanda, Angola
1935

SEPARATION BETWEEN A mother and child happens more often than we care to admit. Women give up their babies for different reasons; some women cannot cope with raising children due to stress, and others have their babies taken away involuntarily, sometimes at birth, sometimes later.

My name is Rosa Soares, and I was born in Novo Redondo, Angola on March 18, 1929. My mother is an Angolan native, and her name is Antonietta. Although this woman brought me into this world and cared for me for the first two years of my life, she is not a part of my later upbringing. I do not know why or how these events unfolded, but these questions and thoughts remain with me. Through one story, I learn the native black population in Angola does not have as many rights or the same social standing as white people. My father, being white, therefore had more clout over my mother, and so it was more normal for my white father to raise me rather than my native black mother. Although, I still ask myself why she did not fight harder to keep me? I am told these stories over the years, but that is all they remain to me, stories told.

It is said my mother worked for my father at his house. She was a housemaid and took care of the other children, helping with the cooking and cleaning. My father was not married then, but he did have a common-law spouse. As the months passed by, and my mother became a familiar sight around the house, my father fell passionately, head-over-heels in love with her. In the stories I hear, I am told she was beautiful, with long black curly hair, big brown eyes, and dark brown skin. It is no wonder that he was besotted by her beauty, however, these situations never end well, and nine months later, I came into this world.

Children born out of wedlock are frowned upon, and because of this I was not well-received. Major arguments took place in the house even before I arrived, and shortly after my birth, my mother abruptly left. When she left, she did not leave me behind, however. Her leaving is not how we got separated. She left with me, after a loud screaming match between her and my father, most likely over me. I never did find out what happened exactly, but I do wonder if my father's common-law spouse forced my mother to go, suspecting I was his. On the other hand, my mother might have left voluntarily, knowing she was not wanted.

My father was left not knowing where I had been taken for two entire years. He told me he searched for me often, but whether this is true or not, I do not know, and I can only trust his words.

When I was around the age of two years old my father found us, my mother and I. Somehow he was able to take me away from my mother for good this time, probably because of his ethnicity. Thoughts of why she did not fight for me, why she let him take me away, and why she allowed him to rip me from her arms, seep into my mind now, but I was not given the opportunity to ask these questions then, being only two years old and hardly able to speak. I was with my mother one day, and the next day I was not. There was no understanding of what was happening at the time, and I have no memory of this either. My father tells me I barely cried, and the few tears shed are the extent of the emotions I showed on that day.

If I had been older, I might have asked the questions that needed to be asked and perhaps begged her not to let me go. However, by the time I was old enough to do so, she was long gone from my life, and soon afterward my father, brothers, and I moved from Nova Redondo where I was born, to Lobito. This is around the same time as the population of settlers in Angola declines.

What happened to me from the time of my birth until I moved in with my father is, to this day, a mystery. What I do know is everything happens for a reason, and I am a true believer in faith. I was not meant to live the early years of my life with the woman who brought me into this world, that was not God's plan for me.

My father's name is Manuel Domingo Soares, and these are my earliest memories. My father is from the Portuguese mainland, a beautiful town called Espinho, outside of Porto. He moved to Angola many years ago when he was young with his own parents and siblings. There was a good opportunity to prosper, especially if you were educated, for example as a doctor or a teacher. And so many Portuguese mainland residents moved to Angola for an opportunity for a better life. The Portuguese in Angola are referred to as Portuguese Angolans.

Today in the 1930s, Angola is governed by the Salazar government. This government of ours has cut spending on colonization, resulting in less immigration to Angola. The colony's economy is improving, and import tariffs are introduced so that the government can try and strengthen its own country's supply chain and infrastructure. Railways being constructed in Benguela now stretch as far as Dilolo, a town in Katanga Province. This will enable copper deposits there. The colony is rich in diamond, and this industry is now an important part of the Angolan economy. While this sounds romantic, daily life in Lobito in 1935 is not an easy one for the average family, and although my father is well-off, life is still labour intensive for us. Clothes must be hand-washed and hung to dry, and dishes scrubbed by our own callused hands, often covered with sweat and blood that lingers well after the tasks are done. As difficult as life is for us, white families have a better standard of living than the native Angolans, and so for this, I should be grateful I live with my father.

Lobito is a port town located on the coast of the Atlantic Ocean and its harbour is one of the finest in Africa. The weather in Lobito is warm most days, other than during the cooler, rainy season between July and August. If you lift your face up to the wind, you can feel the typical sea air you get with most port towns. Rows upon rows of lush green palm trees in all sizes cover a majority of the landscape. Flamingoes are often found at the water's edge, searching for algae and other plants to eat.

We have a full house, consisting of my father and my three siblings, and so there are four of us kids in total. There is Eduardo, my oldest brother, who is thirteen, and then there is Julio, who is four, and Manuel, whom we called Manecas. He is the youngest of the brothers and has turned one–year-old. Why we nicknamed him Manecas, I do not know, but we changed his name in the first place to differentiate between father and son, as both share the same name.

Most families these days have many children, and there are many benefits to having a big family. Children help with the household chores. The females assist inside with cooking and cleaning while the males are mostly helpful outside around the farms, or just helping with outdoor duties. They chop wood and help with the gardens. It is unusual for women to have jobs outside the home, so most women run the household fulltime. This, too, makes it easier to keep on bearing children. All of us children lend a helping hand, and this creates a smoothly-run household. Since I am the only female, and even though I am young, I learn to cook. Often, the responsibility of preparing the family meals falls onto my shoulders. This means we often eat soup for lunch and supper, as it is one of the easiest meals to prepare.

We attend school, other than Manecas because he is still too young. I enjoy school, even though I do not have many friends there. The friends I do have are close though, and true friends. I confide in these friends often about my dreams for my future as a mother and wife. We often walk home from school together, and I tell them about how I imagine my life when I am older, married to a wonderful man, with lots of children, and a house of my own. This is what I want for my life.

The walk from our house to school is about a twenty-minute walk. Some children who live out in the country must walk much further each day, so I consider myself lucky. I am not lazy, but I do not like to walk much, it makes me tired and I would rather conserve my energy to play.

While I have vivid memories of this time in my life some days are a blur and I do not remember them, but I do remember this one specific visit that changed my life forever.

My family and I finish our supper, and I am now scrubbing the dishes at the sink when there is a heavy knock on the front door. "Father, someone is here," I say from the kitchen.

Until the 1930s, it is not common to have a kitchen and bathroom inside the main house, but my father's house is a new build so we have both incorporated into the house. Wiping my hands on the dishtowel, I peek into the living room and I watch patiently as my father greets a woman and young girl, welcoming them into our home. I am curious who they are. "Pai, quem é essa mulher?" *Father, who is this woman?*

I have not seen her before. Next to the woman stands a little girl, perhaps a little older than I am; this must be her daughter, as there is a striking resemblance in their features. I compare the girl's features to my own. She is fairer than I am, which tells me both her parents must be white. Her hair is not as curly as mine and hangs to past her shoulders. Curious, I walk from the kitchen to the living room where our visitors stand, waiting for introductions by my father. I stand behind the big armchair where my father frequently sits.

"Irmã," *sister,* says my father.

He smiles from ear to ear. "This, my dear little Rosa, is your aunt, my sister Mariazinha, and this here is your cousin Lina. Come forward Rosa, do not be rude to your aunt, come and introduce yourself."

Hiding behind the big armchair brings me comfort.

Mariazinha stands tall, shoulders pushed back, chin raised. "Manuel, it has been so long. How have you been keeping up with this household, and with no wife?" she asks, while raising her eyebrows, prancing across the room as if she owns the house.

My father raises his arms. "Oh, dear sister, we have been keeping up the same as you and everyone else."

He kisses his sister on the cheeks, a Portuguese tradition.

My first impression of my aunt confuses me. As I watch her, I am not sure I want to even know her. She appears overly confident, and this raises my suspicions of why she is here. Her daughter does not say much other than an initial hello. Can she even speak? With Lina, however, I am more comfortable and at ease. She is more relaxed, and not as stiff as my aunt. I examine Lina closely and decide she is the same age as I, or possibly a year older. I back away from my aunt not wanting to get too close, as I am still trying to process what to make of her. Something about her makes me want to keep my distance.

Mariazinha stops walking and sits in my father's chair. "Manuel, we have much to discuss. I am here with a proposal."

My father, the businessman that he is, snaps his head around at the mention of the word proposal. He looks at her intently. "I am curious to know what brings you to Lobito from Luanda with no notice."

"Rosa brings me here."

"What about Rosa?"

At the sound of my name, my ears perk up. So she is here about me? What could I possibly have to do with her visit? She has not even met me before today. This is when my hands become sweaty, so I wipe them on my dress. Mariazinha frowns when I do this; she does not approve of me.

CHAPTER 4

1935

D URING MY AUNT Mariazinha's visit, I learn she is here to take me away to Luanda. She wants me to live with her and her family. When I hear this news, I get the urge to throw up. She cannot force me to leave my home. Or can she?

We have a better life than most natives, but life in today's time is hard, even though we are a white family. Females are cherished and needed to fulfill regular household duties. My aunt is not looking for another daughter, but instead, she is in search of extra help around the house. Another female, even at the age of six, can assist with cooking, cleaning, and laundry. This is my sole purpose, and why she wants me.

Please say no Papa, please, please say no.

I say these words in my head so no one else hears. After a few seconds, I repeat them out loud for my father to hear, but it is as if his ears have closed over and he does not hear my words. My father does more than say yes; not only does he give consent to this outrageous idea of hers, he wears a big smile when he gives her his answer. When he replies with that simple three-letter word my blood feels as if it is draining out of my body. I am not expecting this. Surely he should have said no? Is that not the right thing to do when someone wants to take your child away? I have a family, right here, why would I go to another? At least I thought I had a family, until today.

I ask myself how I am going to get out of this situation and take a few steps closer to my father, hoping for a private conversation with him. "Papa, I prefer to stay here with you and my brothers. Please do not send me away."

His reply is loud, so loud I am sure the neighbours can hear his words. And so, even if my part of the conversation was kept private, surely now my aunt knows what I said to my father.

"Nonsense, you will go with your aunt to Luanda. There is more opportunity for you there in a larger city, more to do and lots to see."

"But Papa, I do not want to go. Please do not make me."

"Rosa, do not be difficult. You might not see the benefits now, but someday you will."

My father turns to my aunt, who stands tall and waits. "When are you heading back to Luanda?"

"I expect to be on the first boat in the morning. That should afford Rosa enough time to pack her things. I fear, my brother, you must accommodate us for tonight."

"Certainly, dear sister. Rosa, show your aunt and your cousin to your room."

"Where am I sleeping tonight?" I ask.

"You can sleep in the living room," says my father, before turning and walking away without a backward glance.

The fight is lost, if there ever was one to begin with. I am going to Luanda, against my wishes. I hang my head and walk away, my aunt and cousin following close behind me as I lead them to my room. The room I will not get to sleep in anymore. I reach down and pick up my pillow and bury my face in it, committing the softness of the fabric and the familiar scent to memory.

My aunt looks around my room and frowns. "Well, the bed is small, but I suppose you and I can manage for one night," she says to her daughter, looking at me. "Rosa, hurry up, and get your things packed up, I am rather tired from the boat ride, and need my rest. I cannot have you packing while I sleep."

I quickly gather up the belongings I am bringing with me to Luanda and, with a frown, leave my bedroom.

That night while I lie on the couch, I place a towel under my face so as not to wet the fabric with my tears. I am resentful at my father for allowing this to happen to me, and I wish to never speak to him again. Sleep does not come to me, and after a few minutes of tossing and turning, I walk into his room, one last time. I try to talk to him again, to have him understand and consider my feelings, but it is no use. He has made up his mind and is sending me away. There is nothing I can say to change this. I must come to the realization I have no choice in the matter. There is nothing I can do, and I am far too young to be on my own.

Everything is changing so fast, my mind is whirling, and my emotions are unable to keep up with what is happening. Early the next morning, we are at the port, and I do not know how we even get here, because during the journey I became lost in my own thoughts, oblivious to my surroundings. Soon the engines of the boat roar to life and the vessel begins to move, picking up momentum. Through the window I watch my father and brothers waving goodbye.

We are now officially off to the vibrant and lively big city of Luanda, Angola's capital. I have never been to Luanda, but I am told stories of its grand landscape filled with tall buildings, shops, and many people. I should have an open mind and keep my thoughts positive, as my father says, Luanda is full of possibilities, and all I must do is embrace them. But first I must learn how.

As much as I try to be positive, this adjustment is difficult. I am young, naïve, and I want my father back, and the comforts of the only home I know. Strength is a trait I must now learn to incorporate into my daily life, and that needs to happen straight away. If I am not strong, I will lose my purpose, my passion for life, and my soul. I must learn to protect myself; there is no one else here to protect me now. I did not even get an opportunity to say goodbye to my few close friends from school. I miss them already. Will they wonder what has happened to me? Will they miss me too?

Sleep consumes me for most of the journey, thankfully pulling me into my own world. The boat ride is not long, approximately two-and-a-half hours, and I sleep heavily, tired from the events of the night before. When the boat comes to a complete stop and docks, I open my eyes and look around at the new landscape. There are many tall buildings here, many more than in Lobito, and so the stories are true.

There is a vehicle waiting to drive us to the house, and it makes its way through the streets as I stare out the window at the unfamiliar surroundings. My thoughts remain in my head, I do not want to share them, and so the thirty-minute drive is made in silence. When the vehicle slows and approaches a driveway, I know this is the house I should call home.

"We have arrived. This is your new home."

Aunt Mariazinha declares our arrival with a big smile on her skinny face, making me feel tiny, and a long way from home.

I am not sure what to say, or what to even think. I am lost in my own thoughts again, trying to process the fact that my father sent me away, and the arrival at this place, and my aunt's words are like a knife being pushed into my heart. Staring at the big house from the outside, even with the windows in the vehicle rolled down due to the extreme heat, I still get shivers that run through my body.

Aunt Mariazinha opens the car door and climbs out. "Rosa, did you not hear me?"

"Yes, Aunt Mariazinha, I did."

"Well, answer me the next time I speak to you."

Answer her? She did not ask me a question that required a response back. She reaches out to take her luggage from the driver and pays him, and my bag is on the driveway for me to pick up. "Well, let us not waste time, pick up your bag, get inside, and get to work, there is much to be done around here, and the floors will not clean themselves. Let's hustle. I have already wasted a day having to go to Lobito to pick you up."

I did not ask her to come for me, but somehow even that seems to be my fault. There is no warm welcome for me, but that is all right, I do not need one. I am strong now and I remind myself of this often, hoping that reminding myself will make it true.

CHAPTER 5

1935

AUNT MARIAZINHA'S HOUSE is located on Rua De Mutamba, a quiet street with only a few houses nearby and not many kids out playing at this time of day. My spirits sink as I take note of the lack of children, but then my eyes are drawn to the many plants, flowers, and palm trees surrounding the house. There is a pleasant new scent in the air, and I take a deep breath to saturate my lungs. Something smells sweet, and I wonder what is growing in the lush gardens.

The house is larger than my father's, and the bedrooms are more spacious. Aunt Mariazinha has four children. There is Carolina, whom we call Lina, the cousin who accompanied her mother to my father's house only yesterday — and her three older brothers: Julio, Alexander, and the oldest, Ricardo. Aunt Mariazinha's husband passed away some time ago. The family does not talk of him much, and I wonder what sort of man he was. So, for now, it is my aunt, my four cousins, and now me living in the large house.

The house consists of three bedrooms, and a spacious family room where we gather at night to pass time. There is also one small bathroom complete with a small sink and a tub we fill for bathing once a week. Indoor plumbing is new to me. The kitchen, in the centre of the house, is larger than I am used to, and it is here meals are prepared. There is a large wooden table where we eat our snacks and meals. The floors throughout the entire house are planked in dark wood. They keep me awake when they creak at night, and during the day I get slivers on my feet when I slide over them with no socks. The off-white walls are bare, save for a few paintings randomly hung in the living room, and thick light-coloured curtains block out the hot sun during the summer months. Each table is littered with ornaments, small things such as figurines and statues, making it difficult to dust the tabletops. Since the house is wrapped in blooming gardens and the aroma from the plants is sweet-smelling, I often open the windows to let the wonderful scent in. I did not have this opportunity at my father's house because we did not have many gardens there.

Since there are only three bedrooms, I share a room with Lina. The problem is there is only one bed in this bedroom, and the bed belongs to Lina. Sleeping on the hardwood floor my first night results in muscle aches the next morning. I complain to Lina, and the next night there is a mattress under the blanket I slept on the previous night. Lina is so friendly to me and never makes me feel unwanted or unwelcome. It is Lina who asks her mother for the mattress, of course. My cousin is quiet, and I learn it is not only me she does not talk much with. I never see her carrying on a conversation with the others. She prefers to keep to herself, and this is fine by me. I also want my own space to think and to allow my mind to wander. We complement each other this way. I think about my father and what he is doing now. Is he missing me the way I miss him? Are my brothers behaving now that I am not there to break up their fights? I think of my room and I miss its smell, my old bed, and the belongings I was forced to leave behind.

Aunt Mariazinha expects things to be done when she wants them done, and she wants things done right the first time. When I think

I've finished a task, I know it's best for me to go over the same job again to avoid her telling me to redo what I have just done. Nothing ever seems good enough for her, and she never gives out compliments or words of encouragement. She expects nothing less than perfection from everyone.

I have my share of dirty and time-consuming household chores to do every day. My aunt has money — do not misunderstand me, we are not poor. My father sends money, along with other things such as clothes and soap to help pay for my keep, as if the work I do around here is not payment enough. Using the money my father sends each month, my aunt can hire daily help to assist with cooking and laundry; she insists on putting me to work, however, often saying hard work is good for me.

"Rosa must learn the value of hard work," she says one day to the hired help.

I had gathered clothes to be washed and the maid had offered to do it for me. My aunt is not pleased by this; she expects I should do the work regardless of whether there is hired help or not.

The hardwood floors throughout the house soon end up becoming my nemesis. I must use a thick wooden-handled heavy brush to get the floors as shiny as my aunt expects. My cousin Alexander, who is kind and soft-spoken, often tries to protect me from his mother, recognizing she often overworks me. But he never wins the argument, as she is a strong-willed woman who usually gets what she wants.

When Alexander notices me on my hands and knees scrubbing the floor, sweat pouring down my face, he asks, "Mother, must she work so hard?"

Aunt Mariazinha is busy folding clothes when she hears these words leave her son's mouth. She is double-checking that the corners of the shirts match up precisely, but with his words she stops folding, and looking up at Alexander she says, "She will thank me one day for making her work hard." She continues to fold the laundry. "Vocês todos verão isso um dia." *You will see this one day.*

CHAPTER 6

1935

.

ATTENDING SCHOOL IS something I must still do, even though I am also expected to keep up with the housework. School is an outlet, and I do enjoy it, but it's challenging to keep up with the work expected from teachers and the household chores. Each morning upon waking, I have a list of jobs I must complete before leaving for the day. My morning routine begins with my aunt complaining I am slow and lazy. Each morning I must hand wash the bed sheets from each bed and hang them to dry, help with breakfast, and wash the dishes. Most mornings, by the time I get to school, I am already overwhelmed with exhaustion. I am often late for school — the morning chores are extremely time-consuming.

The evenings are no easier, consisting of hard work that does not get done in the mornings, such as washing the floors and the rest of the laundry. So, evenings leave me little time for school work. Most days, my teachers do not ask me for the homework assignments, as they soon learn I seldom complete them. Maybe they are trying to save me the embarrassment, or perhaps they understand my situation at home.

The weekends are no better due to the amount of sewing that must be done to keep up with clothing a large family. And so, sewing is a big part of our weekends. Each school-aged family member owns two sets of school uniforms. School uniforms are mandatory. The girls' uniform is called, 'batas' a shapeless white dress resembling a sack. The boys wear grey slacks and a collared, button-down white shirt. We each have two sets that we alternate each day.

There are constantly items to be mended, buttons to be sewn, and holes to patch. This is not all the sewing that must be done, though. To bring in extra to pay my way, I also sew for others including neighbours, family friends, and acquaintances. This extra money goes a long way in supporting myself.

Chores are a seven-day-per-week routine, and if my aunt catches me not cleaning or working, she becomes furious, forcing me to redo the work I have already done. This at least is slightly easier, as it's much faster to wash a clean floor or dust a dust-free table than a dirty one. I do not complain, not ever. I do as I'm told, day in and day out. Inside, I want to yell and scream, I am not a maid! But I keep these words safely secure inside my head where no one can hear them but me.

I thank my lucky stars for Alexander; he is like an older brother to me now, protecting me when I am vulnerable, and teasing me the rest of the time like older brothers do. Despite the age difference between us — Alexander is a teenager, and I am only six — we get along well. He is my much-needed rock when the ground softens all around me.

CHAPTER 7

1936

OVER THE COURSE of the year, I try to be optimistic and embrace things as they come. One of my goals is to try and enjoy the good around me because it is not all bad. Some days, but not all, do bring moments of enjoyment. There are a few times a month when my cousins from across the street come to visit. It is during these visits I am afforded leisure time to play and enjoy my childhood. These small moments are the highlights of my time in Luanda. I adore these cousins, and we get along well.

We play in the large gardens between our houses for as long as we are allowed. There is not much to do here in this neighbourhood, but we fill our time together with joy and pleasure nonetheless. My cousins are kind and always cheerful when they come around. Our group is not big, there is Lilly, Belita, and Jorge, and we are around the same age. Belita and Jorge are a few years older than Lilly and me. There are four other cousins, whom I also become close to, Thomas, Mimi, Zack, and Manuela, but they are older and married, so I don't see them as often because they are busy with their adult lives.

It is during one of these late sunny afternoons when we are together playing that I almost lose my life.

It is a weekend, and I am trying to finish the household chores so I can join the others out in the gardens. From my window I watch them happily running around like carefree children, and it is only a matter of time before they come knocking to get me to come out to play with them.

I answer the door covered in dust, and there stands Lilly, laughing at me.

"You look silly."

"I am cleaning," I say, lifting the dusty mop for her to see.

"You poor thing. Can you stop for a while and come outside? It is time to have some fun. We are having a good time, but we miss you."

"I miss you too."

"Then come!"

"Do you know how much trouble I will be in if I leave?"

"Will you join us when your work is done?"

"Yes, I am almost finished. I have one more bed to make after I dust, and I will be right outside. Now you must go before Aunt Mariazinha sees you and gives me more work to do. I promise I will be done soon."

"Okay, I am leaving. If there is any chance I will run into her, then I am out of here."

"Bye!"

I wave as she walks away. She is already halfway across the front lawn, eager to join the others, when she yells back, "Nao demores muito," *Do not take too long*.

I hurry and finish my chores so I, too, can go out to play. Once finished, I make my way to the group, hoping my aunt does not notice I rushed — she probably will, so I'll have to deal with her later.

There is more traffic on the streets than usual, but I pay little attention to the traffic, or anything else. I ignore the vehicles zooming by and set out for an afternoon of fun. The others are already engaged in a game of hide and seek when I join them. Soon we are running around, chasing each other like the children we are.

Cars are moving faster than they normally do, and it is probably due to my excitement and attention to the game that I do not notice the blue vehicle that comes speeding towards me. There is a sudden flash from the vehicle's headlights and blindness takes over, preventing me from moving out of the vehicle's way. I freeze as still as a statue, my feet pinned to the dirt road. Death is imminent, and I have no hope for the future. Out of nowhere, Lilly is running towards me, and her face reveals the true danger I am in.

She screams, "Prima!" *Cousin!*

She jumps towards me, putting herself in between me and the moving vehicle. She pushes me out of the way with so much force and with no more than a split second before impact. I fly through the air, landing hard on my back on the side of the road. I smack my head on the curb, and blood spills over the concrete. Lilly remains where I was a second ago. The driver sees her and stomps on the brakes in time to slow down enough, but Lilly still gets hit. She is now the one screaming in pain, even though the impact is not at full speed. She is lucky because if the driver had not applied the brakes when he did, Lilly might not be able to scream right now.

Belita and Jorge are at her side as she continues to scream. "My leg, I broke my leg! Ouch, my arm! It all hurts!"

I do not move for a few minutes — I do not think I can, even if I try. How is it possible I am still alive? Lilly pushed me out of the way and saved my life, this is how. If it had not been for Lilly, I would not be breathing now. I have a much smaller frame, and I am more fragile than my cousin. The driver had not seen me, and so if Lilly had not jumped, the impact would have occurred at full speed. Most likely crushing me to death, of this I am certain.

The driver, an older man, about my father's age, appears to not be hurt. He is pacing back and forth between Lilly and me. "Are you all right?" he says to me. "When that girl jumped out in front of you, I was startled back to reality, causing me to apply the brakes, and diminishing the impact greatly. I am so sorry miss; I did not see you before the girl jumped out."

I ignore him and crawl to where Lilly and the others are, holding my head. Blood spills over the road, but I do not know if it is mine or Lilly's. We stare at Lilly in horror, and then Jorge runs home to get their mother. I remain with Lilly and Belita at the scene, as Lilly screams in agony.

"Eu vou morrer?" *Am I going to die?*

I cannot blame Lilly for worrying. "I do not think so," I say.

I try to convince her that she is all right. Other neighbours are now forming a circle around us, but the driver is nowhere to be seen.

A few minutes later, my aunt, Lilly's mother is running down the street towards us, arms flapping in the air. "O que aconteceu?" *What has happened?* After looking at her daughter, she turns pale. "Oh, my goodness! Good Lord! My daughter, my poor daughter. What have you done to her Rosa?" she says.

She places her hands over her head, with the fear of seeing her daughter hurt. Of course, she is blaming me for the accident, saying I am responsible, and that I caused it. I am not sure how a seven-year-old girl caused a car to drive into her daughter, but I stand silent, not wanting to bring attention to myself. The last thing I want is to make things worse for myself or for Lilly. My cousin is a big girl and her mother cannot carry her alone, so Jorge and Belita help her. My poor cousin's mother half carries her home, while I limp behind them. I am still in pain, and I can barely walk myself, but nobody helps me. I am on my own as usual, but it is all right, I am used to it.

Back at their house, the doctor is called for, and after thirty minutes he arrives to examine Lilly.

He takes ten minutes to perform the physical examination. "She is a lucky girl, considering what the outcome could have been. Her leg, left elbow, and wrist are broken based on my tests, and she has many scratches, and scrapes, but that is the extent of the damage. The leg and arm will heal within twelve weeks."

"Twelve weeks, oh dear God," says Lilly's mother, hands raised over her mouth.

"Yes, and it could have been much worse," continues the doctor. "I am sure your daughter will be back to running around the neighbourhood, aimlessly, and causing trouble in no time."

My aunt narrows her eyes at the doctor's remark. "My daughter does not run around the neighbourhood aimlessly, nor does she cause any trouble. It is her cousin Rosa that gets her into trouble."

"Regardless, both her arm and leg are in a cast, and I will return in twelve weeks to remove them. Now, I must head out to see the next patient who is waiting. Here are painkillers she can take once a day. Keep the leg elevated to avoid swelling. Do you understand these instructions?"

"Yes Doctor, thank you for coming on such short notice," says my aunt.

"Well, have a lovely day."

The doctor tips his hat and walks out the door before my aunt can ask any more questions.

My own recovery takes much less time and I am back to normal within a few days. I suffered a bump on my head, a few nasty scratches on my legs, and of course, my back is tender from the fall. My aunt expects nothing less than perfection during this time, and I continue with the housework as best I can. The next twelve weeks I try to help Lilly often. I owe her my life, so I bring her food and keep her company. It is the least I can do for her.

Each night when I lie in bed, I think of the day of the accident. In my head, the vehicle speeds towards Lilly and me. When I fall asleep, the vehicle continues to come towards us at full speed, only now, the image is in my dream. Upon waking, I repeat the same words, "The accident is not my fault." There is no one listening when I say this, and I am only trying to convince myself.

❧

Twelve weeks later, Lilly's casts are removed. She says she needs moral support, so I go to her house, even though I am getting in the way. But Lilly insists I stay, and so I do. I have done a lot for her over the last three months, and still I manage to keep up with my chores at home, both before and after school.

I walk home tonight exhausted. Hopefully, now that Lilly is back to normal, I will have time to rest. I am sitting outside on the front veranda for a few minutes, trying to steal a moment of peace. The second I walk in the door my aunt will put me to work, so I need a minute of silence, a moment to myself.

From within the house I hear a raspy voice and I know instantly it's a voice I recognize but do not like. It is my cousin Ricardo's voice coming from the living room. "Please do not come out here," I say to myself. Ricardo is the last person I want to see tonight. He opens the door to the veranda, looks around, and his eyes lock with mine, so I look away. He shuts the door behind him and walks to where I am sitting on the step, cross-legged, with my dress over my knees. What is he doing here? What does he want from me? Ricardo does not like me, and he has not liked me since I moved here, so this is more than a social visit.

He does not sit, but towers over me. "Where have you been this entire time?"

"Helping Lilly, she got her casts off today."

"Mother wants you back in the house. Get inside now."

Aunt Mariazinha probably has work she needs me to do, so my break is over. I get up off the step and wipe my dress of the dust I sat on. Looking up at Ricardo, I am shocked to see he is still staring at me. He looks much different today, his eyes are squinted, and his brow is more creased than usual, but then he does something strange, and he smiles. This smile is not a happy, warm smile, but rather a small smirk and, combined with his squinted eyes, his look gives me the chills. Ricardo is not one to smile. In fact, in an entire year, I have never seen him smile, not once. I cautiously walk past him, keeping some distance between us, and look back over my shoulder as I open the veranda door, before stepping inside. As I look back, he still wears that bone-chilling grin on his mysterious face.

CHAPTER 8

1936

NOT ALL MY cousins are as kind and gentle with me as Lilly and Alexander are. While I have Alexander to protect me from his mother's hard ways, and Lilly to protect me from fast-moving vehicles, I must learn to live with Ricardo.

There are not many people Ricardo likes, but he treats me worse than others. This creepy cousin puts me down often, is rude, and obnoxious. The looks he gives me frightens me to my core.

Ricardo has mental health issues, this I am certain of; although I do not know what his problem is, but there is definitely a problem. He has been involved in encounters with the law. He steals money from his mother, from neighbours, and from stores. He talks back to his mother often, he bullies his siblings, and he never feels remorseful.

Aunt Mariazinha must know what he is like, but I think she chooses to ignore his behaviours, so she does not have to deal with him. Her ignorance to the matter gives Ricardo ammunition to continue this way, he knows there is often no consequence.

Aunt Mariazinha is preparing to leave for the night, she is going to the cinema to watch a movie with some friends. She does not go out often, so when she does, she looks forward to the outing.

She has fed us dinner, and we are expected to retire to our bedrooms for the night. Ricardo is not present when his mother delivers these instructions, and I look around for him but do not see him. If any of us needs a reminder, it is Ricardo. He is most likely the one to cause trouble and break the rules.

My aunt applies a final coat of lipstick and says goodbye. "I expect no trouble from any of you tonight. I shall not be too late. I do not want to see or hear any of you when I return. I expect you all to be asleep."

She walks out the door, putting the lipstick tube back in her bag, and we are left alone.

Later at night, I am lying on my mattress in the room Lina and I share. I lie quietly on my mattress while Lina snores loudly in her soft and comfortable bed. She has a big window next to her that she keeps open most nights to let in some air. The fresh breeze cools the room significantly. I have fallen asleep, but I wake up startled with the sounds of footsteps approaching. Someone is stomping their feet causing the thick floorboards to rattle and shake. There is moaning, but I am not sure to whom the voice belongs. The person's words are muddled, and they are not speaking coherently. I sit halfway up with elbows on my mattress as I wipe the sleep from my tired eyes and concentrate on trying to place the voice. Recognition of the disarrayed voice sets in, and the speech becomes clear as glass. I know it is him. A moan escapes from my throat as I whisper his name, "Ricardo."

He is yelling, and he sounds as if he is in a rage. "Where are you? Rosa, you cannot hide from me."

I place my hands over my ears to block his voice. The bedroom door bursts open, so he must have kicked it hard. It swings back and slams into the wall leaving a hole behind as evidence. Lina is now awake.

"Encontrei-te." *I found you.*

He sounds surprised to find me in Lina's room, as if he does not know this is where I have been sleeping for over a year. With a hunched back, he leans over and tries to grab me from the mattress, I slide back as far as I can before my head hits the wall. My eyes are wide open in alarm, and as he approaches I count the seconds until he reaches me, not knowing what he wants, or what he will do. I smell wine on his breath; pungent and stale. He reaches out with his big long, arms and grabs me with both of his strong hands, lifts me, then throws me down, my back slamming into the firm mattress. I scream and kick as hard as I can. My flailing arms are trying desperately to swat at him, but his eighteen-year-old body is no match for mine.

We remain in this fight, him trying to hold me down and me trying to get away, for what feels like hours, but it is only seconds.

Lina remains still, making no sound, so I look over to her hoping for help. Our eyes meet for a split second, and then she pulls the blanket up over her head. She must be scared also. The security of our bedroom has turned into a battleground for nightmares. My mind is racing, and I am petrified. I consider my options and reach out to grab anything I can use to hit him over the head with, but my hands come up empty.

With his left-hand, Ricardo unbuttons his pants and pulls them down, exposing his penis, and his right hand continues to pin me down. This is my first time close to a naked boy, and I do not like it. What is he planning to do to me? I try to kick him with my legs, but they do not touch him as he is now on top of me, so I grab him by the penis, and I squeeze hard. He cries out in pain, and I pull and squeeze with all my strength.

I must be pulling hard enough to hurt him because he screams again, "AHHHH, stupid bitch."

Good, I am causing him pain.

"Bitch," he says again.

I continue to squeeze and twist it until he cannot scream anymore. He holds his breath and his face turns blue.

I am gaining control over him, and this is my opportunity to end this. "If you ever lay your hands on me again, I will squeeze and break your penis in half. I will also tell your mother you attacked me, and I will tell her other things too."

I give one extra hard tug, to prove my point.

"Okay, okay, I promise. Let go, I cannot breathe, you are hurting me."

"Am I?" I pretend not to notice his pain.

Ricardo continues to beg me to let go, and the moment I release him he is off me, limping out the door. I look over at Lina, but she is still covered by the blanket head to toe. I do not think she saw anything.

The next morning during breakfast, Ricardo's mother comments on how proud she is of us. She has no idea what her son has done.

"I came home last night to a quiet and clean house, and I was able to head off to bed right away. Thank you for behaving, and not causing any trouble."

I listen, saying nothing and wonder if she truly believes her words. Lina remains quiet also, not saying anything to me or to her mother about last night. She did not see much but she heard the dreadful exchange.

Looking over at Ricardo from the corner of my eye, I cannot help noticing he is squirmy and moving a lot in his seat. A small smile forms on my face, because I know I am responsible for his pain. Nobody else in the room notices my smile except for Lina, whom I think returns a smile of her own. I contemplate telling Alexander about what his brother has done, but then decide it is best to keep this a secret. I do not want to bring more attention to myself.

Less than a week later, Ricardo disappears from our lives. He vanishes one morning without a word to anyone, not even to his mother. His leaving brings me relief as I no longer peek into a room before entering in case he is there. I am relieved knowing he will never lay his hands on me again. While Ricardo is gone, he creates an imprint in my memory, one so deep I cannot erase. Because of him, I am haunted in my sleep each night.

I was right when I said the bedroom would be grounds for nightmares, because one week after Ricardo disappears the nightmares plague me.

He has come back, he is in the house looking for me, and calling my name. He says my name with vengeance, accentuating the syllables, saying I cannot hide from him forever. I am in my room hiding behind Lina's bed, and hoping he does not come in here again. The stomping of his feet grows louder, and I hide inside the closet now instead of behind the bed, fearing I need more protection.

I waken throughout the night, and I sit up quickly as I sense a presence around me. The fear pulls me out of the nightmare. It is too dark for me to see well, but I look around nonetheless. My eyes focus on a dark image at the foot of my bed, and for a moment I think it's him. I scream, then place my hand over my mouth as I realize it is not Ricardo after all, it is only my imagination.

CHAPTER 9

1938

SCHOOL CONTINUES TO be a struggle, but I am determined to persevere despite the hard work at home. I am keen on learning about most subjects and I love books and reading, eager to discover the world through them. School provides me with this opportunity.

One day, my teacher assigns an out of the ordinary homework piece. The class is going on a school picnic at a local park, and each student is assigned a meal to cook and bring to the picnic to share with the class. I am assigned a chicken, but this is not a problem for me, because I have lots of experience cooking at home. I tell my aunt about the picnic assignment, but initially she questions me, unsure if I am telling the truth.

"I am not making this up, the chicken is a school assignment."

"I do not believe you, I think you are lying to me," she says.

"I promise it is not a lie."

I lift both hands up, face my palms out, and wiggle my fingers to show they are not crossed.

For a few days, she remains skeptical and does not know whether to believe me or not. It takes some convincing, but eventually my aunt is on board with the school assignment. She believes education is important, even if it means cooking as part of the education.

"Fine, if the chicken is a school assignment, you have permission to use the kitchen. I will even buy you the chicken."

"Oh, thank you so much." A big smile forms and I jump while clapping, planning what spices to use on the roasted chicken. My mouth is watering, and I can taste the juiciness of the meat in my mouth.

The day prior to the picnic, my teacher announces the picnic is postponed due to inclement weather. I am busy writing when she speaks, but upon hearing her words, I stop moving the pencil and look up with a frown.

"That is terrible," I say. The entire class hears me, and many heads turn to where I am sitting.

The picnic cannot be postponed — I had already purchased the chicken and marinated it this morning before leaving for school. I am prepared to cook the chicken tonight as soon as I get home. Because of my excitement, I decide on a whim not to tell my aunt the picnic has been deferred. Instead, I go along with the original plan and pretend the picnic is still happening. The chicken is worth the risk I am taking lying to my aunt.

I leave school at the end of the day, skipping along with one of my friends, Ines.

"That is sad news about the picnic, I was looking forward to it," I say to my friend as we continue to skip down the street.

"It is not that big a deal," Ines says, as she wrinkles her nose.

"Oh, it is to me."

"Why? It is just a picnic. It is of no importance. If we have the picnic tomorrow or next month, what difference does it make?" she asks shrugging.

"Hmm, well none I suppose," I lie.

I arrive home from school a little tired from skipping, but eager to get started on my homework assignment. I examine the already marinated chicken and add a little more salt, a dash more of thyme, and one more squeeze of lemon, to enhance the spices for the perfect flavor. I want to eat the chicken at school and share it with my friends because a roasted chicken is much more of a delicacy than the bun with cheese I take for lunch each day. I would much rather enjoy a juicy, spicy chicken leg than a boring cheese sandwich, and so, food is my only motivation for this lie. I do not even feel bad about lying, and as I wait for the bird to cook, the excitement of taking this roasted chicken to school has clouded my better judgment.

The next morning I take the roasted chicken to school, already precut, and I am surrounded by other kids as they crowd around me. I share pieces with the hungry children who, today, are my friends.

Three days have passed, and Aunt Mariazinha and I are walking to the local grocery store to buy food for tonight's supper. Ines is across the street waving to us, so I cross the road to say hello to her, my aunt following close behind me, already reaching out her hand to introduce herself.

"Well hello, who do we have here? You must be a friend of Rosa's from school?"

"Yes Madame. I am Ines."

My friend introduces herself politely knowing all too well who this woman is, as I have spoken about her often. My nosy aunt proceeds to ask more questions. "You must be here to replenish the food that got used for the picnic?"

"Er, no," says Ines, as she pinches her eyebrows together.

"I am not sure what these schools are thinking, going on picnics. Time is much better spent in the classroom, learning from books. How was the picnic anyway, and what did you have to cook for it?"

At the mention of the picnic I freeze, and my face must be white as I feel the blood draining from my cheeks. I am speechless, and I try to give my friend a warning with my eyes, by raising my eyebrows and opening my eyes big. I am willing her to read my mind, but she gives me a crooked smile. She does not understand my facial cues and turns to my aunt.

"Oh …ah, we did not have the picnic, it got postponed."

"Postponed?" My aunt turns her head to me, and I get an overwhelming feeling in my stomach.

"Ines!" someone calls her name from up the street, a woman I do not recognize.

"Oh dear, I must run, Mother is calling. It is a pleasure to meet you. Good day," says Ines, as she runs off to meet her mother and leaves me with Aunt Mariazinha alone. This is a dangerous situation and I am afraid to look at my aunt, fearing I will see steam coming out of her ears. I am annoyed at Ines for not covering for me, but then I realize this is not her fault, she was honest because she had no idea I needed her not to be.

I steal a quick glance at my aunt, and she looks at me with fire in her eyes. She crosses her arms over her chest and sighs heavily. After a few seconds, she grabs my right ear, pinches tight, and pulls me along the street. As soon as we arrive home, I run to the washroom and stuff several towels under my dress and into my underpants. I know what is coming next. I have been here before, and so this time I prepare for the lashing. From within the washroom, I hear my aunt calling my name as I stuff one more towel down my back-side. Luckily my school uniform covers most of the bulk.

Leaving the washroom, knowing full well what to expect, I almost crash into Aunt Mariazinha. She waits outside the washroom door, and when she sees me, she reaches down and removes her slipper and whips me with it. I pretend to cry out in pain, the towels stuffed under my uniform helps to soften the blow on my bum, so there is not much pain. My aunt grounds me, preventing me from playing with my cousins for three weeks. During this time, Aunt Mariazinha does not speak to me, and the silence scares me more than the beating.

A few weeks later, the picnic is rescheduled, and I convince Aunt Mariaz-inha I am sick and she believes me. I cannot bear to go to school and face humiliation for not having food to share. I know this is another lie, and I also know it is wrong to lie, but I convince myself this is necessary, to save myself the embarrassment.

Adults often say it is okay to make mistakes, but only if something is learnt, and I can most certainly say I learned from this incident. Next time I decide to lie to my aunt, I am going to tell my friends about it so I have a backup in case there is another encounter such as the one that blew my cover.

CHAPTER 10

1940

THE 1940S IN Angola are still peaceful times and the country is sheltered from the raging war as Germany attacks Western Europe. There is an increase in the white population in Angola, but overall this only amounts to approximately two percent of the entire colony's population, with the remaining population being black native Angolans.

It is during the end of 1940 that my aunt makes a big announcement; "We are moving to the metropole."

She says this so casually as if she is announcing that we are moving down the street. There is confusion on my cousins' faces, and doubt sets into my mind as to why she wants to move so suddenly. Lisbon is the city in Portugal she tells us we are moving to. Portugal is in Europe, west of Spain. When referring to the Portuguese mainland we often use the term metropole.

"Does this move include me, or just your family?" I am eager to know the answer, and I secretly hope I am excluded from this family move.

"Well of course it includes you. Have you not been an equal part of this family for the past few years? Have I not clothed you, educated you, and put food on the table for you?"

"Yes," I say.

"Well, then of course you are coming. We must make the necessary preparations as soon as possible because I want to leave by the end of next month."

"Have you informed my father?"

"No, not yet. I shall write to him today."

I am not moving; no way am I going to move to Portugal and living further from my own family. My heart races and sweat accumulates on my forehead. I reach up to wipe it with my sleeve before anyone notices. I need to figure something out, and fast. What excuse can I possibly use? If I do not go, where will I live? I think about this even more and realize if I do not go to Portugal, then possibly I can return home to my father. This gives me hope that had been long lost.

The same night my aunt writes to my father, informing him of her wishes to take me to Portugal with the rest of her family. I am hopeful my father will decline her crazy request this time, and I wait patiently for weeks for the reply to come by post. I hardly eat or sleep while I wait for his answer as I am consumed with worry. Life in Portugal is not a life I have considered for myself. I am an Angolan girl after all, and I do not know anything about Portugal.

Each day I wait for the post to arrive with news from my father, growing more and more anxious until it is finally here.

"Mama, post arrived, and there is a letter from Uncle Manuel addressed to you," says Julio one afternoon.

"Give it to me Julio, I must know what my brother's response is to my inquiry about Rosa."

My palms are shaking as I try to grab the letter, but she slaps my hand away. "What does it say?" I ask.

Aunt Mariazinha remains silent for the next few minutes as she reads the letter, occasionally stopping, looking up and mumbling then continuing to read. I stand by her side, peeking over her shoulder.

"Rosa, have some respect. I shall inform you of the decision when I am finished."

"I am sorry, Aunt Mariazinha."

I apologize only to stay on her good side, although I am not sorry and wish she would hurry up and read the darn letter. It feels like she has been reading for an hour, and the letter is only one-page long. She must be stalling and making me wait on purpose, to torture me.

"It is settled."

She says this so confidently, folding the letter in half and slipping it into the pocket of her skirt.

"What does that mean? What is settled?"

"The move is settled, you are coming with us. Your father gave his consent."

"Oh shit."

"Rosa, get to your room! You watch your language young lady, or I will wash your mouth with soap."

I run as fast as I can out of the living room, and the tears are pouring down my face like a waterfall. I am a disaster, hair flying over my face, snot running from my nose. My world as I know it is coming to an end … again. How can he do this to me for a second time? How can he send me away again, and so much further? No, I will not go. I refuse to go. I will run away if I must. I am not the scared little girl I used to be. I am now eleven years old and I should have a say in this decision. Surely, I can get a job now if I need to. In a few years, I will be of marriageable age, so I only need to hold out a few years longer, and I will be free to do what I want, free to get married.

I have deep conversations with my cousin Alexander about my anguish. He listens to me for the next few nights, holds me in his arms, and attempts to comfort me. He assures me everything will be okay, patting me on the back, trying to soothe my nerves.

"But I am scared, so scared Alexander."

"I will talk to my mother and see if I can convince her to change her mind. Although, I want you to come with us, and I will miss you dearly my cousin."

"Thank you, Alexander, you are wonderful to me. Please do talk to her. I will miss you the most."

Alexander comes to my aid again and convinces his mother to not take me with them. I do not know how he manages this arduous task as she is so set in her ways, but he does convince her. When he gives me his news, I throw myself at him, wrap my arms tightly around his neck, and kiss his cheeks incessantly.

"Rosa, you need to loosen your grip, I cannot breathe," Alexander says.

"I am so sorry, I got overly excited," I say.

"You are not out of the woods yet, another letter must be written to your father. He ultimately has the last say. My mother says, as long as your father wants you back, she is fine with you not coming to Lisbon."

My aunt writes the second letter, and after two weeks, the response arrives containing news that I am to return home to Lobito. I am the happiest eleven-year-old girl, and I give a loud shriek when I learn this. I had given up on my father, believing he had forgotten me. But after all these years, he wants me back; finally, I am going home. A father's love is never forgotten after all.

The happiness fades as the day for me to leave approaches; I am suddenly frightened to face my past. Am I taking a step backward going home? Am I am making the right decision? My life is at a crossroads, and depending on this move, whether to move to Lisbon or go back to Lobito, will set the course for the rest of my life. How do I make this difficult decision?

***

When I reflect on the last five years at Aunt Mariazinha's house, I am overwhelmed with emotions. The time spent here was difficult for me, but it has also changed me. I have learned a lot in the past five years. I understand because of my stern aunt, I am not the same girl I was when I arrived. The past few years taught me many lessons, shaped the way I handle situations now compared to then, and changed the way I interact with people who enter my life. I reflect on what I want for my future, and my conclusions are still the same, family and security; these two things mean the most to me.

I ask God for help and reassurance that I am making the right decision returning to Lobito. I want a sign moving back with my father will give me the love and security I so desperately seek, but God is silent tonight when I pray, so there are no encouraging signs received from Him today. And so, it is with a heavy heart I board the bus back to Lobito on the second day of January, 1941.

I sit on the bus shaking with nerves. The seat to my right is unoccupied and I stretch out a little, listening to the loud engine roaring to life as the bus moves. I think back to five years ago when I made this trip to Luanda by boat, and now here I am, years later, returning. I look out of the window to my right — between myself and the window is the empty seat next to me, then an aisle with another set of seats. Sitting in one of those seats by the window is a boy. He looks to be a few years older than I am. His glare is serious, and he does not take his eyes off me. He has dark, semi-wavy hair, and piercing brown eyes that stare at me until I get shivers. I look away right before he smiles, and I decide the view to my left, while not the most spectacular, is the safest, and this is where I keep my gaze for the entire ride home.

PART THREE
1941-1947

CHAPTER 11

Lobito, Angola
1941

MOVING BACK TO my father's house is not the sweet home-coming I had dreamt of for so many years. I have been away far too long for that type of welcome and spent most of my impressionable years away from what I once considered my home.

Things have changed, a lot. For starters, my brothers look much older than I remember. The house itself is different, both in spirit and décor. There is new white paint on the walls, and different couches occupy the space in the living room. Some of the old neighbours have moved away, and new neighbours now occupy the same old houses.

I also have a little sister, her name is Manuela and she is four years old. Jealousy consumes me when I first meet her. I am cheated out of a father now that he has another daughter to take my place. I have my father back after all these years, so why now must I share him with a sister? I complain to myself when she looks at me with wide eyes, so I come to conclusions about Manuela, conclusions that make me not like her.

However, as time passes and I get to know her, Manuela proves to be nothing like what my first impression was of her. She is sweet, kind, and loves me from Day One. She clings to me often like a lost child, and I to her like a fierce, protective mother. We form a strong bond that cannot be any stronger had we grown up in the same house for the past five years. Within time, I get over the terrible jealousy that consumed me to begin with, and I learn to embrace my new little sister with wide open, loving arms. I do not know who Manuela's mother is and my father does not say much about her. All I learn is that she is a native woman whom he had relations with, and then left after Manuela was born, so Manuela stayed to live with my father. This story sounds a little too familiar.

One month after my arrival, my father announces he found someone to share his life with. He has been courting her for six weeks, since before I came back, and he is in love. He brings this new woman to our home for the first time tonight, and I am surprised by her beauty. She has light coloured skin, she is taller than most women I know, and her body is so slim that I cannot but think that she does not eat much. Her hair is chestnut brown, wavy, and falls below her chin. She has a round face, and lips so full I cannot help but stare at. Her name is Victoria Silva, and her name rolls off my father's lips when he introduces her to me, like music to my ears. He does not say the name, Victoria, but sings it with a melody so sweet I hope it matches her personality. The way my father looks at her suggests Victoria is a special soul. My father announces Victoria is to live with us, starting now.

Another pang of jealousy overwhelms me, so I ignore her at first. Soon I discover Victoria is friendly and has a nurturing way about her, so I open my heart, a little. She is soft-spoken and has a sincere smile, even when she is not looking at me, which puts me at ease. She is patient and sweet with both my sister and me and spends plenty of time entertaining Manuela.

Victoria teaches me how to make new clothes. I am used to mending and sewing from my time with Aunt Mariazinha, but I have never sewn an entire outfit on my own. My wardrobe expands to include different pieces, and I soon learn to mix and match articles of clothing. She teaches me new recipes and shows me how to get the silverware polished to perfection with little effort by placing it in a pot of boiling water.

My father and Victoria are not married, and I pray she will one day become my mother. I am transfixed by her, and I hope she will be staying for the long run. She has no children of her own and soon we become a family, Victoria treating us like we are her own.

Victoria and I develop a close friendship; she is my confidant, my therapist, and my main support for all my needs. I tell her personal things I do not tell anyone else. For example, she is the only one who knows about Ricardo, and how Aunt Mariazinha treated me. Manuela is too young to confide in, and it is embarrassing to discuss certain things with my father.

One month after Victoria moves in, something unusual happens to me, and I worry I am either sick or dying. Victoria notices my discomfort; she is in tune with my feelings and my state of mind. I do not leave my room all day, so she comes in, sits on the edge of my bed, and rubs my leg.

"What is troubling you child? Come, tell me, I might be of some help."

"Nothing."

"I know it is something, you have not left your room all day."

I take a deep breath and decide to be honest with her.

"Eu não sei," *I do not know.* I try to cover my face with the blanket. Victoria pulls the blanket away so she can see my face. She leans in and wraps her arms around me. I let the tears fall, freely.

"Do not cry, it is all right child. Has someone hurt you?" She wipes my face.

"No." I manage to say between sobs.

"Then what is the matter? I cannot help you if you do not tell me what is wrong."

"I am hurt, or sick. Oh, I don't know. Maybe I am dying."

"Why do you say that?"

"I noticed this morning there is blood down there."

"Down where?"

"Down there," I say again pointing to in between my legs.

"Oh."

She stares at me with a quizzical look. She understands the problem. Her face softens, and her smile widens.

"Rosa, my dear child, you are not sick, and you are certainly not dying."

"I am not?"

"No, trust me child, I know about these things. I am a woman also, and I was once your age. What you see is blood, but not because you are hurt or sick."

"What then?"

"You are becoming a woman."

"A woman?" I ask confused.

"Yes, this is nature's way of communicating that you are no longer a child."

I stare at her with my lips twisted in a half frown, trying to understand her meaning.

"Are you sure I am not sick?"

"Yes, child, I am quite sure."

For the next hour, Victoria tells me about the human reproductive system, and how a woman's body works. As I listen, I cannot help but wonder if becoming a woman means I can no longer play outside. Victoria stays in my room for the next hour, and after talking things through, she convinces me I am not dying.

This is only one of many situations I go crying to Victoria for and weep in her comforting arms. She has a magical touch that makes me relax. When I rest my head in her arms, I know everything will turn out all right.

～

She and I often sit on the bench of our front porch, and she tells me stories from when she was a little girl. I listen, glued to her every word.

"What would you like to know today? What stories do you want me to tell you?"

"Tell me everything."

I want to know all about her life, her parents, her siblings, and upbringing, and she tells me everything I want to hear.

She is from Portugal and moved to Angola with her father when she was a teenager. She grew up in a loving household with three brothers, like me. She was close to her father, until he passed away a few years ago, and her mother died when she was young. She has always longed for a mother figure but grew up without one. This makes sense and explains her loving nature. She does not have children because she never found someone special enough to want to start a family with. She is younger than my father by ten years. During these conversations, I get to know her well, and I grow to love her.

We talk about my time spent with Aunt Mariazinha, my upbringing so far, and we often discuss my own mother. She never mentions specific things, but she does bring her up often. Sometimes, she asks me if I have any desire to meet my mother, if she were alive. I reply, I do think of my biological mother often, and I do wish she were in my life now. My father told me several times she died, but he does not have any specific details about her death. Victoria knows this, so I am confused about why she brings her up, but I do not question her.

～

Victoria is with our family for three months when my father brings up the subject of school. I have not attended school since my return and he wants me to start again, soon. He says it has been a long enough time for me to have adjusted, and he is growing concerned for my future. He wants me to further my education, so I can one day become successful. I oblige, and shortly after, I start school once again.

This time school is easier because I do not have as many chores as before. I am afforded more time to study and Victoria encourages this. I still work hard around the house, but now I work hard because I want to, and not because I am forced. I find school easy. I am a bright student, and I do well and receive good marks in return. My teachers adore me, I am often referred to as a model student, and this is different from my school days in Luanda. They do tell me I am too shy and I need to put in more effort to make new friends, so these are things I need to work on.

I have come a long way from when teachers stopped expecting me to hand in assignments, like they did when I lived with Aunt Mariazinha. I never look back though, not ever. I only look forward to the future, and the future is looking bright for me. I have a good home, a new sister, and I have my father back. I also have a kind and gentle mother figure in my life, something I never had before. I have high hopes and dream nightly of a secure future. I am one step closer to my life's plan and reaching my goals.

CHAPTER 12

1941

MY FATHER HAS another sister and Rita is her name. My Aunt Rita lives in Benguela, another city in Angola, and not too far from Lobito, on the west side of the colony. Benguela is a twenty-minute drive from Lobito. I visit Aunt Rita's house often, and soon I am spending my summer holidays there at her house with her and her family.

Aunt Rita is kind and possesses a much different demeanor from her sister, Mariazinha. She welcomes me each summer with open arms, making me an equal part of her family.

This aunt of mine has four children of her own: two boys and two girls. There is Joseph, Liberto, Natércia, and Lila. Uncle Arsenio, Aunt Rita's husband, also lives here as well. He is a hardworking man and often comes home late at night, tired. His children speak nothing but kind words about their father. He pays lots of attention to his wife, complimenting her often.

Aunt Rita loves to knit hats; knitting is one of her favourite pastimes. She knits two hats for me each summer. This is my parting gift from her. She says she wants me to have warm hats to keep my head insulated during the cool, dry weather.

Red is my favourite colour, but she makes me a blue and white one. Those colours of yarn must be more available. I wear the hats often, even to church, and sometimes the hats accompany new clothes that she also gifts me. No one has ever given me new clothes before, so I am spoiled when I leave her home with my bags fuller than when I arrived.

Aunt Rita often comments there is a school across the street from their house. She has high hopes I will attend this school and remain with her and her family during the school year. This is opposite of our current situation, but I am not thrilled with this plan. As much as I enjoy my time here, I have already been away from home too long, and I am not interested in going down that avenue again. I am happy to come to Aunt Rita's every year and spend the summers with her, but I do not want to make this my permanent home. I am afraid to tell Aunt Rita my true feelings, and I worry she will misinterpret this as ungratefulness, which is not the case.

"Está tudo bem," *It's all right,* she says when I summon the courage to tell her I do not want to attend the school here. She takes the rejection well, and I am relieved. I like Aunt Rita and I do not want to offend her.

Once the idea of me attending school here is out of Aunt Rita's head, she thinks up another idea for me. She always has thoughts forming and makes plans for others. She has good intentions and is only looking out for my best interest. One day during supper, she announces she wants me to learn to play the piano. I choke on the food in my mouth when I hear her words.

"Rosa, every young lady needs to know how to play the piano. It makes you a more dignified and accomplished young lady in society."

I swallow the food in my mouth before responding. "Oh, so I am not dignified and accomplished if I do not play the piano?"

"No, you are not."

I frown when she says this.

"But I do not wish to play the piano. I have zero interest in it."

Upon hearing my response, she shrugs to show she is not pleased. This is a difficult situation to get out of; there is a piano here at my disposal, so I have no excuse.

"I do not want to hurt your feelings Aunt Rita, but I do not have any interest whatsoever in learning the piano. My fingers, you see, are not long enough to stretch across the keys."

I reach my hand out so she can see my fingers wiggling. "I will sound horrible, and then how dignified and accomplished of a young lady will I be while playing the wrong notes?"

"Do not be crazy," she says. "Anyone can learn how to play the piano; it takes hard work and practice."

She is adamant, so for her I try. It takes me a few practices to have my initial thoughts confirmed. I am not interested in the piano at all. I do not understand it, and my fingers refuse to stretch as far as needed. Aunt Rita's children play the piano, and every young lady she knows also plays the piano, and she expects the same from me. She wants the best for me and believes this skill will help me in life. She encourages me for a few more days, until she finally gives up on her plan of having me play the piano.

We make it a family tradition each week on Sundays to sit outside in the yard with our lawn chairs and enjoy the air. Vendors gather on the street on Sundays to sell food to the neighbourhood. This includes: fresh produce, fish, meats, and eggs. We set up our chairs in a row and watch buyers haggle on the streets over meat and fruit.

Most nights after supper, we go for a long stroll and look at houses. I ask if we do this because we are nosy, and my aunt smacks the back of my head every time I ask this question. These nightly walks are a treasured family pastime. Uncle Arsenio stops working in the yard and joins us most evenings. Aunt Rita and Uncle Arsenio are about family time and bonding, and this I embrace with all my heart.

Before long, summer comes to an end, and I return home. That first night I have a dream about endings. The emotional pain from this dream is so real, I wake up alarmed. Am I having this dream because my time here is ending, or does this dream have further meaning?

CHAPTER 13

1942

IT IS JANUARY, the middle of the school year, and I am back at my father's house with my own family. Manuela is always so happy and excited when I return home. She shouts in my ear that she is glad to have me back. I tease her and say she only wants someone to play with. She is not lonely; there are many neighbourhood children her own age she plays with. So, I know she truly misses me.

It has been a long week, and I am glad it's coming to an end. I am looking forward to two days to myself. My weekends are relaxed. Other than helping around the house, I do not do too much more. We do laundry twice a week, on Mondays and Thursdays, and the only chore that takes a bit longer is ironing. We do not have electric irons, so we use an iron heated with charcoal to remove the deep-set wrinkles from our clothes. There is the odd trip into town to pick up food and other supplies, but sometimes we have fresh meat and fish delivered to the house. My father owns a store now, and the store is prosperous, so my life is promising.

One Saturday afternoon, I am strolling along the street on my way to the market. The tropical sunshine hits my face, and the cool sea breeze blows my hair when I spot him for the first time from the window. A cute, tall, dark-skinned, sweet-looking boy is stocking shelves. I blush, and I am sure my cheeks are crimson red. I look away rather fast, hoping he does not see me staring at him. My eyes dart back to his, and again I look away. He stares back, my heart is racing, and I notice sweat patches under my arms. Good Lord, what is wrong with me? What on earth am I doing staring at a boy! As I walk away from him, I glance over my shoulder and his eyes are still on me. My face is burning and sweat drenches my shirt. Panic sets in, so I run away in the opposite direction. Wanting to get as far away from him as possible, I bolt and trip over my own feet outside of the market. He walks out, looks at me on the ground and smiles. The sun blinds me, so I must bring my hand up to block the rays. He stands in front of me, hands outstretched.

"Miss, are you all right? Take my hand. Let me help you up."

This cannot be happening — he saw my dreadful fall. What thoughts of me run through his mind now? He must think I am immature, clumsy, and a silly girl. Surely I am not the dignified, accomplished young lady Aunt Rita speaks of. If only I learned to play the piano, then I might have conducted myself in a more proper manner. What would Aunt Rita say if she saw me now? My mind is racing with thoughts as I sit on the ground, covered in pebbles and dirt.

"I am fine. It is nothing. I thank you for your help, but as you can see, I do have things under control."

"Yes, I can see you have things under control," he says, arms still extended.

"I do, so you may leave now."

He chuckles as he stares at me. "Please miss, take my hand. It is the least I can do."

I hesitate, but reach out with my sweaty, dirty hand and let him lift me off the ground. Once I am on my feet, I turn away and run in the opposite direction again. Determined to not make a fool of myself this time, I slow my pace while in his presence. Once I am out of his view,

I run faster, and my knees hurt by the time I get home. There is no looking back at him this time. He must be laughing at me and thinking what a fool I am. Panting and out of breath, I walk in the front door to find Victoria staring at me. Her arms are full, holding jars of canned food she is going to use for dinner.

"Oh, Victoria, you are home." I manage to get these words out, even though I am still out of breath.

"What on earth happened to you?"

She treads over to me as if I am about to attack her. I do not blame her for being cautious, my curly hair is disheveled and dirt covers my dress. I cannot imagine how hideous my face looks.

"Nothing."

"Nothing?"

"I said nothing, what else do you want me to say?"

My responses come across rude, and she does not deserve my poor attitude. This retort is out of character for the type of person I want to be, am supposed to be. I am not usually impolite, and I respect my elders, most of the time. My insides are still a jumbled mess, and my face must still be red from seeing the cutest boy I have ever set eyes on. Letting my guard down, I let the tears fall. She leads me to the kitchen and prepares tea for us. My story spills out in between sobs, but Victoria says it is not a big deal. Of course she would say that, she is not the one who went through the embarrassing moment I suffered.

Victoria hints at my dirty appearance while we drink tea. So, after tea I head straight to the washroom to clean up. She helps me fill the basin with water and brings me a new bar of soap from my father's store. The water warms my skin as it makes contact, so I sit in the basin, soaking in the warmth. As I scrub my dirty skin, I cannot help but think about the cute boy from this afternoon. It is then I remember that I did not purchase the milk I set out to get. This thought brings a smile to my face. It means I must go back tomorrow since we need milk. Water spills over the basin onto the floor because I splash a little too much over excitement. I am elated at the prospect of seeing my first love once more.

⚜

The next day is Sunday, so we go to church as a family. After church, I decide there is no better time than now to go back to the store for the much-needed milk. My father looks at me with narrowed eyebrows.

"Are you not going to change out of your church clothes?"

I am almost out the door when he asks me this. Darn.

"No Father, I am in a hurry, we need milk. I will change when I return, and I will make sure not to get my dress dirty."

"No need to leave the house, we have milk. I picked some up early this morning. Victoria mentioned we were out."

Looking pretty in my church dress, I stand frozen at the door. I am trying to think up another excuse to leave the house. Victoria senses my discomfort as she knows why I want to go back to the store dressed nice. So, she comes to my rescue and gives me a reason to leave the house.

"We need bread for dinner, so please go pick that up," she says, as she winks at me in a way only I can understand.

"Of course, I shall be back soon."

I walk out with a huge smile on my face, head held high. My goal today is to act more ladylike and dignified around the boy.

Outside the store, my eyes scan each corner, but I do not see him at first. When I spot him stocking shelves, my spirit lifts. This is not my father's store, but rather a market. My father's store is a multipurpose store where you can buy both food and household supplies.

I take two deep breaths to calm my unsteady nerves. Straightening my dress hoping to smooth out wrinkles, I open the heavy door and walk in. He notices me right away; his smile widens, and he drops a package.

"You are back."

"Oh, hello."

I try to sound casual, as if I only noticed him for the first time.

Sweat forms under my arms again, and I hope it does not stain my dress this time. I say nothing more to him, and without meeting his eye I race past him to the counter. I am afraid to speak; I do not trust my own voice. When I approach the counter, I tell the lady standing behind it what I need.

"Pão por favor," *Bread, please.*

"All right miss, shall I charge your father's account?"

"Yes please, that would be most convenient. Thank you."

The store clerk hands me the loaf, and I take it from her, eager to leave. Realizing I am holding my breath the entire time, I allow myself to breathe only once I am outside.

For the next few weeks, I make up excuses to go to the market often. Each encounter is much the same; the boy smiling when I come in, and me pretending I do not care for his existence. Each week our vocabulary with one another increases, one word at a time. Our conversations soon evolve from a basic greeting to a friendlier style of talk. We introduce ourselves to each other, and I learn his name is João Batista. João is eighteen, a few years older than I am. After our initial introduction, we engage in real conversations, however, conversation proves to be difficult when he is working. We must keep our encounters short, so we try to find spare moments to talk whenever possible. I go to the store often to buy bread and milk, and my father comments why we have so much supply of both. Victoria and I both shrug at his questions. I tell Victoria everything, so she knows about João, our conversations, and I admit to her that I like him. My brothers are oblivious to the situation, as most boys are.

CHAPTER 14

1942 - 1944

BEFORE LONG, IT is clear João likes me. His feelings for me show on his face; his cheeks become crimson red when I am near, and soon a courtship between us inevitably develops. When his eyes set on mine, his expression changes. His smile widens when I walk into the store, and he often puts items on the wrong shelves. I distract him without meaning to, and this makes me giddy. One day, I stand behind a shelf faking interest in a loaf of bread. I watch as he places a jar of jam preserves on a shelf meant for flour. He is focused on me and does not pay attention to what he should be doing, and this fills my heart. No other boy has ever had this effect on me, and I smile more since meeting him than I have all my life. I long to be with him every day, and my chest tightens when we are apart. I go into the store almost daily now, for no reason but to see him, and I leave empty-handed. The store clerk, who happens to also be his supervisor, knows I come to see João and not to purchase anything. He is a generous man, allowing João to take his lunch breaks during my visits so we can have some time alone.

During João's lunch breaks we go to the park across the road to talk and enjoy each other's company. We discuss many things: our families, politics, and even religion. I love sitting on the bench and listening to João tell me stories of his childhood. I love his stories, and if the words come from him, I am happy to listen to anything he says. João is gentle, kind and considerate towards me; he lays his handkerchief down for me to sit on, so I do not get my dress dirty. He opens every door I walk through and gestures for me to go through first. He holds my hand and gives it a gentle squeeze, letting me know how he feels. He is a real gentleman, the kind most girls can only dream about. We continue to meet in secret for many months.

My new love lives with his mother, a few blocks away from the store where he works. His father has lived in Lisbon since his parents separated years ago. His father left his mother for another woman, a younger version of his mother. He corresponds with his father often through the post. His father owns a few businesses in Lisbon and is a busy man, so he has not returned to Angola since he left three years ago. João and his mother are close since they only have each other.

We keep our relationship quiet, for no specific reason. The only people who know of our growing romance are the store clerk and Victoria. I do not know why the store clerk never mentions these encounters to my father, and I worry he will someday. But so far, he has not spoken a word to anyone.

After a few months, João begins to write me letters. The store clerk offers to deliver them to me in private whenever possible. Sometimes he stops by the house and makes up an excuse why he calls. Other times he delivers them to my school. Each letter is full of emotion and his declaration of love for me. I reply to each letter with an open and full heart, declaring my love in return. I am only thirteen years old, but I am convinced I know true love and that I am in it.

My father becomes suspicious, so I face many questions every time I leave the house. To ward off further suspicions, I bring my sister with me on my visits to the store and other outings. Manuela is young enough to not comprehend the situation I bring her into, so I do not worry about my secret being revealed. João also brings a friend with him, and this is to keep Manuela entertained, so he and I can be alone.

We decide one day to go to the local beach for an afternoon of fun, but the only way I can go on my own is if Manuela accompanies me. My father thinks if I take my little sister with me nothing bad will happen. We have a wonderful afternoon, running in the hot sand and shore of the Atlantic Ocean. We link hands and wade into the warm water, splashing one another. João continues to hold my hand tight, and we jump the waves as they crash into the shore. The water is rough today, and the waves are crashing hard against some rocks nearby. The crashing sound is loud, and we can hear it from where we are. I do not mind rough water; the higher the wave, the more fun we have. When our hands are shriveled up, due to staying in the water for so long, we go and sit on the beach for a while. We lie with our faces towards the sunlight, toes buried in the white sand. It is a marvelous afternoon of freedom, and I do not want this day to end. João reaches up to touch my face and turns my head around, so we face one another.

"What are you thinking about?"

"You."

"I cannot be the only thing in that pretty head of yours?"

"You fill my days, and my heart."

He leans in close and plants a kiss on my forehead. Manuela is still at the water's edge, she is too interested in looking for seashells to pay us attention.

"We need to leave soon. If you do not get home before suppertime, your father's suspicions will grow. I do not want to be responsible for you getting in trouble."

"Yes, I suppose we must go."

Our relationship continues with these secret rendezvous until 1944. We do not have a reason to hide our relationship, and I am not sure why we feel we must be discreet. But we both agree it is best for now, although we never do anything scandalous. It is acceptable for a gentleman to court a girl my age, if he does so in good moral standing. And so, we discuss this further one afternoon while João is on lunch. I wait for him on our usual bench at our regular meeting place. He leaves the store with a frown, but it turns into a smile the moment his eyes lock with mine. He walks over, sits beside me, opens his sandwich bag and offers me a piece. We eat and sit together for the rest of the time that remains of his lunch break. Anxiety builds for both of us, as we know we soon must part. João's arm rubs mine as he shifts in his seat to get closer to me. He is fidgety today, and I notice a bead of sweat on his forehead, even though it's a cooler afternoon. A few times he opens his mouth to speak, but no words come out. A few minutes later, he tells me what occupies his mind.

"Rosa, I love you. I never thought I would love someone as much as I love you. You have brought happiness to my life, and I want you to be my wife one day. I want to talk to your father. It is time, so I will ask him for your hand in marriage. If you will have me?"

I am caught off guard as I was not expecting this now, someday yes, but not now. I answer him almost immediately, even though this proposal comes as a surprise.

"Yes, of course, I will be your wife. There is nobody else I would rather spend the rest of my life with."

"That makes me the happiest man alive."

"You make me the happiest girl."

We discuss our plans in more detail that afternoon and decide to wait another year, until I am finished school, by then I will be sixteen. I have found my first love and the one I dreamed of since I was a little girl.

That afternoon João returns to work an engaged man, and I skip home with a grin on my face. At night, I dream of the wedding day, and the next night I dream of the children we will have. By the third night, I name each child, and in my mind, I am already raising a big and happy family with João. Then on the fourth night after our engagement, I have another terrible nightmare.

We are back at the same beach where we spend our precious afternoons together. The beach is empty, and the sand that is usually light in colour is dark brown. It is foggy, and there is a mist over the water, almost eerie-like. João is standing at the water's edge looking out onto the ocean, and I make my way to him. I call out his name, but he does not answer me. He looks like he is in a daze. He does not hear me approach him, and I reach out my arm to hold on to him, but he drifts, until I can no longer reach him, until he is swallowed whole by the ocean.

I wake up in a sudden panic. This feels so real, like João is slipping away. I then tell myself, it is only a dream. Only a dream indeed.

CHAPTER 15

1944

ONE MORNING, I receive a letter from the store clerk to meet João at the park after my lunch with my family. This request is not unusual, and so I skip along on my way to meet him. When I arrive, he is sombre, his head is hung, and he will not look at me.

Dreams can be our subconscious mind trying to tell us something, however, dreams can also be a representation of our deepest and darkest fears. Sometimes they do not carry any meaning and we dream random and meaningless thoughts only to fill the void at night. This dream, however, was a sign, and the dream from my last night at Aunt Rita's house was a sign also.

João does not have the opportunity to discuss marriage with my father as we planned. Unforeseeable circumstances happen and derail our future, like my dreams tried to warn me.

"Rosa, my sweetheart, please do not cry."

João wipes a tear that falls down my wet face.

"I promise, I will come back to you. This is not forever. I will be back before you know it, and then I will marry you. You have my word.

I have not given any woman my word before, only you. You must know this and believe me."

I shake my head, indicating I understand, unable to respond.

Things have been going smoothly for so long, but now everything is ruined. João's father has died, and this changes our plans. I remain silent for a long time, and a few minutes pass before I find my voice.

"I know you will come back to me, João. It is just hard to know you will be so far away. Portugal is another world. We will be almost six thousand miles apart from one another. I do not know if my heart can take it."

Because João's father has passed away, he must go take care of his father's affairs: the funeral, inheritance, and other personal matters to do with his business. João is the only son, so this burden falls upon him entirely. There is no one else to take his place, and even if there were, it would not matter. His father's younger wife, the one he left João's mother for, has since left him, so this leaves João the only person in his father's will.

João's father had been sick for a long time, and João has never left Angola to visit him. I suspect that was because of me, therefore, I am in no position to prevent him from leaving now. I understand he needs to take care of his father's affairs, even if it kills me for him to do so. I have been strong before, so I must be strong once again. And I need to find strength once more.

"It is only for a few weeks you said, correct? And then you will be back?" I manage to ask through sobbing and tears.

"That is right. It is only for a few weeks my love, I promise."

"Write to me, every day while you are away."

"Every day, I promise," he says, as he kisses my forehead.

We say goodbye that afternoon as he is to embark in the next couple of days on a boat that will take him to Lisbon. There is no further opportunity for us to meet before his departure. I look deep into his eyes, and I can see from his face he truly does not want to leave me, and this realization brings me comfort. Knowing he loves me provides me with hope that he will soon return. His words, promising me he will come back, are the words in my head day in and day out after he leaves me.

~~~

I am miserable over the next few days. I refuse to eat anything, and I do not even want to leave my room. Days turn into weeks before I finally receive the first letter from João. He is gone five weeks by the time the first letter reaches me.

Dearest Rosa,

My love, I cannot begin to express how difficult these past weeks have been without you. I have grown so accustomed to seeing your bright smiling face and dark shiny eyes every day. I have become used to your touch when you gently place your hand on my elbow. I love hearing your soft-spoken voice. I am in agony here without you, but I must do what I can to get my father's affairs in order.

I arrived in time for his funeral, so it was a good thing I made the arrangements beforehand. It was a large funeral, my father had lots of friends and work acquaintances attend. There was not much family present though, so the seats were taken up mostly by friends. I hope he is pleased with the outcome as he looks down upon us from above while we grieve for him.

I am working fast to settle his accounts, so I can return to you. Until then, remember the promises I made to you and you only.

With Love,
João

I place the letter under my pillow that night after reading it over and over the entire day. My pillow is my safe place, my haven where I hide my secrets. Each night when I lay my head on the pillow, I reach under it to feel for the letter and hope it is not there. I pray this entire month has been a dream, so I reach under the pillow hoping to find empty space between my pillow and mattress, but the space is not empty. The letter is always there filling the gap, as a reminder that João is gone for real.

Another month goes by, I receive more letters, and I respond to each one in turn. After three months, I have bad thoughts that he is never to return to me, and I grow impatient.

Dearest João,

Love of my life, please hurry, come back to me and marry me. I am being patient here, but it's now been three months. When will you be finished?

With love,
Rosa

How long can it take to close out a few accounts and settle someone's belongings? It's now five months later, but the letters provide no indication of his return.

I try to make new friends this year as my teachers once suggested, and so I befriend a girl my age named Liza. This new friend of mine has recently gone to Lisbon with her family, and when she returns she calls on me, so we can talk. I let out a shriek as I open my door and see her standing here. She gives me a big hug and I invite her inside. I offer to make us tea, she accepts, so I get to work as she sits at the kitchen table. She crosses her hands on the table, takes a deep breath in and slowly lets it escape.

"Rosa, I am sorry I must be the one to tell you this …. It might be nothing, but I do not know."

"What is it, Liza?"

The water boils and as I pour it into the mugs, I spill it over the counter. "Merda!" *Shit!*

"While in Lisbon, I …I think I saw João."

"Oh, did you talk to him? Did he see you?"

"No. We did not speak, he was rather … occupied."

"Occupied how?"

"He was walking with another woman, and he had his arm on her back, and they hugged."

A hard jolt of pain fills my stomach, I drop one of the mugs I am carrying, and it breaks into pieces when it hits the hard floor. I have an unsettling feeling in the pit of my stomach I cannot shake for days, so I write to João asking him about this woman.

Dear João,

I hear you are rather occupied in Lisbon, not so much with your father's affairs but with your own. You see, my good friend was there not long ago, and she saw you with another woman. Is she the reason you have not returned to me? Is she the reason why you left in the first place? Liza, my friend, says she saw you with your arms around this woman. João, I trusted you, and you betrayed me. How could you?

Sincerely,
Rosa

Consuming myself in misery, I wait for his reply to come, and when it arrives, my hands shake as I open the envelope.

My Dearest Rosa,

I do not know where your mind has gone. The woman your friend saw me with is my cousin.

You must not push me; I am not ready, as there is still work here to be done. My father was involved in many businesses and I have yet to complete the necessary preparations for the future of the business. I will be back, soon. We will marry upon my return. I gave you my word once, and I told you I have never given my word to any other woman. Rosa, this should be enough for you for now. There is no other woman, but you.

Do not give up on me; do not give up on us. I beg you.

Love Always,
João

Relief washes over me when I read his words, but I am still not one hundred percent convinced about the woman. I do not give up on him though, not yet, but after six months of absence, I do become devastated. The more time passes, the more I am convinced he is never to return. He is my first love, and the loss of a first love is always the hardest. My clothes now drape like a curtain from not eating, and I am forgetting basic things that I should remember.

I contemplate my future as I am not getting any younger, and I must come to a decision soon. I have no other prospect for marriage, and at fifteen, I am at a marriageable age.

A month later, Liza tells me she has an idea she thinks will help lift my drowning spirits. There is a gentleman, Vintoro, who has been courting her for the past few months, and he has a friend who wants to meet me. Liza arranges for the four of us to go out one night for coffee.

"It will be good for you to get out of the house, put on a nice dress, put up your long hair and meet someone. I promise he is a gentleman, and his name is Pedro Melo. Please come."

I hesitate at first, but she somehow convinces me to go along with this plan of hers. The meeting is set to occur the following Sunday afternoon, five days from today. So, I still have a few days to think things through and have time to get out of this situation if I so choose to. "Fine, I will go, but please do not push me. My heart still belongs to João," I say.

My head has moved on, but my heart remains still, locked in the past.

"When will you realize João is not coming back for you?"

"Of course, he is. He promised me."

"If I had a penny every time I heard a broken promise such as this one, I would be a rich girl."

She runs her fingers through her hair. "Hmmm, you know if I was rich, then I would not have to depend on a man to carry me through life."

"João is different."

"That is what women say when their eyes are tainted by love and they cannot see reality clearly."

Her last comment gives me something to think about.

"Do you know how often men go to Portugal to seek a wife and return married?" She is now standing over me with hands on her hips. "The women left waiting end up with no suitor because all others are turned away while they wait for their men to come back. You do not want this to be you, Rosa. You are much too strong a woman, so do not allow a man to fool you this way. It's time for you to face reality and move on."

These are harsh words, but the more I hear them, the more I am convinced what she says must be true. I need to move on with my life, and I am not sitting around and waiting for João to return married to someone else. This is not going to happen to me, I will not be that girl.

Although I am nervous, I still look forward to the meeting on Sunday. I plan what to wear days in advance. I inform my father of my plans and he approves, but only because it's a group outing.

When Sunday arrives five days later, I am ready for a new beginning. I receive one more letter from João, but I do not reply to it. This last letter contains much of the same arguments as the last few letters. He writes that he is still working hard, he is still coming back to marry me and misses me. I read this last letter with a different outlook than the other letters. This one does not even make it under my pillow with the rest. I toss this one into one of my drawers, convinced he is lying and not wanting to read another word. As I place my beaded pearl necklace from my father around my neck, I am reminded about what I am to do today. With no further thought of João or his letters, I make sure every strand of hair is tidy, and my dress is well-pressed. I run my hands down the front and enjoy the smooth silk touch as the fabric clings to my fingers. I am ready to impress Pedro.

Within the hour, Liza calls on me. "Rosa, you look beautiful," she says when I open the door. She has never seen me in my fancy church dress and my hair so perfect. I smile back at her, nod my head, and together we march arm in arm down the street, eager to get to our destination.

CHAPTER 16

1944

WE ARRIVE AT the coffee shop a few minutes later, and Liza points to where the gentlemen are sitting. Pedro sits with his back to the door, facing the counter, so he does not notice me at first. We make our way to their table, and there are two empty seats they reserved for us. Pedro turns his head and opens his mouth, dropping his jaw. He stands and watches me fidget with my dress in front of him. When the wrinkles in my dress are smooth, I look up at him and recognition sets in. I remember him from almost five years ago on the bus in Luanda. The man standing before me now has the same dark, semi-wavy hair and piercing brown eyes the boy from the bus had. I hold my breath for a few seconds as I realize without a doubt this is that boy, but now a grown man. I cover my mouth — I am afraid to make an embarrassing sound. This is a sign, and one so big, not even I can miss. Liza looks at me, startled, and then she introduces us.

"Pedro, this is Rosa."

Pedro takes my hand into his and brings it up to his lips. He kisses the top of my hand letting his lips linger on my skin, longer than necessary.

"It is my greatest pleasure to meet you my blooming Rose."

He does not remember me, or at least he pretends to not recognize me, and I go along with this. When I first set eyes on the boy on the bus all those years ago, a dark and unsettling feeling washed over me then. But years later, that boy now a man, has charmed me. My cheeks are burning, and as I notice more of his appearance I admire his broad shoulders and his square jaw. He stands about a foot taller than me, and he might even be taller than João. The moment that name enters my mind I push it away and bury it. Pedro pulls out a chair and gestures for me to sit. I graciously fan out my dress over the chair, cross my legs and place my hands on my knees. I try to remember to keep my back straight. We engage in some interesting conversation right away and find we have a lot in common. I tell him about my love for books, how much I like to read, and he tells me he likes to read as well. When I ask him about his favourite books and his most read authors, he changes the subject, but I do not care because his charm has enticed me.

We spend hours drinking coffee but after my third cup I switch to tea, fearing I will be up all night. Pedro orders sweets for us to share, and we indulge in delicious chocolate cake and sweet bread. The evening cannot be more perfect. Once our bladders are full and our stomachs cannot take any more cake, we decide it is time to leave, and the four of us take a walk.

"A noite é jovem!" *The night is young!* Pedro proclaims to us. We agree, and Pedro insists on paying the entire bill. We leave the café, and Pedro walks close beside me, never leaving my side.

Pedro extends his arm so I can wrap my arm around his.

"Please, if you will?" he says.

He is a real gentleman, and so I slip my arm through his.

The night is indeed young, it is early evening, and the weather is exceptionally warm. We walk around town for an hour, Pedro always close at my side. Liza and Vintoro walk up ahead, arm in arm. When it is late afternoon, we head back to the café. The café is close to my house and Liza and I are to walk home together from here. I do not want Pedro coming to my house, not yet. Before the gentlemen leave, Pedro asks to speak to me in private, and so Vintoro and Liza leave us alone outside the entrance of the café. My hands are shaky, and my knees are weak. What does he want to speak to me about?

He reaches for my hand and pats it a few times before speaking. "Rosa, never in my wildest imagination did I think I would meet someone like you. Marry me? Please. Do me this honour in allowing me to be your husband. You will want for nothing with me in your life," he says.

"Pedro, I don't know what to say, we do not even know each other."

"Exactly, and a lifetime as husband and wife will allow us to get to know each other more."

"I do not know, I must think about this."

"What is there to think about?"

I remember the encounter on the bus all those years ago. "Nothing, I suppose. All right, I will marry you."

I am blown away by his proposal, but I am also impressed by him and I tell him he must discuss marriage with my father. If my father agrees to the union, then I will marry him. I am thinking this is fate, it must be fate. Pedro must be the reason why I was in Luanda to begin with, and it starts to now make sense. God has planned and mapped out my life for me, and the encounter that we shared all those years ago was meant to be. It is because of that encounter I accept when he asks for my hand in marriage.

The next day, Monday morning, there is a loud and steady knock on the front door.

"Rosa, please answer the door," Victoria yells from the kitchen where she finishes breakfast. The room smells of freshly baked bread as I walk past her to the front door.

I open the door slowly, and before me stands Pedro. In his arms is a bouquet of red roses. I take the flowers from him, thank him and invite him inside. I tell him to sit and wait while I go and get my father. My heart is racing and beating fast, and I cannot believe he is here. He told me last night he would pay my father a visit and ask for my hand in marriage, but a part of me did not believe him. I was already lied to by a man I once loved, still love, and so I did not think Pedro would follow through with the promise either. But here he sits on my couch, waiting for my father's permission. I wander out of the room, with my head held high, not wanting to reveal my excitement. Once I am out of his view, I sprint. "Father, Father, Father, come!"

"Rosa, what is it? Why are you acting as such?"

I must catch my breath before I can speak again. "Father, there is a man in the living room. He wishes to speak with you at once."

"Very well."

He walks into the living room, sees Pedro sitting in his favourite lounge chair and looks back at me with a stern look. At the sight of my father, Pedro stands and reaches his hand out to greet him.

My father introduces himself and the two men exchange pleasantries for a few moments. Pedro announces he wishes to speak to my father privately. My father asks me to leave the room, so the men can discuss business. I do not go far, though, and remain within hearing distance down the hall and around the corner so I can stay hidden.

"Mr. Soares, I am here to ask for your daughter's hand in marriage."

Upon hearing these words, I gasp and cover my mouth with both hands. He did it, and my father gave Pedro his blessing. I am promised to be married, and I clap my hands gently, not wanting to be heard.

Victoria walks over within moments, so she too, heard the news. My father calls me back to the living room and Victoria follows. She gives me a questioning look, because she knows I am still not over João. I look away not wanting to reveal my true feelings to her, or to myself. Victoria knows me, and one look into my eyes is all it will take for her to see the truth. Victoria invites Pedro to stay for breakfast, and he accepts the invitation eagerly. Pedro has everyone laughing for most of the meal. He is a real sweet talker, and even Manuela warms up to him. I am on cloud nine, oblivious to his smooth ways and charming smile. My father seems pleased also, and that is enough for me. The only person who keeps a distance from Pedro and questions him a lot is Victoria. For some unknown reason, she is more distant towards him than the rest of us are.

Pedro finishes his meal, thanks my father and Victoria for the hospitality, and shakes my father's hand as he walks toward the door. He leans into me close, kisses my cheek, and says he will call tomorrow. As I close the door behind him, he says, "What a splendid day."

He seems pleased, and why shouldn't he be? He has secured himself a wife, and I have gained the opportunity for a family of my own. I now have security.

CHAPTER 17

1944

AS PROMISED, PEDRO calls every day, and he wants to get married right away. But over the course of the last few days, different thoughts consume me. I still believe seeing him on the bus was a sign from God, but I cannot get João off my mind. And so, I try to convince Pedro there is no rush in marriage. I do not love him, so for me, this marriage is about convenience and security, rather than love. I don't understand his urgency, and I say this to him, but he tells me he loves me and is eager to start our life together. He puts pressure on me and asks me daily if I have changed my mind. I have not had a change of heart, but I do try to keep myself busy until I can become more comfortable with the idea.

Victoria tries to convince me to wait and not rush into this marriage. It is because of her advice that I do wait. My caring stepmother and I remain close over these years. She is still my confidant and the one I run to when I am upset, hurt, or need company.

One morning, as she and I walk to the market, she brings up the subject of my birth mother again. We often talk about her when we are alone. We walk side by side on the sidewalk, and my stomach growls, so I pick a banana from a nearby tree. I peel back the still yellowish peel when she tells me about my birth mother. She says she knows her, and I almost choke on the banana when she says this.

"You can't know her, she is dead," I say.

"Rosa, please believe me, I do not know who she is. But I do know of her through acquaintances. She is still alive."

"That is impossible. My father told me she died."

I stop walking and throw away the remainder of the banana; I am no longer hungry.

"Your father wants you to believe she is dead."

"Why?"

"To avoid questions. He is trying to protect you."

She reaches out to touch my arm. We are standing on the side of the road.

"How long have you known?"

"For a long time, since I met your father."

She takes my hand in hers to encourage me to continue walking. I pull away, and she respects the distance between us.

"She asks lots of questions about you, I know this through my acquaintance. She found out where you live, and she wants to see you. This is what my friend tells me."

"Which friend?"

"That is irrelevant, and you do not know her. Rosa, I have not met your mother, I give you my word. If you decide you want to forget we had this conversation, I understand. I promise to not bring up the subject of your birth mother again if that is what you prefer."

"No, I do not want to forget this, I want to know more."

"Do you want to know her name?"

My breath forms a knot so big I cannot swallow. I must remind myself to breathe, something that under normal circumstances comes naturally.

"I already know her name, my father told me once."

"So, you know her name is Antonietta."

"Yes, that is the name he gave me when I was little."

"Rosa, you must understand, I have been dying inside keeping this from you. I was waiting for the right time to tell you."

She tries to look at me, but I cannot meet her eyes.

Growing up not knowing my birth mother left me with many questions: do I look like her; do I have her smile, her eyes? Do I laugh the same way she laughs? I have asked myself these questions for sixteen years. Am I now, after all this time, going to have the opportunity to find out for myself? That same thick knot forms in my throat again.

Over the years I have tried to ask my father about my birth mother, but to no avail. My father always says she died and does not know how or when. He promised me on several occasions that he knows nothing more about her, so is this a lie fabricated to protect me?

All these years she has been dead to me, when in fact, she is alive, well and wants to know me. A sudden rush of emotions flows through me that I cannot control. The blood inside my veins burns like I am on fire. I tell Victoria I forgive her and do not blame her for keeping the truth from me. I also tell her how appreciative I am of her and all she has done, not only for me but also for my family.

I want to meet Antonietta, of this I am sure. Victoria tells me my father wants nothing to do with my mother, and he does not want me knowing the truth. My father knows about the information Victoria holds. They have spoken about this, but he demands she remain quiet and this concerns Victoria. We resume walking and approach the market's entrance, so Victoria lowers her voice to keep the conversation private because we see people we know here.

"Rosa, if I do this, you must promise me one thing."

"Depends on the promise you need me to make."

"You need to promise to not tell your father. This is important, and you must promise before we move forward with any plans."

"Okay."

"I need you to promise and say those words; otherwise I will deny having this conversation. It pains me to say this, but your father's feelings and faith in me are important."

I contemplate this for a few minutes, so I do not answer her right away. My knees are shaking, and it takes me a couple of minutes to regain my composure. I pretend to look around the shelves, but I am a bundle of emotions inside. If I make this promise, it means I am lying to my father. I walk back to where Victoria stands and give her my decision.

"I promise. My father will not know. You have my word."

"Pronto," *Very well,* she says.

She tells me she will be in contact with her acquaintance to determine how to proceed. "It might take a few days to arrange the meeting," she says.

I do not care how long it takes; I am thrilled at the prospect of meeting my mother, finally. My mother is alive. The outlook seems surreal to me and fills my thoughts, so I do not think of Pedro or João all day.

In the days leading to the reunion, Pedro calls daily, telling me we must get married right away, but I still do not understand his urgency. My feelings toward him are uncertain, to be truthful. I do want to marry him, but I do not feel with him what I felt with João. I keep waiting for the feelings to come, but they never do. I try to ignore this and tell myself it does not matter, Pedro will be a good provider and that is more important. I also remind myself about the sign from God, and a union with Pedro is my destiny, but for now I focus on the reunion with my mother. I am scared and excited about the meeting, and I am overwhelmed over the situation. I must ask Pedro to give me some time to work this out. After this is settled, I will marry him as planned. A few weeks are what I need from him, a few weeks to get through meeting my mother and to deal with any aftermath. Pedro and I have only known each other for three weeks, so we can afford to wait for two or three more. It is ironic to consider a reunion with my birth mother a settlement, but that is how I view the situation — I am getting closure.

I ask Pedro to be more patient with me, and his reaction does not surprise me. "You have made me wait weeks already; I will not be here forever. You better hurry before I change my mind."

I do not know him well enough to know if I should be concerned about this threat or if he is bluffing. Nonetheless, as unhappy as he is, he does agree to give me space for the next few weeks, and I receive no visit or note from him during this time. I wonder if he, too, has broken the promise like João.

João's letters have stopped coming altogether; I have not received another letter from him since the one I threw into my drawer. João must have concluded I am on to him about the other woman. He broke his promise; he must have, why else have the letters stopped? There cannot be any other explanation, and I am too stubborn to listen to any other reasons.

I wait patiently over the next few days for word from Victoria's contacts about details on the reunion.

"Está tudo resolvido," *It is settled,* says Victoria.

She informs me a day later, right after my father leaves for work. "We are to meet your mother on Thursday, two days from now. Arrangements are made for you to meet her at a busy park not far from here."

"Why a busy park?"

"It is more natural, it will not appear as if you are trying to be secretive."

"What if someone recognizes me?"

"They will think you are out with a friend. I hear your mother looks young."

"So, this is happening?"

"Yes. Are you ready for this Rosa? This is a big day and a huge step. If you are not ready, you can still back out. I support you no matter what decision you make. But you must remember the promise you made not to tell your father."

"I understand, and yes I am ready." I lie to her about being ready, but the promise to not tell my father, I will forever take to my grave.

As the day draws near, my anxious feelings subside, little by little. I become more comfortable with the idea and by the night before, I am emotionless. I now view this reunion as any other meeting, and the overwhelming emotions I was feeling before are no more. I do not know why I view this differently now, and I think in part the change of heart is to protect myself, so I put up a barrier. If I do not care, then I cannot get hurt again.

Thursday comes too soon, but I am prepared and trying to keep myself emotionally uninvolved, so I do not get hurt. My barrier is up full force.

Victoria accompanies me on this day. "Are you nervous, Rosa?"

"No." I am nervous, so I lie.

"You must be a little nervous?"

"Not at all." More lies.

"Ok, I understand. You do not want to talk about it and that is fine. I am here for you though, so please remember that. I will not be too far away." She gives me instructions on where to go once we enter the gate, and she also tells me where she will be waiting for me. "Take as much time as you need. I will be here when you are ready."

"Thank you for everything Victoria."

She embraces me in one of her warm hugs and holds me for an extra-long time. I wonder if she feels like she is losing a daughter now that I am meeting my birth mother. I hope she knows that no one, not even this Antonietta woman can replace her. I should tell her this before I go, but I do not say a word and keep this to myself. I leave Victoria and head down the path following her clear instructions. I am ready to face my past, eager to meet my mother, and am armed to ask her the questions I wanted to ask for sixteen years.

CHAPTER 18

1944

THE PATHWAY LEADING to the opening of the park has flowers of all colours and sizes running along its sides. The path reminds me of the gardens at Aunt Mariazinha's house. As I walk through the clearing at the end of the path, there is a woman about the age of thirty. She does not look much older, there are no wrinkles on her face, and her shiny hair displays no grey. She is youthful looking and beautiful. Her skin is flawless, and her eyes remind me of a china doll, big, dark, and piercing. She has an aura about her that makes me want to approach her; although my internal guard warns me to keep some distance. So, I do not approach her right away, instead I stare for a few minutes from afar. Her hair, straight posture, slim figure, and beauty captivate me. This is not a dream, this is real, and this here is my real mother.

After a few minutes, I clear my throat to alert her of my presence. I do not want to startle her; it is awkward standing here staring for so long. She takes a graceful turn towards my direction and whispers my name with so much passion. I have not heard my name spoken like this before, "Rosa!"

She says nothing else for a minute. I want to speak, to ask her the questions I came to ask, but I am at a loss for words. We both stand to look at each other, not knowing what to do next or what to say. Tears flow down her perfectly sculpted, oval-shaped face. She wipes the tears with her sleeve and pulls out a colourful handkerchief from her bag to gently blow her nose. I note the handkerchief's colour, my favourite colour, red. We must have this one small detail in common if nothing else. She adjusts her immaculate dress, straightening the front, and takes a step toward me.

She suggests we sit on the old cement bench, it's big enough for two, but I remain standing. A group of children laugh and play on the creative while their mothers sit a safe distance away, watching. How different my life might have ended up if I was raised by my mother, but I will never know.

"Please Rosa, sit. We have much to talk about. I am sure you have many questions for me."

I gather enough courage to say, "Hello Antonietta."

This is all I can muster out of my lungs at this moment, and I cannot bring myself to call her Mother, she is no one to me. My fingers are busy playing with the hem of my dress, legs swinging rhythmically. I cannot stay still. Antonietta notices my discomfort, tells me to relax and places her hand on my knee. "I am happy you came," she says.

She speaks first of the past and how she never wanted to let me go. She talks of the long, lonely years without me, and how she longed to hold me in her arms and care for me.

"Your father tore us apart, Rosa. He stole you from me. I did not want to let you go but I was young. I was only fifteen. Your father was much older, more powerful, and had more connections than I ever will. You see, he is white and I am black, and that gives him more power and more privileges than I could ever dream of having. What else was I to do? I was a young unmarried black girl with no future and no rights to you."

She stops speaking for a minute to give me an opportunity to say something, but I remain quiet.

"Please understand the situation I was in," she says.

My legs stop swinging, but I am still playing with the hem of my skirt. "He told me you died."

"I know he told you that. He does not want us to reunite."

"But why?"

"It must frighten him for you to know I am alive. You will ask questions and might even search for me. Your father loves you, that is evident. I have never doubted his love for you. He does not want to lose you."

"How would he lose me?"

"He is afraid of losing you to me," she says.

Antonietta suggests we take a walk, so we do and then return to the same bench. We fall into a comfortable ease with one another, and we talk for the next two hours. The children that were here earlier leave and laughter that filled the air is replaced with a new group of children.

My mother wants to know about my upbringing. She asks many questions of me. Was I treated well? Am I happy now? She asks the expected questions a woman would ask her child after sixteen long years of absence. She cries a lot during our conversations, and I fear she will soon run out of tears. She reaches for the red handkerchief often to blow her red nose.

I do not look at the time, but it must be late because my stomach growls. I know we must end this meeting soon. Victoria is still waiting for me back on the other side of the pathway. Antonietta and I say goodbye, but we agree this will not be our only meeting. My mother tells me she wants to see me again soon, so we plan to meet the following week.

I stand to leave, but she remains seated, watching me. She most likely is hoping I will not leave, but knows I must.

"Rosa, I cannot tell you what today means to me. To lay my eyes on you after all this time, my sweet daughter. I never once forgot you."

I smile back, but I do not respond. I turn away and begin walking up the path I walked down two hours earlier. I do not dare look over my shoulder, not even once. I am afraid of what I might see if I do. I am terrified I will see my mother, still sitting, watching me and weeping for the daughter she never had the opportunity to raise. This image would break my heart, so I would rather not witness it.

Once I pass the clearing at the end of the path, Victoria is waiting for me as promised. I run straight into her arms and weep like a baby.

The next day, Pedro comes to the door. He has a stern look on his face, arms crossed, and he stands before me waiting for answers to questions he has not asked.

"Pedro, please be patient with me," I plead. "You must understand, I am going through family issues. This is an emotional time in my life, please give me space."

I have not told Pedro about my mother because I do not know if I can trust him, so he does not know what the family issues are. He exhales loudly, says not a word, and storms away. I am too concerned with Antonietta to care at this point, so I let him go and shut the door once he is out of view.

Antonietta and I continue to see each other often, but this, of course, is in secrecy. My father can never know about our rendezvous, I promised Victoria, and I intend to keep that promise. We meet at least once a week, and we get to know each other well during this time. I learn a lot about her childhood, and she learns about mine. We share memories, stories, and dreams with each other. We continue to see one another weekly over the next few months. Victoria encourages our relationship, and she is happy for me, for us. With such an emotional part of my life under control, I daydream about my future once again; the future involving my fiancé and our upcoming marriage. I am now able to move forward with the decision I once made to marry Pedro.

I am ready to become his bride.

CHAPTER 19

1945

AFTER THE SECOND World War ends in Europe, things change for our colony. There is a sudden increase in the demand for coffee in the world, and this includes Angola. The coffee industry rises, and this increases the coffee production for Angola exponentially. Most coffee is produced on larger plantations owned by white settlers, however, in the north, some coffee is still grown on smaller plots of land owned by African peasants. Coffee becomes a welcomed and regular part of our daily lives.

I am sixteen years old, soon to be married. This still does not seem real to me. When I say this out loud, I have a hard time believing my own words. Pedro surprises me, but not in a good way. He does not seem pleased when I tell him we can proceed with the marriage plans. He is quiet when I give him my news, has a faraway look, and does not pay me much attention. I notice changes in him these past few days, but my mind is still too preoccupied with Antonietta to notice anything alarming. He is much more demanding, short, and rude when he speaks to me, and he does not smile anymore. It is peculiar, as if he has lost his charming way. He becomes more accusatory and he never believes what I tell him anymore. His visits are now less frequent, but when he comes, he questions me on my whereabouts the evening before, not trusting me.

We are sitting outside on our front porch one early morning. He stops by before work a few times a week now rather than daily. I clench my cup of coffee in my hands as I brace myself to ask him about his mood.

"Pedro, what is wrong? What have I done to upset you?" I ask, but I know I have not done anything.

"I do not think I can marry you anymore," he announces.

I shift in my seat to get a better look at him. I narrow my eyes, forming a new wrinkle on the bridge of my nose. "Why?" I am not sure where this comment has come from.

"I have my reasons."

I raise my eyebrows and move in closer to him. "You were in such a hurry before? Please tell me. What changed?" I ask, curious to know.

"If you must know, then I will tell you."

"Yes, I must know."

"I do not believe you are a virgin," he says, but he does not look me in the eye.

Not a virgin! What on Earth is this man talking about? I am as innocent as a newborn baby, raised well and with good morals. I have not done anything more than hold hands with João, so his words stir up odd feelings inside that I cannot explain. My eyes well up with tears. Perhaps Pedro has found out about my past relationship with João? Is this possible? I have not told Pedro about him yet.

I gather my courage to respond to his harsh accusations. "Pedro you must speak with reason. Please tell me, what got into you? What compels you to say such horrible things about me?"

He continues to avoid looking at me when he answers. "I have ears you know, and I heard the rumours."

"Really, what rumours exactly did you hear? Because I can assure you they are only what you said, rumours."

He storms off the porch. I let him go and do not go after him. Perhaps my mistake is not being open and honest about João. He must have found out I was previously engaged, so he is furious.

Pedro stays away for the next three days, but when he returns he comes with the same accusations. This time though, I am determined to know more about the rumours he is worried about. "Please, Pedro, let's talk this through. I need to understand why the sudden change in your attitude."

His nostrils flare. "My attitude towards you? Rosa! You have some nerve! Speaking like you are a virgin when you and I both know that is not true."

"Of course, it is!" I say defensively. I am now yelling back at him.

"I have been cheated out of a wife who is innocent and pure. I do not know if I can marry you under these circumstances. I thought you were a virgin."

"Pedro, you are not being fair!"

"You are the unfair one here, not me," he says facing away from me.

I do not know how to answer him anymore. No matter what I say, he is too stubborn to listen. Then I decide on the truth. "Pedro, please, you must understand while I did have a fiancé before I met you, we never did anything more than hold hands. My father does not even know about him. He is gone, never to return to my life again," I say calmer this time, hoping to reach him.

He whips his head around to face me, and his eyes are open wide. "Lies, more lies from you are all I hear."

Hmm, he does not know about João based on his reaction to my confession. My chest feels tight. Am I too young to have a heart attack? I take in a deep breath and clear my throat before I speak again. "I am most certainly a virgin; I have never been with another man before. It is your choice if you choose to not believe me."

I manage to get these last words out without choking. Pedro does not reply, but he storms off to work, leaving me feeling as if the wind is blowing right through my centre of gravity and knocking me off my feet.

We continue to argue over João for the next few days. He still accuses me of not being a virgin, and I try desperately to convince him of the truth, that I most certainly am.

I do not understand why he keeps coming to see me if he has already told me he cannot marry me. His actions and words are not aligned, and I do not understand why, in fact, I do not understand him. If he does not want to marry me anymore, why does he keep coming back to badger me? I ask myself this often, but I do not dare ask him why, afraid of what ludicrous answer he might give me.

Towards the end of the week, I decide I need to be even more straightforward with him and put an end to this nonsense. He comes to see me again in the morning before work. He does not knock, but rather remains outside expecting me to come out. Out the window, I see him pacing, so I prepare us both coffees. He is sitting on the porch step when I bring him his cup. I sit next to him and gently place the mugs on the top step, not wanting to spill the overflowing liquid.

"Pedro, I do not know how we are going to fix this. What do I need to do to prove my innocence to you? Please tell me and I will do it."

For the first time in weeks, his eyes brighten. "Well, there is one thing you can do for me," he says.

"Tell me, I will do anything."

I am desperate at this point.

"You must go to bed with me. This is the only way to settle this matter. I must know before we get married if I am marrying a virgin. There is no other way to know. I will be able to recognize a virgin."

It is not even a full second after he finishes speaking that my eyes well up with tears. I turn my face away, so he does not see me crying. All my life I knew I would wait until marriage to go to bed with a man, but before me sits my future husband demanding otherwise. If I refuse, he will call the wedding off, so I am trapped. Sharp pains in my heart return. The pain is so deep it pushes my heart into the cavity of my chest. I bring my hand up to my chest to soften the blow, but it does not help. I have no choice but to do what he demands. As I contemplate his threat, I ask myself why I care so much if I do not even love him. But the answer is simple, I do not want to disgrace my father by having to tell him the wedding is off, and especially why. Pedro will spread these horrible rumours faster than the plague. What difference does it make anyway, if this man is to be my husband, then I should follow through. Nobody needs to know it happened before the wedding and not after, the way it is supposed to be, is meant to be, between husband and wife.

Pedro has an apartment of his own, but I have never been to his apartment before. An unmarried couple should not socialize together at a man's apartment. That is not lady-like, and I am a lady despite what Pedro thinks. The next day, I walk to his side of town. He does not live too far, but by foot it still takes thirty minutes. I arrive soaked in sweat and run my fingers through my hair to try to smooth the frizz. I knock lightly, secretly hoping he does not answer, but he opens the door a little too eagerly.

"My Rosa, you have arrived on time. Please come in," he says, as he steps to the side to give me room to enter.

He is much happier today than he has been the last few weeks. He is nice to me again, and his voice is soft, like in the beginning when we first met. He takes my hand in his and leads me into his apartment. It is a small space, one bedroom, tiny kitchen, and I wonder how any meals can be cooked in here, it is that small. There is clutter on the counters, dirty mugs with coffee stains and dirty bowls in the sink. The floor needs sweeping, and as I step over crumbs, they crunch under my feet. To the right is a small living room containing only a couch and coffee table with no room for any other furniture. Off to the side of the living room is a small bathroom. I notice the lack of closet space. If we live here after we are married, where in this tiny closet will I fit my clothes?

He tells me to sit in the living room and offers me a drink. "I have tea, coffee, and red wine, what would please you, my dear?"

Did he just offer me wine? I have never had wine before. I do not think today is a good day to start. "Nothing right now, thank you though." My hands are shaking, and I try to hide them by placing them under my legs.

"Very well then, shall we get on with business?"

Business? This is how he refers to our first night together as man and wife, like business? I am not prepared to stay the night, my family is expecting me home in a few hours, at least before it is dark. I have not told Pedro this, but I assume he knows and I expect him to understand.

"Well, come with me," he says smiling again as he leads me into his bedroom. My hands are no longer the only part of me shaking. I am petrified of what is happening and want to get this over with. I have information on what to expect when a man and woman go to bed, but sweat still accumulates under my shirt, staining my blouse.

"Will this hurt?"

"Hurt? No, of course not, silly woman."

"Okay, this is good to know."

His bedroom is small, with only enough room for a tiny bed, intended for one, or possibly two skinny people. It is a good thing I am small, or we would not both fit. He keeps the windows open, and the fresh sea breeze whips through the long curtains as they fly through the space between us. The curtains blow around the room, tickle my arms, and I get the shivers from the curtains' touch rather than from the breeze.

I ruminate back to earlier today, while at my father's house. I had tried to dress nice for Pedro, and so I put on my church dress. This had caught the attention of my brother Julio. "Where are you going dressed like that Rosa?" He caught me before I walked out the door. I ignored him, not saying a word and kept on walking out into the street.

Now that I am here at Pedro's apartment, I wonder if Julio suspects where I am. There is heaviness in my chest again. Pedro is sure to cause me a heart attack soon if this keeps up.

"Relax, Rosa."

He strokes my arms, my legs, and then pushes me flat on my back onto the bed. He is not rough with me, but he is not gentle either. I have an image in my head, as most girls do about their first time with a man, and this is not how I picture my first time. My vision of my first time is pure, sweet, a loving moment between my husband and me, opposite what I feel now. I must get this over with, then we can be married, and I can start my life and have a family of my own. I dream of the many children I will someday have.

Pedro is mistaken; it does hurt, a lot, and I bleed, too. This must be the proof he needs to know I am still a virgin, or rather was one before now. When it is over, we lie on his bed in silence. I whisper in his ears as if I am afraid of anyone else hearing me, even though we are alone. "Pedro?"

"What is it?"

He seems annoyed now judging by his tone.

"Do you believe me now about being a virgin?"

He clears his throat. "Rosa, do you think I ever thought you were not a virgin? I would not be courting you or asked your father for your hand in marriage if I thought otherwise."

He says this while not even looking at me. Why can he never look me in the eye when he speaks to me anymore? My heart beats faster and faster as I listen to him speak the truth for once.

"So then why force me to go to bed with you?"

Is this man using me? He does not answer my questions directly.

"You are so young and so naïve. You have much to learn yet."

He is right; I do have a lot more to learn about life and especially about men. He has been lying on his back, but now turns away from me, avoiding me. I remain frozen, on my back and trying to understand the situation I am in. Oh, dear God, what have I done?

CHAPTER 20

1945

HOURS LATER, I wake up with a foggy head — we fell asleep. The room is silent and there is no noise coming in from the open window. No voices linger from children playing in the streets, and no radio sound comes out of the speakers. Complete silence fills the small room. I look around at my surroundings, but it is so dark I cannot make out my own shadow. I search for the window with squinted eyes and I am met with darkness outside, too. The sun set hours ago, and I jump from a lying position when I come to this startling realization.

I am not sure what time it is, but I know I am expected to be at home with my family. I try to speak, but I am mumbling. I attempt to stand, but my legs will not move. It's like a nightmare when you are chased and your legs are glued to the ground. I look over to the right of me, Pedro is sleeping and snoring. It must be the snoring that wakes me, as I am a light sleeper. "Pedro, Pedro, wake up," I say when I can speak. He does not wake up, and so I shake him. "Get up now, I am serious. Get up NOW!"

He stirs at my rough touch. "What the hell is wrong with you? Why are you yelling?"

"Pedro, we fell asleep."

"So?"

"So? That is all you say. So? Do you understand how much trouble I will be in when my father realizes I am not home? He will kill me and you too. So, if I were you, I would figure out how to get out of this mess soon. You need to get me home fast and before …"

The sudden pounding on the apartment door cuts my ranting short. I put my hands on my head. "Oh God, that must be my father."

Pedro jumps out of bed, pulls on his pants while trying to walk, trips, continues to fumble and runs to answer the door.

"Where is she? Where is my sister? I know she is here." My brother Eduardo's voice echoes through the apartment. I am paralyzed with fear. It is not my father, but my brother is as bad. He storms into the bedroom as I gather my clothes and throw them on to cover myself. He becomes stiff when he sees me. "Let's go, now."

Tears cloud my vision as he drags me by the arm and out of the bedroom.

As he continues to drag me out of the apartment, there is more pounding on the door. The door bursts open with more force than needed. Before me stands my father with anger blazing from his fiery eyes. I look over to Pedro who stands beside the only small window in the room watching us. He scratches his chin and avoids eye contact. I do not argue with either my brother or my father, because this is not the time or the place. I pick up my things as fast as I can, but I fumble and drop items onto the floor. I am trying to hurry, but I cannot figure out which shoe goes on which foot. When I get my shoes on, my father grabs me by the elbow and escorts me out. I leave shamefaced and embarrassed with my father and Eduardo close by my side. They do not say a word to Pedro the entire time; it is as if he does not exist.

&

We make the short two-minute drive in silence, and when we arrive home my father does not say a word to me. I expect a lecture, yelling, or worse, but he does none of these things. Silence is the worst kind of punishment. Victoria looks at me with a solemn expression, and she shrugs when I look back at her. She cannot help me this time.

At night, I cry myself to sleep, but I do not sleep much. I wake twice through the night to change the pillowcase because it is wet with tears. The next morning my father storms into our bedroom, Manuela is still asleep. I am yet to fall asleep and have been up all night. It must be early still as the sun has not risen yet. My head is pounding at the front of my forehead above my eyes. "I want you downstairs, ready to go in ten minutes," he says too loud for my aching head.

"Where are we going, Father?"

"Não perguntes," *Do not ask*, he says.

He storms out while flapping his arms behind him. I still do not know where we are going, but as tired as I am, I get myself out of bed. I tiptoe to the washroom so I don't wake anyone else. I peek into the basin to see if there is water left from the night before and use what little there is to splash over my face. This is an attempt to try to conceal my puffy, swollen eyes, but the cold water does nothing for my appearance. I am a mess today, but I do not care. My head continues to throb, and as I rub my temples my father's voice blasts from the living room; so much for trying to not wake the rest of the family. I tiptoe back to my room and select a dress to slip over my head. The dress is grey, simple, and a representation of what I hope the day brings — a sense of simplicity.

I walk downstairs and meet my father at the door; he is already waiting for me, keys in his hand. I got ready in less than five minutes as I want to have a few moments to grab a piece of bread to eat, but the moment my father sees me, he grabs my arm and walks me out to the car. I am still oblivious to where we are going, and do not ask out of fear. He drives to a factory, and I presume this is where Pedro works. He gets out of the car and tells me to wait inside. From the front passenger seat I watch him approach some fellows that are on their break, and I spot Pedro amongst the crowd. My father heads toward him, arms swinging at his sides. When Pedro sees my father, he becomes fidgety and looks around. I struggle to roll down the window using both hands and all my strength, the window is difficult to maneuver, but I am desperate to roll it down because I want to hear the words exchanged between the men.

Both men are yelling, sometimes they take turns, and other times they yell simultaneously. My father tells Pedro he must come to City Hall to marry me today. He is insistent and says he is not accepting no for an answer. Pedro refuses this request at first, but then glances over at me. He looks deep into my eyes, and this is not something he has done in a long time. His expression softens when our eyes meet, and he has fewer creases on his forehead than he had a minute ago. I almost see the Pedro I once knew, the Pedro from when we first met, but only for a brief second.

He looks away from me and turns back to my father. I shudder when he speaks the words. "Fine, I will marry her."

"Very well," says my father.

He returns to the vehicle alone, leaving Pedro standing by himself with a frown. My father climbs back into the car and tells me Pedro promises to meet us at City Hall. As we drive I keep my head bent and my hands pressed together in a prayer formation. Rather than listening to my father ramble about the mess I created, I pray to God asking for help to get me through today.

One hour later we stand before the justice of the peace answering the popular question asked of many young couples in love. But I am not in love, so I answer this question with an empty heart.

"Rosa, do you take Pedro to be your husband?"

With my head still hung and looking at my feet, I answer, "I do."

There is no kissing of the bride, no flowers to decorate the room, and no white dress for me to wear. There is no celebration, no congratulations, and no words of encouragement from anyone. There is no other person at the wedding, other than my father, there is just me and my new unloving husband.

CHAPTER 21
1945

PEDRO AND I have been married for two months, and I can now say the man I first met is not the man I married. To shine a light on small stuff is to look for things that should remain hidden, and that is what I did not do; I allowed his truths to remain buried. I learned lots about life over the last few months. If I knew then what I know now, I would have made different decisions, I would have shined the light. If I had gone to live with Aunt Mariazinha and her family in Lisbon, I would not be in this marriage today. In fact, if I never left Lobito, I would not have seen Pedro on that bus in Luanda and would not have agreed to this union. I thought seeing him on the bus all those years ago was fate, a sign from God. Maybe it was, but not the sign I interpreted it to be. Perhaps it was a warning sign, warning me to stay away. I should have paid more attention and asked more questions. I am still learning, I am young, and trying my best despite my situation. I try to be the best daughter, best sister, and best wife, but the latter proves to be the most challenging.

Married life is nothing like I imagined as a little girl while dreaming of a white wedding and the life after. There are no kind words, no soft touch of the arms as he walks by, and no encouragement of any kind. Instead, he is cold, rude, and ignores me most days. He has never laid a hand on me, but he uses words to hurt me. He calls me lazy and stupid almost every day. For the most part, I learn to ignore him. This is the best approach and avoids arguments. Sometimes though, his words are so harsh they cut right through my heart.

After only being married a short time, I come to discover Pedro has an unpleasant past. I learn this from my brother Julio, as he too discovers Pedro's true character. This husband of mine is running from the authorities and has spent most of his teenage years on the run from the police. This is the reason he was in a hurry to marry me. He was hoping marriage would disguise his identity as the authorities are looking for a single man, not a husband.

The police are after Pedro for theft, and other criminal acts I am not even sure of the details on. He has already spent time in jail, and he is now wanted before the courts again. I am disappointed in myself for learning this now and not before. They say you do not know someone until you live with them and this is true in my situation. I only learn of this now, after we are husband and wife and when it is too late.

If the news about my husband is not heart-shattering enough, I also learn I am with child. It only takes once for this to happen, and it was on that dreadful day my brother and father came barging into the apartment. For the first two months, I have no idea why my body is changing. It is at eight weeks gestation that I understand there is a child growing inside me. The symptoms at first are new to me, and I do not know what changes my body is going through or why. I am not able to recognize the symptoms at first. I have not had a menstrual cycle for two months, but that does not alert me to anything because this is a normal cycle for me. The first few weeks I wake up nauseated and cannot eat as it makes my nausea much worse. I start vomiting about a week later. I lose weight and am tired all the time. I do not want to get out of bed, sleep is all I crave morning to night, and I have no energy. This is also about the same time when Pedro calls me lazy.

The first trimester is the most difficult, but after three months there are marked improvements. My nausea subsides a little, enough so I can now function. My belly expands, and I outgrow my clothes. Overall, my pregnancy is nothing out of the ordinary, at least when I compare to other women I know.

Even though I do not love my husband, I am not sorry I am pregnant. I am already imaging feedings, walks, holding the baby and soothing her. Somehow, I know in my heart this baby is a girl. When I tell people I am having a girl, they ask me how I can say this with such certainty, and I tell them the truth; I have a strong insight, but I know because of another dream.

As the morning sickness improves, I allow myself time to wallow in my own self-pity. How am I to handle a baby in an empty marriage with an unsupportive husband? I do not know if I am strong enough, but then I remember those difficult years spent in Luanda and how I survived them. I survived many things then: Ricardo, separation from my family, and hard work. I was weak, naïve and inexperienced, and while I am still those things, I am stronger now. What would my life be now if I had gone to Lisbon? It occurs to me for the first time that if I made a different decision then, I would be with João in Lisbon. Could that have been the destiny we should have had? I will never know.

It is a weekend, and I am walking to the store to purchase some needed things: sugar, bread, cheese, and milk. I cannot carry too much due to my burgeoning belly, and so this is a trip I now make several times a week. It is easier to buy a few items at a time to reduce the load I must carry.

As I walk to the store the sun shines, and I look up to the sky to feel the warmth of the sun on my face. When I bring my head down, my glance shifts, I think a ghost appears, but it is no ghost, it is my first love. It's João. I am six months into the pregnancy when we run into each other for the first time since he left. The dreadful day back in 1944, almost three years ago, rushes back to me. And now here he is in Lobito, standing right before my eyes once more.

He is on the sidewalk looking at a newspaper, my breathing quickens, and I wipe my eyes with my hands thinking my vision is blurry. I close both eyes and leave them shut for a few seconds before opening them again. On the corner of the next street, about a block from the store where I am headed, he stands tall and handsome as ever.

I am transported into one of the nightmares I get often that paralyzes my legs. As much as I try to move, I cannot as I am frozen here on the spot. He is here in front of my eyes, all this time later, why? How can this be? Why has he come back now? Has he come back for me? I do not know what to do, so I watch him like I did the first day we met. He looks up and turns his head over to my direction as if he can somehow sense me looking at him. He appears serious, his lips are tight, and he has a crease between his eyes. But the moment our eyes make contact, he smiles as recognition sets in. He drops the newspaper, runs to me and pulls me into a big embrace. He holds on to me for a few seconds longer than I am comfortable with. I try not to look at him so he does not see the tears forming in my eyes.

His arms are still around my shoulders when he speaks. "My Rosa," he whispers close to my ear. "I am so sorry, I know you are another man's wife now and I cannot call you my Rosa any longer." He stops speaking for a second and looks at his feet. "I received word about your recent marriage, and I also know you are with child."

"What are you doing here?" I gasp.

"I came back for you."

"João I …" I cannot finish the sentence. My voice is cracking. I try again, this time with more of a whisper so the effort in speaking is less. "João, I cannot believe it is you. You are here." I take a step back from him, there are many people on the streets, and I am uncomfortable with our proximity.

"Of course I am here, I gave you my word. I made you a promise to come back, only you forgot that promise, or you did not believe me."

"You were gone for so long. What was I supposed to do?"

"You were supposed to wait for me. I always told you I would come back, but you moved on without me. I had wanted nothing more than to come to you, to surprise you, marry you. But that is no longer possible. You are no longer mine."

At his confession, I am unable to hold back the tears any longer.

"I have only arrived three days ago, and I went to your house to see you. Your father answered the door, and he told me you were with your husband. Victoria must have heard my voice, so she came running to the door to see me, and she told me you are with child. Rosa, I do not know what to say, I have never stopped loving you. But now I must leave. I cannot stay here any longer. There is no place for me here."

"Oh João, I am sorry."

"Rosa, you must know the truth. She was my cousin."

My heart is broken into a million tiny pieces, smaller than a grain of sand. All the memories of us together come rushing back. I have been so careless, thoughtless, and I rushed into a relationship I do not even want. What led me to make such rash decisions in my life? I was in such a hurry to leave Luanda, to return to my normal life and start a family so I grew impatient. Patience is a virtue I do not possess.

João proceeds to tell me he thought the letters were getting in between us. He says at first the letters were special and warm, and then changed. Yes, that makes sense, and it was most likely around the time my friend put ideas in my head. He says he felt an emotional distance, so he decided to stop trying to convince me he was coming back. His business in Lisbon took a turn for the worse and ended up taking much longer than he imaged it would. He says he only hoped I would wait for him, which, of course, I had not. I moved on thinking he was not coming back for me, thinking he was being unfaithful and now it's too late.

We do not talk for too much longer as we both agree it is best to part ways soon, so we say goodbye. He walks away but stops on the other side of the road and turns his head to say one last thing. "Take care of yourself, Rosa." He blows me a kiss, and I watch him walk away from my life for the second time.

I am distraught, so I walk back home and completely forget why I have come here to begin with. I cannot see well, my vision is blurry from the tears.

When I arrive at Pedro's apartment with no groceries, he searches me for the bags I am not carrying and frowns. "This is why I say you are stupid. You leave the house to go to the store and come back empty-handed. You stupid, stupid woman."

It is only now I realize the silly mistake I made. "I am sorry Pedro, I was not feeling well, and so I decided it was best to return home. I need to rest."

I walk away with my head hung and go straight to our bedroom. I want to be alone with my thoughts, my memories, and misery that I created.

CHAPTER 22

1946

THE LAST THREE months of pregnancy pass with no further incidents. João leaves town, and I must move on. I cannot afford to look back, so I focus my energy on my pregnancy. I am healthy, gaining more weight than I should, and my belly is growing both outwards and sideways. A woman's body is amazing, and females make such sacrifices to grow life inside. I am more tired now than during the middle of the pregnancy; the baby must be using more of my energy.

Pedro is not home much anymore, especially not when I need him most, so I spend a lot of time at my father's house with Victoria and my sister.

Antonietta calls on me at the apartment often. She says she likes to check in on me to offer help in any way she can. When she is here visiting she makes tea and we talk for hours at a time. I tell her about my absent husband, my fear at becoming a new mother and she listens with an open heart. I also confess that I ran into João, and I can tell by the way she shrugs and places her hands on her face that she, too, regrets the decision I made.

"Where do you suppose Pedro goes all this time?" she asks me curiously.

"I do not know, and I do not care." This is the truth. I have become accustomed to the fact that while he is my husband, we do not live as man and wife.

"Do you think he has taken on another lover?"

"I suppose so, that is in his nature after all," I admit this to her, and to myself for the first time as I have ignored the rumors until now.

"Perhaps when the baby is born, he will come to reason."

"I am not counting on that." Part of me hopes he will, for the baby's sake.

My father still does not know of these visits I share with Antonietta. We keep our relationship a well-hidden secret. I am thankful to have Antonietta in my life during a time when I need the support. Being almost nine months pregnant is not easy and it's taking a toll on me. I am not sleeping well because it is too difficult to find a comfortable position. I try putting the pillow in between my knees, but that only makes me more uncomfortable and I end up throwing the pillow across the room through the night. Antonietta cooks for me, she cleans the apartment and even helps me get dressed towards the end as it becomes difficult to put on a skirt and tie shoes. I can no longer see my feet over my swollen belly, and I forget what they even look like. Antonietta has the personality of someone who gets things done. She always makes sure to come when I am alone. She has not once made the mistake to call when my family is here. We worry my family will show up while she is here, but we take chances and seem to be getting away with it for now. I do not know how we get so lucky in that regard, but Antonietta always seems to know things.

***

The day I give birth, I am alone in the apartment. I wake up early in the morning and something wet is against my legs. I gasp at the thought that I wet my bed, and I am embarrassed even though I am alone. I am unaware I have broken my water, thus, I do not think that I am in labour, so that thought does not cross my mind. The next thing that happens out of the ordinary is the staining on my underwear. I worry about what this means. I am not in any pain yet, so I still do not associate these oddities with labour. It is not until a few hours later when the pain starts that I realize I am having the baby today. So, *this* is what labour pain feels like. I am in so much pain, but I manage to crawl to the neighbour's door to ask for help. This neighbour is not one I know well, but she is friendly, so I ask her to go and call for my midwife as I am incapable of doing so myself. The pain grows stronger by the minute, and I wince as I place my hands over my belly.

The midwife arrives less than one hour later, and I am by now unable to walk due to the piercing pain. The labour is long, and I suffer hours of sharp, excruciating misery. My mother is here with me, and she is the one to stand by my side and hold my hand through the birth of my child. She places a cool, wet washcloth on my forehead to wash away the sweat from the effort of pushing. My insides are exploding, and I am sure I am dying as I scream in agony. Six hours later I hold my baby girl in my sweaty arms for the first time, like in my dream. I had not decided on a name, but the moment she enters this world I know she is Tavina.

"She is beautiful, so exquisite," says my mother.

She brags with a wide smile as she stares at me holding my new daughter, her first grandchild.

I count the number of toes and fingers and relax when they are all accounted for. Exhaustion sets in, I cannot keep my eyes open, but I do manage to speak a little.

"Thank you, Mother." This is the first time I call her mother. Up until now, I refer to her as Antonietta. I place Tavina on my breast and begin the bonding experience of breastfeeding. This is painful at first, because getting her to latch is not easy. However, it is a rewarding feeling knowing my body is responsible for feeding my child, like in the womb. A woman's body is true magic.

Pedro does not come home today, and in fact, he has not been home for weeks. He is now a father, and he is less the wiser. I do not know how many days go by before he comes home, but when he does, he reeks of alcohol. He looks at the baby lying in her bassinet and complains about the timing of her birth. He is selfish if he thinks I can choose the day my baby decides to enter this world. Nevertheless, he is still her father, so I try to get him to bond with her but without great success.

"Pedro, hold your daughter."

"I am not sure how."

"Try, it comes naturally. It did for me."

I try to pass Tavina to him, but he refuses to take her.

"Por favor," *Please.*

After much hesitation, he takes her from my arms and holds her, but his arms are shaking while she is in them. He must be afraid to hold a baby, afraid he might drop her, so I take her back less than a minute later. He is too quick to hand her over and lets out a loud breath as he passes her to me. I tell him to give it more time, and that they will bond soon enough. But to form a bond you must put in an effort, open your heart, and be present, and Pedro does none of these things. Instead, he complains when she cries, he is cold towards her, and often not even around. Tavina will never know the love of a father, but at least she and I have each other, and this needs to be enough.

I adapt well to motherhood over the next few weeks, and I fall into a comfortable enough routine. The most difficult thing about motherhood is the lack of sleep, and I am positive any new mother will say the same. I must force myself to rest when Tavina sleeps during the day rather than clean and cook. Naptime is the only free time I have to do these things. Pedro must get used to this whether he likes it or not, so it's a good thing he is often not home.

Tavina cries only when she is hungry or has a soiled diaper, and the remainder of the time she sleeps. I have only enough cloth diapers for a few days before I must hand wash each one. This is challenging, and sometimes I find myself with no clean diapers. This happens when Tavina gets diarrhea, as she often does. When this occurs, she goes through more diapers in a day than normal. On these days it is difficult as I must leave her unattended while I scrub her soiled diapers by hand. If I wait until she naps, then I must forego the much-needed sleep for myself, a constant battle fighting with time.

Manuela and Victoria visit often, and so do my father and brothers. They bring food, so on those days I do not worry about cooking. Manuela helps with laundry, especially the diapers, and this is such a tremendous help.

With the increase in visits from my family, Antonietta worries they will see her here, so she stops calling as often. I miss her when she does not come. I am torn between my families, but I cannot have them all. It is either the mother I have not known all my life but have grown close to, or the family I know and love. I understand the risk, so I comply with her decision to stay away, even though I do not like it. Family should be united; family should be one. So why must I choose?

Tavina is four weeks old now and growing lots each day. She and I have yet to leave the house, so today I decide is the special day. I pack up Tavina, extra diapers, and place her in the buggy my father gifted me. Together, she and I head out to my father's house to visit with my family.

It is a day like any other, the middle of the week, skies are blue, and there is a light wind as we walk down the street. The familiar house peeks through palm trees as we get closer. It is exhilarating to be outside after a month of seeing only the inside of the stuffy, small apartment. Even with the thick heat, I am happy to be outside. I am so excited to show Tavina off to the world. "We are almost there my sweet baby girl,

Mama can see the house now, and it shall not be too long," I say to Tavina, as she sleeps in her buggy.

It is a hot day, but despite this I still have her bundled up in a blanket. My neighbour from the apartment building once said, "You must always bundle her up when you go outside. This is how babies get sick otherwise." I am inexperienced, so I do what I am advised to do by the more experienced mothers around me. I take all the unsolicited advice I receive, the crazy suggestions and all.

As I approach the front door, Manuela comes running and almost crashes into Tavina's buggy. She is happy to see us both. "Finally! You have come. I waited for you all afternoon and was hoping you would come today like you mentioned yesterday. Would you care for some tea?"

"I would love a cup, thank you."

"We expected you sooner."

"It took me longer than expected to get Tavina ready."

"Please, come, let me take the baby from you. How exhausted you must be, my dear sister. I cannot imagine what it must be like for you having to care for a baby. Are you tired? Here, let me get you a chair."

"Manuela, please you must not fuss, I am fine, and I slept this morning while Tavina had her early morning nap. I am well rested today."

"Nonsense, you must sit."

She proceeds to drag a chair over to where I stand still with Tavina in her buggy. The chair is heavy; she struggles with it and drags it on its back legs so it makes a scratching sound. It is a rocking chair and made of solid wood. I have always wanted a rocking chair, but we have no room for one at the apartment. It looks old, unstained, and there are pieces of old wood chipping off the arms. It is an exquisite chair, and I love old furniture, so I can't help but admire it. The chair must be new here; it is not a piece of furniture I recognize, so they must have purchased it for me.

"Here, sit. I will take Tavina and get you your tea."

I take a seat in the rocking chair and realize I am more tired than

I thought. Manuela disappears with Tavina into the kitchen to prepare the tea. The rocking chair is unstable, but I continue to rock back and forth. The swaying motion is relaxing and almost puts me to sleep. I enjoy the swinging motion of the chair so much that I do not realize I increased the momentum of the swing. The last swing I take is too hard; the chair flips over from the front onto the back and crushes me underneath. As I flip backward my head slams into the steel table next to the chair. There is a loud crashing sound as my skull hits the table, my head pounds and throbs. My skull must be splitting in two. I yell loud enough so others can hear. Until help arrives, I hold my head as I lie under the chair, trapped and unable to move.

Manuela comes running into the room after hearing the crash. "Rosa, dear God." She runs over to me. She tries to lift the chair off me by herself, but it is too heavy for her small, weak arms so she runs to get my brothers to help, leaving me alone again.

Julio arrives with her less than a minute later and helps her lift the chair off me.

"Are you all right Rosa? Take my hand, and let me help you up," he says.

I hold on to his arm as instructed, and he lifts me off the floor. There is no visible blood, so my head is not cut open. I am not too concerned about the fall, other than the pounding inside my head.

"Where is Tavina?" I ask.

I do not recall if I was holding Tavina when I fell, and I panic over the fear that she was in my arms when I took the tumble.

"Tavina is fine Rosa, she is in the kitchen, still in her buggy. I left her in there while preparing our tea."

I am relieved to know she is safe. Tavina is not yet baptized, and I worry about something happening to her prior to baptism. Once baptized, she is welcome into the house of God, so I make plans for her baptism the following week.

After standing on my feet for a minute my vision blurs and the room spins. I place my hands over my head to stop the pounding.

"I must go home. I need to rest."

"Of course," says Manuela.

"Can Tavina stay here with you for a while, so I can get some sleep?"

"Are you all right?"

"I will be okay; it is only a bump on the head."

"Yes, please go home. We will take care of Tavina, no need to worry. Victoria shall be home soon, and I will send her to the store to buy milk as soon as she arrives. She is in good hands. Go and rest."

I leave my father's house empty handed — my baby stays behind. I am not thinking straight. I am so tired, disoriented, and nauseated. I need sleep, and a nap is all I crave. I do not even remember getting home; the walk from my father's house to the apartment is a blur.

I do not know how much time passes, but the next thing I remember is someone standing over me, fussing.

"Rosa, wake up. Rosa."

Victoria is shaking me awake, but I do not stir. I keep my eyes closed, listening.

"Is she still sleeping?" Manuela asks with a crack in her voice.

"I do not know. She hit her head hard, she should not be sleeping."

"Porquê?" *Why?*

"She could slip into a coma due to the head injury."

"Oh, I had no idea this is a concern. I encouraged her to sleep."

I try to open my eyes, I want to tell them I am okay, but I am confused and disoriented. My head is heavy and feels like a herd of elephants is sitting on it. When my eyes open, I look around the room trying to place where I am, and I can vaguely make out faces. I know they are the faces of Manuela, Victoria, and Julio, but even their faces are fuzzy. I try to stand, but everyone keeps fussing over me and pushing me down. They say things like: "She needs a doctor," and "We must take her to the hospital," although, I do not know whose voices these are. I am lifted off the bed and carried to the car, I remember my other brother arriving, but I am not sure which brother. Things are not making sense to me now.

We are moving, and someone is driving the vehicle, but I cannot distinguish who. During the drive the same voices speak, but I can only make out single words at a time. "Urgent," one voice says "Die," says another. What are they saying? Am I dying? Is this what death feels like?

The moment we arrive at the hospital, my brother Manecas runs out of the car and heads straight for the entrance. Other people walk by, and I may or may not have recognized them, their faces are not clear. After that it all goes silent and still, and I fall into a deep black hole.

CHAPTER 23

1946

I AM ASLEEP. I remember many things, but others are confusing. Groups of people visit daily, but I do not know who they are. They say they are my family. Their voices are in my head while I sleep. The doctors encourage them to sit and talk to me, hoping that hearing a familiar voice wakes me. They refer to a man named Pedro, and they say he is my husband but that he has not visited me yet. The doctors say I am in a coma, and three weeks have passed. In my dreamlike state, I ponder over the word coma and wonder it means.

It is getting loud, so I try to block out the noise from voices. A man's voice fills my head now.

"There is a specific medication needed to reduce the swelling, but it is rare in Lobito, so it is not available. It is on order, coming from afar. This delay prolongs the swelling in Rosa's brain and causes further damage."

I hear the words, but I have no idea who speaks them or what they mean. And who is Rosa?

"A fall after childbirth has dangerous side effects, causing brain damage and even death. Let's hope this is not the case," says another unfamiliar voice.

Each day I spend in the coma, I receive many visitors. I begin to recognize voices, and soon I even recognize names. I remember the name Antonietta; she is special to me. This is a woman who comes often, but is always alone. She talks to me about a baby — Tavina, she calls the baby. Tavina must be her daughter.

On the day I come to, it is a young girl's gloomy face I first see. She sits at the foot of the bed with a frown and sad eyes, while staring into space. At first, she does not know what is happening, and then she realizes I am awake, so her eyes widen. Her mouth opens ready to scream, she jumps high from the edge of the bed and runs out yelling. "Doctor, Doctor! Come quick! Help!"

"What is the urgency, Manuela?" Someone asks, as they peek into the room. It must be a nurse. She must realize I am awake, and this must be the reason for the young girl's sudden screams. The nurse had called the girl Manuela. When the nurse sees me she, too, yells, "I will get the doctor!" and hurries off, leaving me wondering what the fuss is about. She returns less than two minutes later with the doctor at her side.

I am not myself when I first wake up, and I do not even remember who I am or what my name is. I am confused as everyone tries to talk to me and doctors try to examine me. I become frustrated and scream at everyone to leave me alone.

The people that often came to visit me are here now, fussing over me. This is too much for me to handle. I shut down, remain quiet, and pull the blanket up to cover my ears.

Days go by before I begin to remember names, people, and places. Memories come flooding back more and more with each new day. I remember my family: my father, brothers, sister, and Victoria. I wonder where the Antonietta woman is who visited me often. She has not returned since I woke up. My family tells me about my baby, Tavina, and that she is well cared for by relatives, but I stare at them in awe.

They must be crazy, because I have no memory of ever having a baby. I do not believe I am a mother, and when my family tries to tell me about her, I look away, refusing to believe. The doctors tell my family that talking and telling me stories is helpful in recovering my memory. How is it possible I have a child in this world and do not remember her? This idea is ludicrous to me. Little do I know my brain suffers from severe swelling, and it is I who am the crazy one and not my family.

My hospital stay lasts for several long, lonely months. Little by little, and after months of living in the deep dark hole, I regain my full memory. It is only small things at first that come to mind: memories of walking with my sister and playing with my brothers. I remember the beach, and a boy who makes me nervous, I think his name is João, but I am not sure. My daughter is the last one I remember, but when I do, those memories shake me to the core. When I remember her, Tavina is a full force in my mind. After all these months, I finally remember her. I long for her, to hold her, and ask for her daily. I cry myself to sleep every night. About a week after I regain my full memory, the doctors say it is safe for me to see her. My family makes plans for someone to bring her to me, but only for a small visit, "To test the waters," says the doctor. What are they afraid of?

The next day a man enters my room, approaches my bed, and to my surprise he is holding my baby girl. This man is not my husband; I remember Pedro now as well, and this is not him. At first, I do not recognize this man, but after searching his face for some familiar features, I remember him. It takes me time to place faces as my brain is still recovering from the swelling. I am also on several medications and monitored hourly still.

"Vintoro," I say upon recognition.

"Rosa, I am so pleased you are well."

"Vintoro, what are you doing here? Where is Pedro?"

Vintoro is Pedro's friend; the one Pedro was with the night we met. He spent some time at the apartment at the beginning of my marriage, and he also works with Pedro.

"Rosa, I do not know where he is, I have not seen him in months. I am sorry. This here is Tavina, your baby."

He approaches the bed, so I can get a closer look at Tavina, but I do not recognize her. I remember her, but I have no recollection of what she looks like. She is a few months old now. I hold her in my arms, and it feels like the first time. She is so tiny, and I expect her to be bigger.

"Are they feeding her enough?"

"Tavina is being taken good care of."

Vintoro has always been kind to me. He protected me from Pedro then, and he must feel sorry for me now. He knows his friend well and understands the type of emotional abuse I suffer. We do not visit long today because my nurse does not want me to get too much stimulation. So, Vintoro leaves about half an hour later, but he leaves with the promise to come again and to bring Tavina once more.

Vintoro continues to visit often and, as promised, he brings Tavina with him. She and I start to bond little by little. Within time, I am her mother again. Vintoro brings Tavina regularly until two weeks prior to my release. Then without warning, the visits stop. I grow anxious and wonder why. I ask my family when they visit, but when I ask the simple question, they avoid answering. I look to Victoria for help, she will tell me, but she, too, looks away and remains silent, and this is unlike her.

I am regaining my strength; I am now eating on my own, remembering details and feeling better, but not great. I am still not back to how I was prior to the accident. I was active, full of energy, and now the body my soul is trapped inside of has become fragile and incapable of simple tasks. I hope this is not my new reality. The doctors say I am on my way to a full recovery, but it does not feel like a recovery. I am trapped inside a body I do not know.

CHAPTER 24

1946

"IS IT NOT too soon? Are you sure I am ready?" I ask my doctor.

"Yes, in my professional opinion, you are ready."

He places his stethoscope back around his neck after finishing the examination. I remain on my back as he completes the paperwork.

"I do feel a bit better, but I am not back to normal. I cannot explain this, but something is still not right with me."

He moves away from the bed, and walks over to his chart, picks it up and writes something. "This is normal, you need to give yourself time."

I shift the thin hospital blanket up against my legs, there is a draft and I am cold. "If you are sure, then I trust your opinion. But I think a few more weeks here might help."

He places the clipboard back on the ledge and turns to face me. "Rosa, we have done all we can at this point. It is up to you to return to your normal life now. So go raise your baby girl, go for walks, and do things that bring you enjoyment. You will be back to yourself soon. What you lack now are sun and the cool sea breeze. Remember your medications daily, come see me again next week, and we shall assess things then. It is time you leave this hospital."

He adjusts his glasses and places his hands in the pockets of the white jacket, waiting for me to agree, but I do not. He is making a mistake, I am not better and should remain in the hospital, but nobody agrees with my assessment of myself.

The doctor leaves after he has said his last words, leaving me alone. I make my way to the closet where my bag hangs, and I put the few items I have with me into the bag. My mind is racing, and I contemplate what to do when I get home. Where is home? Is home back at my father's house, or is home the empty and lonely apartment? I am certain I will be alone there; Pedro is still missing and has not been seen since before the accident, months ago. I look around the hospital room, the place I spent the last few months and sadness comes over me. I am empty inside. "Think of Tavina," I say to myself. She will get me through this.

My brother Eduardo picks me up later in the afternoon and takes me back to my apartment. While the doctors think I am all right, I know I am not. The short walk to the vehicle takes out of me everything I have left to give. We are silent during the drive, and when we arrive Eduardo helps me out of the car. When I enter the apartment, I drop the bag on the floor and go straight to my bedroom. With clothes left on, I fall onto the bed, close my eyes and go to sleep. I do not hear Eduardo leaving.

The next morning there is a visitor knocking. The knock is gentle as if they are afraid to wake me, but loud enough for me to hear from the bedroom. I am too weak to get out of bed to answer. When I fail to answer, the unlocked door opens; they let themselves in, and their footsteps approach.

It is Antonietta, my mother. I can hear her calling me from the living room. "Rosa, are you here?" It is no more than a whisper. She must have stopped by the hospital, only to find my bed empty. She must not be sure if I am here or at my father's house. This must be why she is whispering. Her usual demeanor is much louder and more aggressive, but not today. I want to respond, but I cannot find my voice. I slept the entire evening and well into this morning, with no desire, strength, or stamina to get out of bed. I have no energy to speak any words. Speaking takes too much effort, something I lack.

"Rosa!"

She repeats my name a little louder. She peeks into my bedroom and finds me awake, eyes open but otherwise non-responsive.

She stays with me all afternoon, comforting and caring for me. She says she hopes my family does not come, but she does not feel comfortable leaving me alone, so she takes the risk. She knows I am not well.

"Where is your family? Why are they not here with you?" she asks but is met with silence.

She makes me feijoada, a healthy, thick bean soup full of nutrients. Only the soup does nothing for me this time. I slip in and out of consciousness through the day. For the few minutes I am awake, she sits on the edge of my bed with a wet cloth, like when I delivered Tavina. She looks ten years older than the last time I saw her. She has dark circles under her eyes, she frowns, and her lips are set in a tight line. I try to speak to her but fail at the attempt. She says she is staying the night to make sure I do not slip back into a coma. She also says, "A coma could take you from me again, my daughter." I do not think she intended for me to hear the last part.

Two days pass since my discharge. I am not eating or drinking. The moments of consciousness are less and less. I spend more time in the deep black hole that sucked me up once already. Antonietta approaches my bed, leans in and whispers in my ear, "Rosa, I am leaving you for a short while. I will not be too long. I have a friend who is a doctor and he might be of assistance. I am going to call on him and find out if he can help. He owes me a favour. I shall return shortly."

"Hmmm," is all I manage as a reply.

"Can you understand what I am saying?" She says.

I cannot speak enough to say yes, but I do manage to give her a small nod of my head, hoping she understands the gesture.

"Do not attempt to get out of bed; you are too ill and too weak to walk. Even I can see this. I cannot believe those idiots at the hospital released you. Stay strong my daughter, I will be back with help. This I promise you."

She leans in close, kisses my forehead and wipes away the messy hair that covers my face. After she leaves, my eyes remain shut. I fight the deep black hole as it fills my head, takes over my memories and tries to pull me back into its abyss of nothingness. I do not have the strength to pull myself through this, so I allow the deep black hole to take a hold of me once again. The emptiness pulls me in and consumes me whole. Sleep now takes over me as I drift off into the same dark place I was in before.

CHAPTER 25

1946

"M OTHER?" I SAY.

"Rosa, you are awake," says my mother, as she jumps off her chair and runs towards the bed.

Something is different, the fog inside my head is gone and my mind is clear. I have more strength, and I can see straight.

"I am not dead?"

"No, sweet child, you are not."

"What happened? I remember you saying you were leaving to get help. Did you go?"

"Yes, I did."

I look around but do not see anyone here. "Where is this person you brought to help?"

"That was two days ago, my daughter."

My mother pulls the covers back, climbs into bed with me and pulls the covers up to our necks. She wraps her arms around me and tells me her story.

"It was close, Rosa, too close."

"What was close?"

I do not understand anything because she does not make sense.

"I returned with help as promised. I brought with me a gentleman who claims he is a doctor, but he is not a doctor in the traditional sense. He is an old wise man who has cured many ailments in his lifetime. I was desperate Rosa; I did not know what else to do. I did not want you returning to the hospital, they already released you too early once. They missed something grave in your diagnosis. This friend of mine was our last hope."

I listen with my ears close to her lips as I stare up at the ceiling while lying on my back. She continues her story. "He used a treatment on you called bloodletting. This treatment pulls contaminated blood from your body and brings out the disease with it. The bleeding was done from your head."

I reach up and touch my head. "He bled my head?"

"Yes, my daughter, he did. He pulled a lot of blood out. I was sure you would die from the treatment, rather than the illness that crippled you. I was desperate and had no other option. You were going to die, so I had to take the chance."

"I am well now, so it helped."

"Rosa, please stay put, you need to rest more, this is imperative to your recovery. Sleep a little longer. I will be here when you wake up."

My eyes are closed before she even finishes, but this time it is sleep that takes me and not the black hole. I sleep for the remainder of the evening and through the night until the next day.

Upon opening my eyes the following day, I test my energy level by trying to get out of bed. I make my way to the window and I come alive when the warm sunshine hits my face. I am a living miracle, a new person compared to two days ago. I do not think I can handle too much strenuous work yet, but my energy is returning. My mind is sharp, I can think straight, and thoughts are no longer jumbled in my brain.

"You are up. Are you hungry?" says my mother sitting on the floor by the bed.

I turn to look at Antonietta, now standing at the bedroom doorway. "I think I am."

"I will be back with chicken soup. It is made, all I have to do is heat it up for you. Do you want to stay here or try to go out into the kitchen? Are you well enough for that?"

"Yes, I am, I will come out."

Ten minutes later, we sit at my kitchen table with a bowl of soup as I try to eat on my own. My fingers have difficulty holding the spoon steady; they shake too much causing the soup to spill, so my patient mother takes the spoon from me and spoon feeds me. I eat the entire bowl, I am famished. By the next meal I hold the bowl in my own hands, the shaking subsides, and I feed myself. This small victory is a milestone. This bloodletting treatment my mother speaks of worked.

The sun has set, it's now late, and I yawn despite all the sleep I have had. Antonietta tucks me back into bed and crawls back inside with me. She must be exhausted from worrying about me.

My stomach is full and, other than needing more sleep, I am healthy.

"The doctor is most likely a witch doctor," I say to my mother.

She raises an eyebrow. "Yes you raise a good point, but does it matter? You are well again my daughter. That is all I care about."

"I do not know how to thank you for what you did. I would have died had you not intervened."

"Rosa, my daughter, it is the least I can do as your mother. I never stopped loving you. We lost many years, but you are still my daughter." She takes a deep breath, sighs and speaks once again. "But, Rosa, you must listen now. I have sad news. I do not know how to say this, so I am going to say it like it is. I must leave you now."

"Yes, I understand, you have been here a long time, go home and get some rest."

"You misunderstand me, and I am sorry. I know this is devastating to hear. But I must go. I have acquired a new job, and it is taking me out of the city."

"Nao!" *No!*

"I will write to you, to notify you of my whereabouts so you can contact me there. It will take a few weeks before I am settled, so do not worry if you do not hear from me right away."

"I do not want you to leave."

My insides are tightening up, I have a ball in my stomach. Before she even finishes her story, tears fill my eyes. "When are you leaving?"

"Soon, my daughter." She reaches out to caress my cheek.

I wipe my eyes with the blanket. I am overwhelmed with the news of my mother leaving. I have only found her a short while ago, and now I am losing her again. Only this time, losing her feels much worse because I know the type of woman she is, and I know what I am losing in my life. I have grown to love her, and I do not want her to go, but I know I have no choice. I fall asleep in my mother's arms while dreaming of her. She stays with me through the night, a few times I wake up and she is next to me.

The following afternoon we talk lots, and both shed many tears. It is time for her to go, and with one last look at me as she walks through the door out of my apartment. She blows me a kiss and says, "Be strong, my daughter."

"I will try, Mother."

"Do more than try, promise?"

"I promise, I will be strong."

CHAPTER 26

1946

DAYS PASS, AND I still do not know where Tavina is. No one allows me to see her, not since before my hospital release. I am well again and almost back to my normal self. My energy level is still not what it used to be, but I am healthy enough that I long for my daughter. I am able and ready to take care of her, and this brings me hope.

The walk to my father's house is one I can manage now, and I plan to go and pick up Tavina this afternoon and bring her home. Tavina's little face floods my memories as I soak in the tub. In my mind, I imagine the days ahead and the time she and I will spend together. After I wash my hair and smell fresh and clean, I pull myself out of the tub. The bar where the towel hangs, aids as a lift, so I do not slip and fall. Dressing takes a little longer than I expect, so I slow down to conserve much-needed energy for the walk.

Upon arriving at my father's house, I surprise my sister when she sees me standing before her.

"Rosa, we wanted to give you some time to adjust to being home."

She opens the door wider to let me in. My family knows nothing of what transpired the last few days and that I almost died. They have not visited since my discharge from the hospital.

"I am better, I had lots of rest, and I have come to pick up Tavina."

I do not reveal any details about the last few days. Partly because I cannot explain my mother's involvement, also I do not want to discuss it. I want to move forward with my life and resume my duties as a mother. I missed many months in Tavina's life already, and I do not want to miss another moment. Tavina is the only thing that matters to me, and I long to hold her in my arms again.

"Where is she, where is my baby?"

I look around the room, but I do not see her.

"She is not here, Rosa."

"Onde está ela?" *Where is she?*

"I do not know, let me go get Victoria." Manuela hurries off, disappears into the kitchen, and leaves me alone to my thoughts.

Manuela returns a moment later with Victoria at her side. Victoria tells me she does not know where my baby is.

"How can you not know where she is? Has she not been here this entire time?" I ask irritated.

"She was here for a while, but not the whole time," says Victoria.

I push further, demanding to know my daughter's whereabouts. "This should be an easy answer," I say.

I grow more and more impatient with them both. They tell me she is with another relative and to be patient. I ask which relative is taking care of my daughter, and again I receive no answer. I ask if she is with my sister-in–law, since she cared for Tavina for some time while I was in the hospital. Again, no response. This is ridiculous. My stomach feels like worms are crawling inside me. I know my family's silence means something is wrong, I can sense it inside my bones.

Everyone tries to avoid me, and this is the reason my family has not visited me since my release from the hospital. Their absence makes sense now, whereas it did not before. They are cold, evasive, not answering my questions and do not look me in the eye. I am annoyed with them all. I remind myself to remain calm before speaking again. "I want you to go get her, wherever she is. Go get her and bring her to me at once."

"Rosa, it is not that simple," says Victoria.

"I am her mother, what right do you think you have to keep her from me? I was ill, and yes, I understand I was not capable of caring for her at that time. But as you can now see, I am well."

My father walks into the room now, a stern look on his face. "Rosa, you must give it more time. You are only now recovering from a difficult illness that almost took your life. Give it a few more weeks so you can be more prepared to take care of Tavina. She deserves that much," says my father. But I refuse to listen, and I will not accept any of it.

I storm out the front door, determined to find her myself. I visit every close relative I know. I go to cousins and aunts who live nearby, and I go to my brother's house and question my sister-in-law. When they open their doors and see me looking frantic, they tell me the same thing. Nobody has seen or knows where Tavina is. This is insane. This is not possible. How can a baby go missing? The worms in my stomach multiply by the minute and eat me alive from the inside. If I did not die from the accident and head injury, the silence shall kill me now.

"Where is my daughter?" I scream into the night, alone. Nobody hears me. I return to my empty apartment and stare at the walls, lost and alone. Where is she, where is my daughter? I now know in my heart something is wrong with her. She must be sick. This must be the only reason why everyone is evasive toward me and not telling me the truth. My family must fear if they reveal the truth too soon it will be my undoing, and they are right. There can be no other explanation for them wanting to keep a baby away from her mother.

Determined to keep up my energy, I tread into the kitchen and find some leftover soup Antonietta made before she left. I warm it up, force myself to eat. It is tasteless now.

My bed feels cold tonight. I get some sleep, but it is interrupted. I dream often of a baby girl, about seven months old with deep, brown eyes, and dark black, curly hair.

She is crying and is in a fast-flowing river and floating on her back. When I wade into the water to get to her, she disappears as I reach my arms to grab her. She vanishes into thin air.

I dream this same dream tonight several times. It is always the same; me noticing the baby in the water, and then me trying to reach her. The last time I dream this tonight, I am startled awake as the tears begin to fall. "Tavina," I whisper to no one, as there is no one here to listen.

CHAPTER 27

1946

MY FAMILY TRIES to reach out to me on many occasions, but I want to be alone, left to my own thoughts and misery. They come to the apartment a few times. They knock, but I ignore it and pretend I am not home. They are speaking to one another from the hallway. "She is out," someone says. It sounds like Eduardo's voice, but I am uncertain. He speaks to one of my other brothers, but minutes later they leave.

Another time Manuela and Victoria are at the door and speak to one another. "Where do you suppose she is this time of day?" Manuela asks Victoria.

"She must be at the market."

"I suppose that is a possibility," says Manuela.

Soon they both leave, and I continue to brood in silence in the empty apartment, alone. I have not eaten all week, save for the small bowl of tasteless soup. Hunger is the last thing that occupies my mind; it takes up too much energy. I have not bathed in days, I am in the same clothes I wore the day I visited my family, almost one week ago.

If they are to see me now, they will run from fear. My hair is messy, I have bags under my eyes, and the apartment smells atrocious. I sniff my underarms to check if it is me and not the apartment, it is both. But, I do not care because there is nothing left to live for. Nothing. I know in my heart my daughter is gone.

My mouth is dry, and I cannot feel my tongue, so I try to make myself a tea to moisten my mouth. This does not go according to plan. I get as far as to fill the steel pot with water and bring it to a boil. I reach into the cupboard for a mug, select one, and whip the mug across the room. It slams into the oil lamp in the living room and knocks it over. I leave the broken glass shattered over the floor, and the knocked over lamp still on its side. I make my way into my bedroom and crawl into my bed with my clothes still on. There is no point in changing because there is no one here to care. Struggling with the blanket, I yank harder and pull it up to cover my body, including my head. All I want is sleep. Darkness and silence are my only two friends.

It is a new week, and this week brings much of the same despair as the last. The only exception is this week I manage to make tea and fill the mug before throwing it across the room. The broken glass accumulates on the floor, and I leave it there again. I step over it and walk back to my bedroom. Back to the darkness and silence that fills my head.

Another week creeps by, and I ignore many more knocks on the door. I am slipping into a dangerous zone and out of reach with reality, so I force myself to get up and do something. Convincing myself this is what I need, I try to clean the apartment, take a bath and change my clothes. This is progress.

While walking into the kitchen, I pick up a letter in front of my door. It must have come by post and slipped beneath the door by the neighbour. Curious on what it is, I bend to pick it up and blow off some glass that got on it from the smashed mugs. I did not get this far in my attempt to clean the apartment today. The envelope is thin, displays my name printed neatly in ink. I assume it must be a woman's handwriting.

Although, I do not recognize to whom the handwriting belongs. There is no return address or name on the top left corner. I open the envelope, slide the piece of paper out and look to the end of the letter to find a signature. But the letter is not signed, so I do not know who it is from. I do not read it right away; instead, I decide to attempt another tea. This time, I get as far as taking a sip from the mug, and I am about to toss it across the room, but I stop myself. I carry my tea and letter to the living room. Curious to know what it contains, I unfold the letter using the tips of my fingers. I am afraid of what it is about to reveal to me. I take a deep breath, and I begin to read.

Rosa,

It is my deepest regret that I must be the one to inform you Tavina died. She passed away while you were in hospital. This was about two weeks before your release. She became ill one day, she caught a fever, and the fever got worse. You must not blame yourself. You were in no position to be able to take care of her. This is not your fault. It is nobody's fault, everyone tried to help. Everyone tried to take care of her for you. I know you must be suffering. I felt you must know the truth, so you can move on with your life and get some much-needed closure.

My deepest condolences go out to you. Rosa, do take care of yourself.

I fold the letter into a small square and slip it into the pocket of my skirt. Standing is a challenge for me again, so I take my time and test the strength of my legs. Once I am convinced I can stand without falling over, I walk into my bedroom and open my top drawer next to my bed. I place the letter in the drawer and slam it shut. The loud sound of the drawer smashing shut does not faze me as I barely hear it. I flip over the covers of the unmade bed, and I slip inside, clothed. I close my eyes and concentrate on my breathing to try to steady my nerves. My hand comes up to touch my face. I expect to feel liquid, but my face is dry. There are no tears yet, and so this must mean I am in shock. I lie on my back in bed for many hours, staring at the walls before me, thinking of Tavina, the daughter I no longer have and will never hold again.

I get an idea in my head that I should talk to her, so I do. "Oh Tavina, I am sorry. There is nothing in this world I would not give to hold you in my arms." I hope she is listening, so I wait for a reply, a sign, anything, but nothing comes.

I must have fallen asleep at some point, although I do not remember when that happens. When I wake up, it is again morning, a brand new day. The sunshine beams into the room from the small window. When I open my eyes, I forget Tavina is no longer alive, but then I remember. The memories of the night before are flooding my brain and make breathing difficult. I remember the words written in the letter. "Tavina died." I become hysterical, and I continue to talk to her, hoping to hear her sweet cry, but I am met with silence once again. I cannot see straight. I try to get up, but I am dizzy, so I fall flat on my face. When I try to get up again, I am certain it is the room spinning out of control and not me. No, it cannot be me. I write Tavina a melody, and on a whim, I sing made-up lyrics.

I will never hold you,
I will never see you walk.
I will never kiss you,
I will never hear you talk.
You are lost to me forever,
Like a dream, I shall forget.
I will never hold you
I will never be your mother ... again.

I sing this song over many times out loud and in my head, and the song brings me comfort. I smell Tavina's clothes, her diapers, her bassinet, but there is no smell of her left. I try to remember her scent, but it is now too faint to recall. It has been so long since she has been here, so I cannot smell her anymore. I pick up her white tiny undershirt and use it to wipe the tears from my eyes.

CHAPTER 28

1947

THE DEPRESSION I go through is deep and painful, and I lose hope for myself. I have lost the one most precious thing in my life. I have lost my daughter. Over the next several weeks I manage the basics, but only enough to keep me alive; although some days I want to die myself. I make a pot of soup and force myself to eat one bowl a day. Through the day, I bring a glass filled with water to my lips to keep myself hydrated. The food in the apartment is running low, I must get to the market, but I wait until the cupboards are empty before I go. Days pass before I bathe, wash my hair and change my clothes. But when I do, I select a plain black skirt and a black top. I run my fingers through my hair to try to smooth most of the curls. There are a few pins sitting on my night table, so I grab them and put them in my hair to tame the curls. This is the first time I leave my apartment in so long. Leaving the door unlocked behind me, I walk to the market and keep my head bent to avoid eye contact. I have one goal today, and it is to walk into the store, grab what I need for soup, and leave. As I pace back home, I remember I left the door unlocked, and I am not gone for any longer than an hour, but when I return, my sister is waiting for me.

When she sees me enter the apartment, she runs to me and places her arms around me, holding me tight.

"Rosa, I am so sorry. You know now, I assume?"

I stare at her with a blank look in my eyes. "That my daughter is dead?" I try to break away from her embrace, but her grip is too tight.

"Yes," she says.

"I know my daughter is dead. No thanks to you for being open and honest."

"Father said it is best we wait, he is afraid for you. He feared the news would kill you."

"Well he is right to worry, it almost did."

I manage to break free from her tight grip. I back away from her, but she reaches out to take my hand.

"Do not shut me out, please."

"I do not know what else to do."

"Try to let me help you. I beg you."

She has bags under her eyes, and her hair looks as messy as mine. I decide to let her in and allow her to try to help me.

"I am making soup, would you like to help?"

Her eyes brighten when I say this. She grabs the bag with groceries from the floor and carries it into the kitchen.

She stays the entire afternoon and helps me make soup the way I like it, the way Antonietta made it for me many times. We eat our soup on the couch but seldom talk. This is the start of my recovery.

Manuela visits every day for the next few months. She sometimes brings food, other times we walk to the market to get groceries, and we cook together.

Many unanswered questions are looming in my head, and I ask Manuela about them. "Who was Tavina with when she died?"

"She was with us."

"Did you write the letter?"

"Qual carta?" *What letter?*

I walk to my bedroom, open the drawer, pull out the letter and hand it to Manuela. She takes a moment to read it, and then says, "No, I did not write this. I do not know who sent this letter."

"Was she buried? Was there a funeral?" I ask.

"Yes, a beautiful one," she says. She sighs, and then continues. "We had to proceed with it. We did not know how long you would be unreachable."

"Will you take me to her, to her grave?"

She reaches out and places her hands on my face. "Anytime."

The next day, and every day after for the next few weeks, Manuela and I go to the graveyard, so I can see my daughter's grave. I sing Tavina her song every time.

A few more weeks go by and I begin to worry about what to do for money. I can stay in the apartment because Pedro has always been good at paying the rent in advance. But today I received notice from the landlord that in two months the rent is due again. I do not know where I will get the money for the rent, so I plan how to track down Pedro. I need to ask him for help — it is, after all, still his apartment. It occurs to me then, he does not even know about Tavina's death, or does he?

CHAPTER 29

1947

ONE MONTH AFTER receiving the anonymous letter, I receive unexpected visitors. The knock is louder than usual, so I do not think it is a member of my family. I hesitate as I open the door and find two police officers standing on the other side. Immediately I narrow my eyes and wonder why on earth they are here.

They stand tall and stern with serious looks on their faces. One of them rests his right hand on his holster; this is the one who speaks first. "Good day Madame, may we come in?"

I do not know what they want from me, but I know enough to be polite and obedient.

"Please do," I say, and step to the side to allow them room to enter. I offer tea, but they decline. "To what do I owe this visit from you officers?" I ask looking at the holster. This is the closest I have come to a gun.

They ask me to confirm my name, and I tell them. They ask about Pedro Melo, and I confirm I am married to him. They ask many questions: how long I've known him, when we got married, last time I saw him, and where he works. I answer the questions, leaving no stone unturned — I have nothing to hide. Both police officers thank me for my cooperation and honesty. We are still standing by the door, so I offer for them to sit. They decline the offer to sit and tell me they prefer to stand. Standing is more formal, so my palms begin to sweat. They inform me they are looking for my husband, but this news does not surprise me.

"I cannot help you, officers, I am sorry, but as I told you, I have not seen nor heard from my husband in months. I cannot tell you of his whereabouts," I say.

We remain standing, and they inform me of Pedro's past, the past I already discovered. I already know he had altercations with the law and spent time in jail. What I do learn is that Pedro is still running from the law today, and that is why he stays away from home. Pedro is not a stupid man, and he must know this is the first place the authorities will look for him.

This is the second time Pedro crosses my mind since Tavina died, the first is when I realize he does not know about her death. How can this even be possible? He is her father after all, or rather was. How can a man walk this Earth and not know his baby girl is gone? Only a man like Pedro can, a man who does not care for his family. The thought occurs that he has another family, another daughter, another son, or both. I do not put this past him. This has me in deep thought and I forget about the two police officers still standing in my apartment.

One of the officers, the taller one, interrupts my thoughts when he speaks again. "If you see or hear from him it is imperative you contact us right away. Do you understand?"

"Yes sir, I understand, and I will."

"Very good," says the shorter police office.

"Will that be all then?"

"Yes, good day."

They bow their heads as they turn around, open the door and let themselves out. At least now I know why my husband is so absent.

A few days later, I receive another visitor, and this time it is Pedro himself who makes an appearance. I am sitting in the living room in the dark and thinking when he opens the door with force. Memories of Ricardo rush back. I tell myself this is not Ricardo but Pedro, not that Pedro's character is any better. The noise startles me as I am used to spending most days alone.

"Pedro, you scared me."

I do not have time to say much to him as he appears to be in a hurry. He runs to the bedroom and gathers clothes into a bag. He does not say anything, and I do not bring up Tavina.

"What are you doing here?" I ask, as I stand by the bedroom door, watching him go through drawers and throw more clothes into the same bag.

"Where have you been?" I ask, but he does not respond. "Are you leaving for good?"

"Would you shut up woman? I have had enough of your lectures."

His reply catches me off guard and I back away a few feet, afraid he might hit me. He has money hidden in one of his drawers, and puts the money in the same bag. Why have I never checked his drawers? Darn, that is money I need now to pay rent, and I missed out on that opportunity.

I continue to watch him in his frenzied state. "I am sorry, I do not want to make you angry," I say in an attempt to keep the peace. "Police have been here looking for you," I say.

"I told you to shut up!"

He does not look at me as he yells these words. After ten minutes there is another hard knock, the same knock I heard a few days prior. I leave Pedro in the bedroom to answer the door. Upon opening it, I face the same two officers who were here days ago. The moment the door opens, they push me aside and barge into the apartment with full force. I almost fall over.

"We know your husband is here, we received a tip. Do not try to conceal him, or we will arrest you."

Oh, dear God no, this cannot happen. I will not allow my despicable husband to take me down with him.

"Yes, he is here," I say right away to show cooperation.

"Where is he?"

"In the bedroom, he arrived minutes ago," I say while trying to stay out of their way. My breathing quickens, and I point to the bedroom door. They disappear into the bedroom, and moments later my husband is in handcuffs and taken into custody. This is my opportunity to tell him about Tavina, but I hesitate and bite my tongue. He is not worthy of knowing the truth, and this is how I justify not telling him about our daughter's death. He was not a father to her anyway, so he does not deserve to know.

Within a few days, I learn from Eduardo that Pedro is at the county jail and will spend up to a year behind bars. This is his sentence for the crime he committed. The crime that I still do not have details on.

One month later, guilt consumes me for not having told Pedro the truth. I contemplate every day whether I did the right thing. While it is true he was no father, he still deserves to know his daughter is no longer alive. What kind of person am I to keep this from him? I will not stoop to his level, no. The thought occurs to me that he already knows, and it is the reason why he does not ask about her.

I decide I must see him and tell him the truth, and this must happen in person. This is the only way to relieve my guilt. A letter like I received will not suffice. Later in the afternoon, I go see Eduardo to ask for help. The prison is far, and I worry about making the trip on my own. I do not have the courage to go alone, and I also have no vehicle. The bus ticket costs more money than I have, so Eduardo agrees to help and offers to drive me. We make the necessary arrangements for two days from today. I give him a kiss on the cheek to show him how grateful I am for his support.

Since the prison is a two-hour drive, we decide to leave early in the morning. Eduardo says he will pick me up by eight. He is punctual and knocks promptly on time as promised.

"Bon dia," *Good morning*, I say.

"Rosa, are you ready?"

"Yes, I am."

"Are you sure about this?"

"Yes, I am Eduardo. I must go see him. He needs to hear from me that our daughter is gone. I will not be at peace with myself until I do this. I am not expecting miracles, and what happens after this is in his hands."

"Very well then, let's not delay this any further."

We walk out to his vehicle in silence. The drive is long, and it is hot and the heat in the car is too much to tolerate, so we roll down the windows. My hair becomes a mess again. I try to contain it with some pins I keep in my purse. I do not want Pedro thinking his disappearance from my life causes me grief, so I try to show up looking put together on the outside at least. Inside, I am falling apart, but nobody needs to know but me.

Later in the morning when we arrive at the prison, my stomach is not well. I am nauseated and worry I will throw up my breakfast. Am I doing the right thing by being here?

The guards search my bags and instruct us to wait in the visiting room. Prior to entering, they announce they must do a physical search, so one guard pats me with his hands, I tense up, but he tells me to relax. As we wait in the visiting area, my palms are sweaty like they often are when I am scared or nervous. A few moments later, two security guards bring Pedro into the room, and again he avoids eye contact. He is thin and appears to have lost thirty pounds, but he is not a heavy man, so this is a lot of weight to lose in a short time. The guards must have shaved his head, and now an irregular scalp displays. He has dark circles under his once charming eyes, and many wrinkles now appear on his once smooth forehead. This new look does not suit him, he looks like a criminal, and then I remind myself that he is one.

His hands are at his side, and when he sees me, he curls his fists into balls. He raises his voice when he speaks, and it echoes throughout the empty room. "What the hell are you doing here? Why have you come? I do not want anything to do with you. Can you not understand that by now woman?"

I stand, to appear more confident, but I brace myself for more of his harsh words. He continues his rant, and my brother comes to stand in front of me in a protective way. I find the courage to speak in between his yelling.

"Pedro, I am here to tell you about our daughter's fate. She died. I wanted you to know, as you are still her father."

"I already know this."

"How?"

"Are you such an idiot that you do not think I know about her death? Of course I know."

"I had no idea you knew, or I would not have come."

"Now you know, so leave, and do not come back again."

"What about the apartment?"

"You may have the apartment as long as you can pay for it. I do not need it any longer. When I am released, in short of one year, I am going to live with my cousin. I have made the arrangements. You will never see me again."

Eduardo begins to speak, and I put my arm out.

"Eduardo, do not bother. I want to leave."

My brother's fiery eyes shoot daggers into Pedro's, but he does not say a word to him. I grab his arm and turn to the guard to let him know we are ready to leave. I walk out satisfied. I have said my piece and done my part. This is the first and last time I visit my husband in prison.

⁂

Eleven months later, there is word that he lives with his cousin and has another woman. Good luck to her — I am glad the woman is no longer me. He never tries to contact me, so to him, I am forgotten.

One day, not too long after Pedro's release, Eduardo comes to pay me a visit. He appears flustered, running his hands through his hair when I let him into the apartment.

"Eduardo, what is wrong?"

He hesitates, and then says, "I saw him today."

"Quem?" *Who?* I ask.

"Pedro, the bastard. I saw him in town."

"Oh, did you speak to him?"

"We said a few words to each other. I told him he has an obligation and duty to you, and that he is a coward and a poor excuse for a man."

"Oh dear."

"The idiot promised me he will come see you, to settle things."

My blood boils, I do not want to see him again. "Okay, when is he coming?"

"He said he will make time to come in the next two weeks."

"I hope I am not alone when he comes."

"Rosa, he will not lay a hand on you, if he does, he goes back to jail."

I am not convinced jail is a big enough threat to keep him from harming me, but I do not tell my brother my fears.

Three weeks go by, and I must be lucky because Pedro still has not come. He must have made the promise only to keep my brother off his back, but I do not let my guard down, I remain waiting and ready in case he shows up while I am alone. Months go by and still no Pedro. Christmas and New Years go by as silent as the night.

On New Year's Day, I have another nightmare. I dream of my father.

He is calling out to me for help. We are in a field, walking, and he is ahead of me calling my name. As I try to speed up, the distance between us increases until he is so far away I cannot see him through the thick fog any longer.

When I open my eyes, it is dawn. I get out of bed, walk to my window and there is nothing but fog outside.

CHAPTER 30

1947

IT IS THE end of 1947, so another year passes, and Europe, including Portugal, now sees the conclusion of WWII. This year brings the beginning of the Cold War, but Angola is still a war-free zone, unlike much of Europe.

My father was unwell over the last year, but it is no surprise. I expect, because of the dream, he will die soon. The dream came to me almost a year ago, but it is still as vivid as it was that night. By the end of 1947, my poor father can no longer hide his agony. My brothers decide to take him to a clinic in Luanda. There is a doctor at this clinic who runs a program that might help. We do not know what ailment he suffers from, but whatever it is, it has attacked his lungs. My father is a heavy smoker and has smoked for most of his entire life. He began smoking when I was young, and I remember my first days after returning home and seeing him smoke. He did not smoke prior to me leaving, at least not that I remember.

He smokes in the house, in bed, and while driving. He always has a cigarette dangling from his lips. To see my father without a cigarette looks odd, and I am not used to the image.

When he becomes sick, he develops a deep, hoarse cough that causes him to bring up phlegm filled with blood. I am afraid he will cough up his lungs as well as phlegm. After the cough comes the back pain, and it prevents him from walking for extended periods of time. Shortly thereafter he develops chest pain that is worse when he breathes deep. Once this starts, he must stay in bed or on the couch. His breathing is the next thing to become affected, and he suffers from shortness of breath. His physical state deteriorates so fast, and this is when my brothers decide he must go to the clinic.

As my brothers place him inside the vehicle, I say goodbye. My father shakes his head, he is out of breath and unable to speak. His silence signifies the end, and he dies one month later in the clinic in Luanda. He is not alone when he passes, Eduardo is with him. He stays with him the entire time, and it brings me comfort knowing my father was not alone.

I am devastated to receive the news, but not surprised; the dream was an omen. I allow myself time to mourn the death of my father, and mourning now comes naturally to me. Losing a child causes the deepest stab to the soul. Once a person goes through this kind of pain, no other tragedy hurts as much, not even the death of a parent.

There are many people I know at the funeral, both friends and family. Aunt Mariazinha, Aunt Rita, and the cousins I have not seen in years are here. My father had many acquaintances from his store, and they are here too. I run into Victoria for the first time in a long time. Her and my father parted ways almost one year ago, before he got sick and shortly after Tavina died. It is bittersweet that we meet again this way, but we embrace and talk for a long time. She gives me her deepest condolences. She asks how I have been since losing Tavina, and she asks about Pedro.

"You know, I never did like him," she says.

"Yes, I know. You tried to warn me to stay away, and I should have listened."

I miss talking to her, especially since Antonietta left. I miss the mother figure in my life. Victoria reaches out and pulls me into another hug, only this time she holds on for longer and hesitates to let go. When she releases me, tears fill her eyes, and while wiping the tears, she walks away and out of my life. Victoria is like a wave I grip tight and ride to shore, only the wave breaks too early and leaves me floating in unknown waters.

PART FOUR

1975 Present Day
1948 - 1974

CHAPTER 31

Lobito
October 4, 1975
Present Day

I MUST HAVE FALLEN asleep. I wake up to the baby, my grand-daughter Telma, pulling on my sleeve. She must be hungry, poor thing. I stretch my arms out to the sides and wonder how long I have been asleep. Has it been one hour, two, or longer? No, I cannot have fallen asleep for that long. Impossible.

I wipe sleep from my eyes, pick my granddaughter up in my arms, and hold her close to my chest for a few minutes. "I know baby girl, you are hungry. Grandma knows your tummy hurts." She tugs on my blouse and moans; her tummy growls and my heart breaks.

I stretch my sore legs because they are numb from sleeping on the floor. I look around the room, and everyone is still sleeping. Something seems different to me today, and I wonder if it's morning. Silence fills the room. I leave Telma sitting on the floor beside Leo as he sleeps, and I walk over to the front window. I push away the couch that blocks the window's view, and I risk a peek, but only a quick one.

As I look outside through the window, I do sense something is different, but I cannot distinguish what it is. There is a sense of calmness in the air. I have not felt this for four days, not since our city went under siege. The radio is not on. Leo must have turned it off so we can sleep. None of us have received a full night's sleep for days. The most sleep we get is an hour at a time, alternating turns, so there are always a few of us awake, in case of trouble.

I decide I have risked this long enough, so I move the couch back into its original place, covering the window. We are once again protected from the outside world, so I walk back to our little haven, our cave. "Leo, wake up, the sun is rising, and it's morning."

He opens his eyes and looks around the room like I did. "Have you been up all night?"

"No, I woke up a few minutes ago."

He sits up, leans back on his elbows. "Something seems different today."

"Yes, I notice it too."

Suddenly I realize what is different; I have not heard gunshots since I woke up. Leo rocks his head back and forth, touching his ear to his shoulder, and then stretches his arms behind his back. Sleeping on the floor four nights in a row is taking a toll on us; we are not as young as we once were.

Telma's stomach is not the only one now growling, mine is too. It is five days now since we ate a proper meal. I am sure I am losing weight, something I cannot afford to lose. I look over to Leo, and he is still stretching. "How much longer do we have to stay locked up inside, prisoners in our home?" I ask him.

"I am turning the radio back on. Let's listen for new information today."

"Okay, I will wake up the others."

"No," says Leo, "Let them sleep a little longer."

I have no energy left. I am spent, defeated and lost. I know I must get to the kitchen to find something for the baby to eat. At this point, anything will do to trick her tiny belly into thinking it is a proper meal.

Leo sees me getting up. "Stay clear of the window," he reminds me. "Yes, I know," I say, as I walk away.

To get to the kitchen, I must walk in front of the big window that faces the backyard and the ocean. I duck as I walk past. When I arrive in the kitchen I am more concealed, so I let my muscles relax from their tightness. I open cupboards one by one looking for food, anything will suffice. I find biscuits I saved, and I am satisfied. This will have to be the baby's breakfast. As I carry the biscuits back to the living room I say another silent prayer to God, begging for help for us all. As of late, I realize I need to make more of an effort to start to pray daily, and not only when I am in need. I recognize that I am guilty of this, turning to God only when I need Him. I make a promise to change this if I survive.

When I get back to the area where everyone is trying to stay alive, Leo is playing with our granddaughter. I am so lucky to have him in my life, and to have this man by my side every day.

He sees me watching him. "We will survive Rosa, I give you my word. I will get us out of this situation. I will get us out of this country, and into safety."

"I hope so."

"Do more than hope, believe."

I remember someone from my past saying something similar about doing more than trying. I reflect on that for a moment, and I remember it was my birth mother, all those years ago. This now has me thinking about my past again, and everything I went through before I met Leo. How did I survive that life without him by my side? I do not think I can go through that again. That was another life, another time, and another version of me.

I sit beside Leo and Telma and I reach out and give her one of the biscuits. Her eyes light up when she sees the food. She chews urgently, despite her only having four tiny front teeth.

I lean back and rest against the chair with my eyes closed; I remember how Leo and I first met.

CHAPTER 32

1948

I DO NOT WANT to go to this party. I would much rather stay home, make tea and curl up with my books. Instead, I am at my friend's house getting ready for a party I do not want to attend. So, I complain the entire time my friend Ana and I get ready.

I met Ana two years ago one afternoon while at church, and we became instant friends. Ana loves parties and tries to get me to come along. I often decline, as I am not into crowds and loud music.

Tonight is different though, tonight is New Year's Eve. Ana is applying her lipstick, and says, "No young woman should stay home alone, not on New Year's Eve."

I sigh and look at her as she smiles back and reveals perfect white teeth. With her dazzling eyes she wills me to comply, so I agree to go to the party.

I stare into the mirror trying to decide if I am satisfied with my hair. "Parties are such trouble. I do not understand why anyone bothers with them," I say.

"Do not be silly, parties can be lots of fun if you let them. You need to open your mind. Who knows, you might meet a gentleman," she teases.

"I would like to see a gentleman try to win me over. I shall give him something to work for."

I act tough, but inside I am weak. I have not gone out since before Tavina passed away. After my father died I moved back home into his house, spending most of my time there, helping however I can. It is a difficult year adjusting to many changes. I still grieve every day for my baby girl, the heaviness in my chest and the feeling of despair will never leave. I shall suffer forever, and do not think it will get easier.

Tonight though, something pulls at me, telling me to go. So, I decide to accompany Ana to this party.

"You are coming?" She confirms.

"I said I will come, and I will."

"Wonderful. You will not regret it."

"But you must get my hair under control," I warn her.

"Oh Rosa, you will not regret tonight. I promise. It is a new year, a new beginning, a new life."

"We shall see about that."

Together she and I set out to my brother's apartment building; the party is in the backyard. We plan on taking a taxi as it is too far to walk in heels. I wear a simple black dress that flares out at the knees. A lurid red belt hugs my hips, and black buttons frame the front. I have a matching hat with a red flower on the side and matching gloves with the same red flower. I put on a little lipstick, which is unusual for me. I have not worn lipstick since my daughter died. In fact, this is the first time I wear any colour other than pure black.

Before we leave her house, I take one last look in the mirror and I am pleased with my appearance. As we arrive, I notice many gentlemen staring at me. I am uncomfortable and not used to the attention since I seldom frequent places like this. I keep my head bent to avoid eye contact, I do not want to give them the wrong impression. The moment we arrive, Ana leaves me. She sees someone she recognizes, and she runs off to say hello, leaving me alone standing by myself with no one to talk to. I pretend to enjoy the music, but I am too shy to dance by myself. The yard is filling up fast with both people and smoke. The bar is busy, and many men stand to wait for their drinks. I notice none, except the one.

His eyes are mysterious looking, brown and radiant. His hair is light brown and parted to the side, revealing a model like handsome face. His nose is perfectly sculpted and centred, he looks like an angel. He has not noticed me yet. To him, I am still invisible. He sits alone on a couch, waiting for something or someone. A man that handsome must have a woman in his life — he cannot be single. He scans the room, I am not sure what or who he looks for. Then his eyes become locked with mine. My breathing stops. I try to shift my focus and look away, but I cannot tear my eyes off him. He has me mesmerized. I straighten my back so I can appear taller. I am not short for a woman, but I am not considered tall, either. As I continue to stare at his handsome face he stands, straightens his left pant leg, and walks toward me. I take a deep breath and hold it for a few seconds. I manage to release it before fainting, and my breathing quickens as he gets closer. I prepare myself. He is near, and so the encounter is inevitable.

I clear my throat to prepare my voice for when I speak because I want to sound elegant and not raspy. "Hello," I say, as he approaches close enough I can touch him. I wipe my palms on my dress and hope he does not notice.

He reaches out his right hand. "Do you care to dance?"

I squeeze the fabric of my dress. "I do not know how to dance."

"I will lead, and you follow," he says, as he bows his head to the side.

"Why then, certainly."

Oh, dear God, what have I said? I am braver today than usual.

I place my hand in his as he leads me to the dance floor, ten feet away from where we stood. He saunters with posture to an open spot.

When we arrive, he places his right arm around my back, his left-hand takes mine and we form a waltz stance. Our bodies glide and shift to the rhythm of the music. Our hips sway and rock back and forth. The hand that rests on my back is warm and heats me even more in the already stuffy air. His eyes never leave mine. We remain in this position until the first song comes to an end, but then we continue into the next song. It is automatic, and he does not ask if I want to dance again. He assumes I do, and he is right. Neither of us wants the music to end.

The third song stops, the band plays another, and we dance to the fourth. When it finishes, there is a pause, so the next song does not begin right away. The band members are now speaking into the microphone and making announcements. My mystery man takes my hand in his and walks me off the dance floor. He asks me if I want a drink, but I decline as I do not drink alcohol. He orders liquor for himself and asks for my name. "Rosa," I say.

He takes a sip from the drink that now sits on the counter. "Rosa, what a beautiful name."

"Thank you."

He sets his drink down again. "You have the sweetest voice."

"Thank you," I say for a second time. I am growing annoyed with myself, and I try to think of something else to say, but I am lost for words. Then I remember I do not know his name, and that is a good question to start with. As I am about to speak, a man I do not recognize appears and pats my companion on the back. "Leo, there you are, where have you been?" says the man.

Oh, so his name is Leo. Now I cannot ask that, and I must come up with another question.

Leo shifts from one leg to the other before replying. "I am dancing with this beautiful lady here."

"I have been going mad looking for you. We must go, she is here. I found her," says the friend to Leo.

"I am not ready. Give me some time," Leo says.

"What on earth do you mean to say you are not ready?"

"I said, I am not ready," repeats Leo giving his friend a look with raised eyebrows.

"You drag me out here to propose to the love of your life, and now you are dancing with another woman?"

I turn to Leo who has a red face now, and his smile fades. He looks at his friend with a hard stare.

"I know what I asked you to do. And it is a mistake," says Leo.

As the two continue to argue, I try to excuse myself. "Thank you for the dance, it was most lovely," I say, as I walk away.

Leo grabs my arm, preventing me from leaving. "Stay," he says.

"What do you want me to do?" asks the friend.

"Tell her I have not come and get her out of here for me, please?"

"You owe me one," says the friend as he walks away, flapping his arms in the air.

"Thank you my friend!" Leo shouts back.

I am left standing alone with Leo in this odd situation. Leo is here to propose to a woman, but he has had a change of heart, and I do not know why. Interesting.

I try once more to leave, and again he grabs my arm. "Please, do not go. Stay with me," he pleads.

"Why?"

"Because I have never in my life been so enamoured over anyone before."

"Oh," I say, not knowing what else to say at this awkward moment. My cheeks burn, but I resist the urge to touch them. "Are you not engaged then?"

I want him to clarify this. He brings his hands to his head and swipes his hand across his hair. "No, I am not. I was going to ask a young woman to marry me, but that was before I set eyes on you. I am now certain of one thing; I cannot marry anyone else."

I straighten the bottom of my dress for something to do. "Well, this is a rather sudden decision."

He reaches for his drink again, eyes on me still. "I have made the best decision."

"One you will not come to regret, I hope."

"Not ever. Now, may I have another dance?"

I smile, he takes my hand, and we dance together for the remainder of the night.

I rarely think of Pedro, but tonight my thoughts drift to him because guilt plagues me. I am still legally married. Although we have not seen each other in almost two years, I cannot help feeling shameful, and I must keep these thoughts in my head. I convince myself there is no harm in this, I plan to leave soon and end the night early. But as much as I want to leave before midnight, we dance until the band counts down.

Leo pulls me in close to him. "It is almost midnight; we are ringing in the New Year together."

I try to back away, but he pulls me in tight. "Leo I cannot stay any longer …"

I am interrupted by the sound of the singer on the microphone counting. "Ten, nine, eight …"

Leo and I continue to dance, even though there is no music playing. He leans in and with a soft voice whispers in my ear, "Happy New Year, Rosa."

He is so close I smell his cologne.

"Happy New Year," I say.

"This is the best one yet!" he says. Although I do not respond, I do agree.

We spend the rest of the night dancing, and by the end of the night my feet are sore from the shoes I wear. Eduardo is across the room talking to a gentleman, and beside him is his wife. I had not noticed him until now, but I am not surprised to see them here as this is their apartment building. Eduardo notices me then waves, so I wave back. He approaches us, and his wife follows with her arm around his. He nods his head towards Leo. "Good evening. You have been enjoying the company of my sister tonight," he says, as he places his hand out to introduce himself.

Leo's eyes widen and he shakes his hand. "How do you do? Your sister is most lovely, if I may add."

"Yes, she is. Please excuse us for a few moments. Rosa and I have some things to discuss." Eduardo grabs my elbow and pulls me off the dancing floor, and my sister-in-law follows close behind. Leo is alone, and this frightens me. Will he decide to marry the other woman now that he knows I have an overprotective older brother?

When we are no longer within hearing distance, I let Eduardo have a piece of my mind. "Eduardo, let go, you are hurting my arm," I say, as I try to break free from his grip.

"I do not care."

"What is wrong with you? Why are you embarrassing me like this?"

I am still trying to break free from his tight grip. He does not let go, and my complaining only makes him hold my arm tighter. I am sure a bruise is forming.

He grabs my other shoulder with his free arm. "What do you think you are up to Rosa? This is not acceptable. You are a married woman and cannot be dancing with other men. This is disgraceful."

I knew this lecture was coming, and I try to plead with him to stop. "Pedro and I have not lived as husband and wife for years. Please, Eduardo, do not be angry with me. I only want to have a little fun. The night is innocent."

"Judging by the look in that man's eyes, still on you right now as we speak, it will not end innocently." He points to where Leo is. "He does seem to like you, so what are your plans? What are you doing to do?"

"I do not know yet."

"Have you told him?"

"About what?" I say, but I already know what he refers to.

"About your past?"

"No."

"I suggest you start with, 'I'm married.'"

"I know I need to be honest with him and tell him the truth. I have not had the opportunity. We have danced, and the music is too loud to carry on a conversation."

His eyebrows are knit close together. "Do you love him?"

"I only met him a couple hours ago."

I cannot help myself, so I look over to see if he is still looking at me, and I find he is. This makes me giddy, and my stomach tingles. Happiness is an emotion I have not experienced in years. I hope he decides to not propose to the other woman and to stay here with me instead. I ponder the question my brother asked, do I love him? I am interested and captivated by him, so I am sure I can love him soon enough.

My brother contemplates what to do next, and then tells me he is going to talk to Leo. "Wait here, and do not leave. I will see what I can do to help you."

My sister-in-law has not said anything and only listened. Eduardo leaves his wife and me alone for a long time. By now the party is over, there is no more music playing, and the band packs the gear. People stack chairs and tables and the cleaning crew sweeps the ground. Eduardo is gone for a long time, so my sister-in-law and I find chairs to rest our tired feet. Her feet too are sore from the uncomfortable shoes, and it is good to know I am not the only one that sacrifices comfort for fashion.

The men are still talking, and I ask my sister-in-law how much longer they will be because I am tired.

Moments later, they walk toward us and my heart skips a few beats. What is Leo thinking of me now? Does he regret the decision he made earlier?

Eduardo says he told Leo the entire story. He knows everything now about my failed marriage, the coma, and Tavina's death. Leo says he feels sorry for me and accepts me nonetheless. He promises to call the next morning, and he remains true to his word. From that day forward, we begin to see one another, and I learn about his life.

Eleuterio Carvalho is from the Island of São Miguel, a city called Ponta Delgada located on the water's edge. He is in Angola with the army. His parents and siblings are back in São Miguel, and they are eager to have him return home. He was stationed in Nova Lisboa when he arrived, and he stayed there for a long time, but not long ago he moved to Lobito. He is twenty-four years old, five years older than I. Every Portuguese man must serve in the army from the age of twenty for a full four-year term. Leo only has a few months left to serve before he is free. With a name like Eleuterio, of course his friends call him Leo.

We see each other daily, and he does not allow me out of his sight for longer than a few minutes. We go for long walks, share many meals, and each time he takes my hand in his, I know I am safe. I long to see him every day, and when our time together comes to an end, there is an emptiness inside. We talk about Tavina, and I confide in him about my sorrows and the heartache at losing her. He listens and caresses my face with his gentle hands, wiping away tears that fall as I speak of my past.

After a few weeks, he tells me he wants to spend his life with me and marry me. When he says these words, I grab onto him tight, afraid if I let go that I will float away as that is how elated I am. I accept his proposal, throw myself into his arms, and he catches me with ease.

We talk about the one problem standing in our way — Pedro. As much as I do not want contact with the man, I know I must search for him. Leo has a strong hatred for him, and I expect this given the circumstances. I need to find him to beg him for a divorce so I can be free to marry Leo.

Without wasting any time, I begin looking for my long-lost husband in the places he frequents. I place advertisements in the local papers, spread the word by mouth, and my family helps to spread the word, also. I write letters to the few relatives of his I know, but I receive no replies from any of my sources. After weeks of trying to find him, I become defeated because this is not an easy task, and we cannot find Pedro as hard as we try. My wonderful brothers assist me with the search, and of course, so does Leo. Leo is the most eager to find him; he has the most to lose if we fail. As hard as we search, Pedro remains a hidden mystery and lost in this world. Another few weeks go by, but still, we cannot find Pedro.

Leo and I are out for lunch one afternoon when out of the blue I get a lump in my throat and cannot stop the tears from falling.

"This is not fair. How can we get married if we do not find him?" I say.

"Rosa, listen to me," Leo says, and lifts my chin as he speaks. "It does not matter to me. I love you, and I want to marry you, but if we cannot marry each other now, then we wait."

I use the napkin on the table to blow my nose. "What are you saying?"

"I am saying you will still be my wife. Even if it is not official."

I fold the napkin and keep it in my hands in case I need it again. "How? I mean, if I am already married, then how can I be your wife as well?"

"It will take time. One day we will find him, but for now, we can still live as man and wife." He reaches out and wipes another tear that falls from my eye. I place my hand over his and squeeze it. I am blessed and lucky to have found this man, but first I must convince my brothers of our plans.

CHAPTER 33

1949

A FEW MONTHS LATER, Leo finishes his term with the army, and we move in together. My brothers put up a fight, but without my father alive to forbid me, they eventually back down.

We live in Restinga, a prestigious neighbourhood in Lobito. This is where rich folks live: doctors, lawyers, and engineers. Restinga is a peninsula with a beautiful, white sandy beach. Leo's work brings him here, so I follow.

He works in a popular restaurant owned by a married couple. We do not have an apartment of our own — we cannot afford one here. But the restaurant owners offer us a room for free as part of Leo's wages. We are happy with the arrangement and able to save some money by not having to pay rent.

The restaurant owner's wife's name is Catarina, and she is the one to show us to our room. She looks at Leo with longing in her eyes, and this makes me uncomfortable. Leo ignores her, but she does not take her eyes off him. She must not know I am aware of this, but I am. I mention this to Leo, and he tells me I am overreacting.

Without warning, one day Catarina's husband leaves for Lisbon to get medical help for their son who falls ill. He asks Leo to run the restaurant in his absence. Leo will be well compensated for the extra work and responsibilities, and we need the money, so this is an opportunity we cannot pass. Tonight, we celebrate Leo's temporary promotion with red wine. This is a new beginning for us, one full of possibilities and a bright future.

With her husband gone, Catarina's true colours show. At first, Catarina comes across as playful, but soon she is paying Leo more attention than she should for a married woman. I do not like the way she carries herself around him and talks to him. I tell Leo, but again he tells me to not worry and to not make any trouble. Leo says the money he makes is worth it, so we need to put up with her ways. I trust Leo and know he loves me, so I am not concerned about his actions, but it is her agenda I do not like and that worries me.

It is painful to witness how she looks at him; how she touches his arm when not necessary and lets her fingers linger far too long. She carries on this way even when I am around, so I cannot imagine what she tries when Leo is alone. Leo ignores her, shrugs off every touch and avoids each advance she makes. The more he disregards her, the harder she tries to seduce him. She continues this way for a few weeks before she comes to understand her actions are not reciprocated. Leo and I have a bond, not even her long fingernails can rip apart.

When her advances towards Leo go unrequited, she sets out to get revenge. She spreads rumours about Leo and says Leo is after her. This is not true, and when the rumours reach me, I must control my temper, so I do not end up yanking her hair from her scalp. I want to poke her eyes out, but Leo says to be careful and that the situation is best ignored. I listen like a good wife.

The rumours circulate for a few weeks, and when customers now walk into the restaurant they give Leo an odd look. This bothers me, but I hold my tongue.

Leo is busy keeping the restaurant running when a letter arrives addressed to him. He comes upstairs and enters the apartment showing me the letter. It is from Leo's boss, Catarina's husband.

Eleuterio,

I write to inform you that you are terminated from your employment at the restaurant. This is effective immediately. Pack your belongings and leave my premises by the end of this week. I will compensate you for the time you put in.

Thank you.
Management

Leo reads the letter out loud so I can hear. I walk over to where he sits on the bed and put my arms around him. "It is for the best."

He gets up off the bed and rips the letter in half. "This is ridiculous, she has been telling lies, and I am the one who gets terminated."

"Eu sei," *I know.*

I try to comfort him by giving him a hug, but he pushes me away and walks towards the window in the small room.

"That damn woman. I want to wring her neck."

"Leo it is not worth it. Remember this is what you told me. Your own words are that the situation is best ignored."

He looks at me with shock in his eyes, surprised I am using his own advice against him. "Why are you always right?"

"So, you admit I am always right?" I say teasing him. He is in a better mood now, so I try to tickle him to make light of the situation. He smiles and wraps his arms around me and carries me to bed where we forget about Catarina.

The letter specifies we need to leave by the end of this week, so this only gives us two days to pack and find a new place to live. Leo gave notice at his old apartment already, so going back is not an option. We search right away and find another apartment, but it is not in Restinga as we cannot afford to live here, but we can afford an apartment in the town near the village. Living near the village is convenient because we do not have a vehicle to get around in. I am sorry to leave Restinga, there was much opportunity here for us, and I fear we will never again get another opportunity like this one. But we do not look back, we have each other, and we look forward to the future together, no matter where that might be.

Two days later, we are in the taxi on our way to our new apartment. This is our first apartment together, and I am ready to start the next chapter of our lives with or without Pedro's help.

CHAPTER 34

1950

I
T IS EARLY one morning, and Leo and I are enjoying each other's company too much to get out of bed. Leo gets up to use the washroom, there is a knock on the door, and I am alarmed because it is so early in the morning. Good news does not start this early in the day.

From the bathroom, Leo yells, "Rosa, are you expecting company?"

"Not at this hour of the morning I am not."

"Who on earth can this be?"

"Eu vou ver," *I will see.*

I reach for my house robe, slip it on and run to the door. It is Eduardo, and he forces himself into the room, out of breath. "Rosa, have you seen today's paper?" He waves the newspaper in front of me.

"No, I have not; we only got up a few minutes ago."

"You need to look at this right now." He throws the paper at me.

"What is it?"

"Just read."

He folded the newspaper in a way that when I unfold it the article he wants me to read is first in view.

"What is this about?" I ask before reading it.

"Will you stop talking for once and read?"

Pouting my lips at him makes him smile. It takes me less than thirty seconds to understand what I am reading. When I finish, I look up with shock, my mouth is open, and I immediately jump into my brother's arms. The newspaper falls to the floor.

Leo walks into the room and sees me in my brother's arms. "Eduardo, it is you. You must bring good news with you to make my wife happy this morning?"

"Yes, good news indeed," says Eduardo.

"Eduardo, I cannot tell you how thrilled I am. Oh, Leo, wait until I tell you the news," I say.

"Well, I am waiting. Are either of you going to tell me what this is about?"

"It's about Pedro, and he is looking for me. He wants to dissolve the marriage."

Leo stiffens at the sound of Pedro's name. "Let me read that?"

Leo grabs the paper from the floor and reads the article for himself. "Why now, I wonder? Why after all this time does he want to find you to settle the divorce?"

"Oh Leo, can you not see why?"

"I would not have asked if I could."

"He is looking for me now, for the same reasons we searched for him," I say.

Eduardo jumps in, "He has obviously found someone himself, and he must want to get married, it only makes sense Leo."

"Yes, yes, I suppose it does make sense," says Leo, scratching his chin.

The article is short, and only contains a few lines with a plea for anyone who knows me to contact him with my whereabouts. His contact information is included. Now I know how to get into contact with him, and I can get my divorce after all these years. I am finally going to be free from the devastating marriage I rushed into long ago when I was young and naïve.

CHAPTER 35

1951

A YEAR HAS PASSED since we found Pedro, but I am still not divorced. We are correct in our assumption that he wants a divorce because he found someone himself. Leo is the one to contact Pedro, and this is a mistake. Once Pedro discovers I have someone in my life, he refuses to divorce me. I should not have expected less from him. Pedro says he wants the divorce still, but he now insists I pay for it. I regret not foreseeing this, I am married to the man, and I know this is typical of his character. I should have contacted him myself, and I should not have brought Leo into this. If I had approached the situation differently and pretended I was not pleased about the divorce, he would have paid for it. We did not think this through. Pedro now knows I have stakes in this, so he forces me to finance the divorce.

A divorce costs a lot of money, something Leo and I do not have much of now. From this day forward, we begin to save most of what Leo earns. Leo contacts Pedro several times to get the process started, but without the money, we get nowhere as Pedro is not willing to pay for it. The money is obviously worth more to him than his new-found love. Throughout this time, Leo and I remain positive, we are stronger together, and this is how we get through it.

We want children, but we prefer to wait until I am no longer married to someone else before starting a family, so we wait. Leo and I are sitting outside at a park near our apartment, people watching.

"It will not be long now my love," says Leo.

"You will marry me yet if it is the last thing you do."

I smile as he reaches over and kisses me.

Leo gets a new job working as a truck driver, he makes a little more money, so we save every penny he brings home and put it towards the divorce. Since we are not married we try to be extra careful, but we are not careful enough, and within a month I discover I am with child. I get a funny feeling in the pit of my stomach when I find out, but Leo says it will work out and is not the least bit worried.

My aunts used to tell me each pregnancy is easier than the last, but I am not so sure this is true. This pregnancy brings more nausea and vomiting than the first. I am reminded of how much the female body must work to grow a human being, and I forgot what this feels like. I was so young when I was pregnant with Tavina, and that seems like many moons ago. How did I manage with no one at my side to guide, protect, and encourage me? But I remember Victoria and Antonietta; I was not alone, I had them both by me, and I miss them dearly.

All I want to do during this pregnancy is sleep. Leo is supportive, bringing me tea, and encouraging me to rest and not work too much around the house.

He peeks into my mug and notices I have not touched my tea. "Rosa, drink this, you need to stay hydrated."

"It is cold."

"I will make you a new one." He leaves with my old mug in hand and returns minutes later with a steaming cup.

"Thank you, but I should get up. I need to clean the apartment."

"The apartment can wait."

He pushes the mug closer so it is within reach. He gives me a nod of the head as if to say, 'Go ahead.'

Each day is the same, and nine months later I give birth to my first son, Carlos Carvalho. The memory of taking care of Tavina those first few weeks of her life comes back in a rush. I know exactly what I need to do to keep my baby safe, warm, and fed. I love being a mother again. Tavina comes to mind every time the baby cries, every diaper change, and at every feeding. I look up hoping she is looking down on me from Heaven, and I pray she knows I am, and always will, think of her.

Leo soon goes through another job change and this brings us to Bocoio, a small village far away from Lobito. The move happens not too long after Carlos is born, and moving is more difficult with a newborn baby. We settle in as best we can, and I do not mind it here in Bocoio too much, but I miss Lobito and I long to move back someday. Lobito is the place I call home.

Less than two years after we move, I give birth to Anabella. Bella or Belinha we call her often. I am still not free from Pedro. Leo has made several more visits to the man, but he still refuses to divorce me, so I pretend that part of my life does not exist. The biggest struggle I have now is watching over a two-year-old while caring for a newborn. Carlos grows jealous of the time I spend with Bella and grows close to his father. When I am looking for Carlos all I must do is find Leo, the two are inseparable.

As Carlos grows older he becomes more rambunctious, making my life much more difficult. He is always up to something, that kid, even at this young of an age. I decide I must keep a close eye on him, always, but today I discover that always is not enough.

We have a part-time nanny who comes to the house a few days a week to entertain Carlos while I am busy with baby Bella. Bella still requires a lot of attention as she is not even one. The nanny's only job is to watch over Carlos, play, feed, and take him for walks. This frees my time so I can focus on nursing, cooking dinner for when Leo gets home, and doing a little cleaning.

It is early morning, the nanny arrives, and I am busy nursing Bella. Leo gets ready to leave for the day as he has a delivery to make for work.

"Come give Papa a kiss, Carlito. I will see you later tonight."

Carlos runs into his father's open arms and clings for dear life, not wanting to let go. "Okay Carlito, I must leave now, you do not want to make Papa late, do you?"

Carlos responds with crying, as he does not want his father to leave. Leo takes him everywhere; he even takes him on some local deliveries. But, this delivery is far, and Leo is not expecting to arrive back home until later tonight. He says he will not be home for dinner and to not wait for him. This delivery is much too far for Carlos, he will become antsy. I sit back nursing Bella, watching the exchange between father and son, and I know I am in for an afternoon of screaming the moment Leo walks out the door.

I shift Bella to the other breast as she is still hungry. "Carlos, let go of your father. He must go to work now," I say.

Carlos ignores me, so I motion to the nanny, who does nothing to help and get Carlos off his father so he can be on his way.

I crinkle my nose at the smell coming from Bella's bottom, she needs a diaper change. I pull Bella away from my breast and lay her over my shoulder to burp while I carry her upstairs.

By the time I come down, I do not see Leo, Carlos, or the nanny, so I assume Leo left and Carlos and the nanny are out for a walk. I go about my business as usual, picking up toys and trying to decide what to make for dinner tonight. I clean and cook lunch since Bella is napping and this is my only opportunity to be productive. Once lunchtime approaches, I look for Carlos and the nanny. They should be back by now — they have been gone a long time. Carlos must be hungry and will want food soon. He has a big appetite for a child his age. I decide it is long enough, so I go outside to look for them. The nanny sits in the garden reading a book without a care in the world.

With my hands on my hips, I say, "Where is my son?"

I do not see him close by.

The nanny pulls his face away from the book and looks up with an odd expression. "I do not know, I thought he was with you."

My heart beats faster. "What do you mean you thought he was with me?"

"Well, he is not here," he says extending his arms.

"He has not been with me all morning."

This kid must be trying to pull a prank on me, but then worry sets over his face and I know he is serious. "When did you seen him last?"

He stands and paces in the garden. "When your husband left. He went outside with his father and waved goodbye to him. I took the opportunity to use the restroom. I had too much coffee this morning, and when I returned your husband's truck was gone, and so were you. I assumed he was with you. The apartment was quiet, so I came out here with a book to read for a while. I did not realize so much time passed, and I lost track of the morning. I assumed if you needed me, you would come to get me. I got so consumed in this book, and it has felt more like five minutes rather than two hours passed."

He is rambling, and my ears hurt hearing his voice. I stop listening to him and look for my son, but my vision is blurry. It is impossible for me to see straight, and my hands are shaking. The realization that my son has been missing for two hours, at least, is unbearable. My thoughts drift back to the horrible day I received the anonymous letter about my daughter's death. I need to do something, but I cannot think. Where is Leo when I need him? Leo would stay calm. Leo would know what to do. I think of where Carlos would go.

"Where do you two go for walks?" I ask.

The nanny is now white as a ghost when he responds. "The park down the street."

"Go, check the park, he must be there. I will knock on neighbours' doors."

He does not move. "Go NOW!" I demand. "What on Earth are you waiting for?"

"Are you telling me, Madame, that Carlos is not with you?"

"Oh, for crying out loud, go and find my son, the one you lost while reading!" He snaps back to reality with my last words because he is now running down the street. I go inside, make sure Bella is asleep, and leave her alone while I go door to door. I manage to get through the entire building before Bella's cry echoes through the halls, so I go get her. I have no choice now, I must bring her with me. It will slow me, but I cannot leave her alone in the apartment if she is awake. I continue going door to door, but nobody has seen Carlos all day, so my efforts are for naught. It is now well after lunch, and my blurred vision is worse, I have difficulty holding the baby in my shaky arms. Neighbours soon arrive to help search. Some walk the streets, while others go door to door as I do. Before long, the entire neighbourhood bonds together to look for my three-year-old missing son.

After an hour, the nanny returns without Carlos. He was not at the park. The search continues well into the evening. Supper time approaches, and I lose hope. Was my son kidnapped? Kidnapping is not common in this town, but it's a possibility. I do not know how else to explain his absence, so I tell myself I must start to face this reality.

I lose more hope with each minute, but then a woman's voice calls my name as she runs down the street towards me. "Rosa, Rosa, come quick, someone has found a small boy and he looks like Carlos. A lady found him, and she is bringing him here now."

"Oh, thank the Lord!" I fall to my knees upon hearing this news. I do not recognize this woman who brings me this news; she must be one of the neighbours helping in the search.

"I was with them, but Carlos is too slow, so I ran ahead to tell you, I can only imagine how you must be sick with worry."

I do not waste another second before running off with a screaming, hungry baby in my arms. There are two people down the road, one is tall and probably an adult, the other is shorter, but I cannot make out who they are. I pray it is Carlos and the woman that found him. I run towards them hoping it is my son. As I approach, his little face becomes visible. He looks worried, cheeks wet with tears. I allow myself to breathe the air trapped in my lungs.

"Carlos!" I yell.

It is my boy; relief and gratitude pass through me. Carlos runs into my arms, and with only one arm I hug him tightly. The other arm still holds the screaming baby. I am on one knee, so we are at eye level. "Where were you? Do you know how frightened I was?"

He nods from side to side. "Where did you go?"

"I go work with Papa," he says in his broken speech. "I follow the truck, but truck too fast. I want Papa."

"You tried to follow your father in his truck?"

"Yes, Mama."

"Oh, thank goodness I found you."

I hug him a little too tight; he complains and asks for his father again. He has not eaten since breakfast, but it is his father he asks for instead of food.

We walk back to our home together, Carlos close to my side. I am furious with the nanny and ready to dismiss him of his duties on the spot. He sits on the front step of the building as I approach, and I do not hesitate before speaking. "We will not require your assistance any longer."

He stands right away. "But it was a misunderstanding, Ma'am please give me one more opp…"

He does not have the chance to ask for another opportunity because I interrupt him. "I do not want to listen to another word out of your mouth. Leave my sight now." He lowers his head and walks away without saying another word. My hope is to never see this nanny again, but I pray the next family he works for does not have the same fate. I pray he is more vigilant with other children than he was with mine. Now that I have both my children in my arms, I relax.

Carlos' stomach growls, and at the same time so does mine. We have not eaten since breakfast, so I better find some food, fast. My vision has not returned to normal, but it is better. My arms are still a little shaky, and I struggle to hold Bella for too long. When we are back inside the apartment, I feed the children first, then myself. A sandwich will have to be it for supper today. I hope Leo is not too hungry when he gets home as this is all I have to offer him. I put the kids to bed, and I fill the tub as I need to soak in a bath.

After my bath, I sit in the living room knitting while I wait for Leo. It's late, almost nine o'clock. Leo is a hardworking man, and after Pedro, I am still not used to his kind and gentle ways. Leo is sweet with kind words, helps me with the children, and I treasure him like a rare diamond.

Nighttime is now upon us, and Leo is still not home. Both Bella and Carlos are asleep, safe, and warm in their rooms. I peek into their rooms every fifteen minutes on the clock to make sure they are still there.

I am almost ready for bed when the roar of the truck's engine pulling up the street comes in from the open window.

In walks Leo. "Rosa darling, where are you?" he yells from the door. He walks into the kitchen where I wait to tell him about the events of the day. He wears a big smile for a man who has worked thirteen hours. "How was your day, sweetheart?" He asks, but before I can answer he continues. "You will not believe the day I had. It was horrible. The drive was long and boring, and I am so glad to be home. I have been thinking about eating for hours, I am starving, what's for supper? I hope it's something good," he says, as he pulls up a chair beside me, waiting for me to bring him his dinner.

I place a sandwich in front of him, and he stares at it for a moment before asking me if this is his dinner. He takes one look at my sad eyes, slumped shoulders and pulls me into his arms. As I lay my head on his shoulder his shirt becomes wet with my tears.

He feels it too and reaches up to wipe my cheek. "I don't mind the sandwich — a sandwich for dinner is great," he says, as he rubs my back.

CHAPTER 36

1955

THE END OF Leo's term with the driving company comes, so we move back to Lobito. I am already with child again and eager to deliver this baby in the town I call home. We make the move from Bocoio back to Lobito early in the pregnancy.

Eduardo has a daughter, Manuela, named after my sister, but we call her Mina to differentiate between the two. Manuela used to babysit her often, but she had to stop as she herself is not well, suffering her own issues.

Eduardo is separating from his wife and moving to Lisbon. He is a soccer player and the team offered him a contract to play for a Portuguese first division team. For this reason, we discuss Mina coming to live with us for an extended period. It is common for children to live with extended family, as I lived with Aunt Mariazinha.

Eduardo and my sister-in-law soon confirm Mina is to come and stay with us, and I am thrilled to have her here. When Mina arrives on our doorstep, she is only a five-year-old little girl. My niece is so kind and sweet looking with her round face and big, dark eyes. I have a good feeling about this as she stands in my doorway when Eduardo delivers her to me. She is a well behaved, polite child, and I know I will grow to love her like my own. She adds a new dynamic to our family, and Carlos and Bella love her like a sister right away.

~∞~

A few months later, I give birth to another son, and I decide to name him João. Our little house is full. Bella is two years old, Carlos is four, and Mina is five. Carlos is the most difficult of the children and continues to challenge my patience.

At the end of 1955 we have enough money saved, so we contact Pedro again to begin the divorce proceedings. He is furious it took this long, but he sticks to his word and grants me my divorce. Towards the end of the year, we receive word from our lawyer that the divorce is final, but there is paperwork needed before I can marry Leo. Despite this delay, this is still a day for celebration. After all these years, I am free from Pedro. I am also more at peace with myself now that I am no longer married to Pedro and living with Leo. I can embrace my life with Leo and my children with no remorse.

CHAPTER 37
1955

I HAVE NOT SEEN Antonietta since the dreadful day when I became sick and she saved me by bringing the witch doctor. She had promised she would send notice by post of where she is living, but I never received any letter. She crosses my mind often over these last few years, but I am so consumed with raising my own family, I do not try to find her.

One afternoon, I go out with the children hanging on my hips to pick up our daily post. In the stack is a letter addressed to me. I look at the return address, and it is her name I read on the envelope, my mother's name. I rip open the letter eager to read it.

Dearest Rosa,

I hope this letter reaches you well. I have written several letters to you over the years, but each one is returned. For the longest time, I did not know you moved out of Lobito. It is only recently I learn you are back. An acquaintance of mine gave me your address.

I am returning to Lobito soon and I long to see you, my daughter. I now have your address, so I will be in touch again.

Love Always,

Antonietta, your mother.

I jump with the letter still in my hands. I thought she forgot about me, but this letter proves otherwise. There is a warm feeling inside knowing she made attempts to reach me before now.

A few weeks later, there is a knock on the door and I run to answer it, eager to see if it is Antonietta. When I open the door, a smile forms, I see the woman who gave birth to me standing before me now. Her arms are full of toys, but she still tries to pull me into an embrace, dropping a few toys in the process.

She pulls away after a few seconds, looks me over from head to toe and pulls me into another big hug. "You look happy, so happy."

"Yes Mother, I am." She backs away and looks at me again and nods her head in approval.

"Come in, you must meet your grandchildren."

"Grandchildren. My, oh my, that makes me feel old. Must they call me Grandmother?" she teases.

"Wait until you meet Carlos. He will think of a few things to call you."

We have a good laugh, and then I call for the children.

Carlos is the first to appear, and he is standing a few feet behind me. "Carlos, come here, come meet your grandmother."

He hides behind my leg. "No."

I reach out to grab his arm. "Carlos, do not be rude, come at once."

He must have been playing outside in the dirt. I am embarrassed Antonietta is meeting him looking like this for the first time. He has grass stains on his knees, and his face is covered in dirt. I turn to my mother. "I am sorry Mother; he is not usually like this," I say lying to her, embarrassed. What am I supposed to say? That he always says no to me and it is impossible to keep him clean? I could tell her the truth, but I want to impress her, I want her to think I have everything under control as she does. So, I lie.

She shakes her head. "Do not fear Rosa, he is only a boy. I will go to him and introduce myself instead."

Carlos runs outside and throws himself on the ground in front of the house, screaming.

We watch this temper tantrum from the door he leaves wide open.

My mother turns to me. "You have your hands full with that one."

When the tantrum is over, Carlos does not pay us any attention. He keeps himself busy taking rocks from a pile that he dug and transports them into another pile. He looks up and smiles with his dirt covered face and missing front teeth. I cannot help but laugh, and my mother joins in the laughter with me. Before we know it we are both outside, dirty, helping Carlos build his mountain of rocks.

CHAPTER 38

1955

I T IS THE end of 1955, and today I receive a letter with a return address belonging to my cousin Liberto. This cousin of mine is Aunt Rita's son, the Aunt I spent my summers with. I rip open the envelope, eager to know what information it contains. It is uncommon for Liberto to write to me, so I am apprehensive about why he writes now. I scan the letter to learn what it is about, and I shed a tear as I read that it contains news about my poor, beloved sister, Manuela.

Manuela suffers from severe anxiety and has suffered for a long time. It is because of the anxiety that she tries extra hard to be more lively and outgoing. She tries to compensate for how she feels inside. Anxiety is not easy to live with, and some people can handle it better than others. Some shut down and become withdrawn, cold, and evasive. While others put on a fake face to the world while they are dying inside. This is how Manuela copes, and she hid it well, most of all from me.

I go back to the beginning of the letter to read it over, slow this time, absorbing every word.

Dearest Cousin,

As you know, over the years your sister has had some physical ailments. Besides anxiety, a couple years ago she suffered from severe stomach problems. Although I can only speculate what her diagnosis was. She had surgery to try to make the pain more bearable. You know my cousin, this was a big deal for her, she was deathly afraid of surgery, and this caused a lot of panic attacks. Despite her grave fear for surgery, Manuela still managed to get through it and survived. Her stomach pains improved, and she left your father's house and moved to Benguela to study nursing.

I am sure you are aware of this my dear cousin, but if you are not, I am giving you the full story. I am the one who helped your sister with the move and assisted her with her studies. I set her up with an apartment, and eventually, she graduated from the hospital as a registered nurse. Shortly after, she found a roommate and even had a gentleman court her and ask for her hand in marriage. Did you know your sister was engaged?

Things did not work out for her, however; because her mood declined. She presented herself as happy and content on the outside, but inside she was falling apart.

As time passed, Manuela became more depressed and withdrawn. She pushed away her fiancé, her roommate, and me. She isolated herself from everyone who cared for her.

You most likely have not had much contact with her over the last couple of years. There were several suicide attempts, two of them to be specific.

I drop the letter when I re-read the words *suicide attempt*. I take a deep breath, pick up the letter, and continue to read. I have a difficult time seeing the words, so I look away from the blurry pages for a few minutes to gather enough strength to read on.

It was late one night, nine o'clock and a new moon phase, so the evening was darker than black itself. Manuela had once again attempted to take her life in her own hands. She was still engaged, and she dressed in her white, flowy wedding dress and walked out in the dark, cool waters of the Atlantic Ocean. Her intention was to keep walking until she could no longer feel slippery sand beneath her feet. She wanted the harsh waves to take her away into God's world. This is what she wrote in the suicide note she left behind, found by her roommate days later.

But this is not how your sister's life ends. I do not know if she had a change of heart, or panicked out in the cold ocean, alone. But she did not die the way she had intended. Instead, she swam back to shore before the waves took her away. She had spent a great deal of time in the ocean, and while this is Angola, and our climate is warm, it was still a cool breezy night, as we sometimes have.

Manuela was found unconscious on the ocean shore, face down. Her body half buried in the dark sand, and still dressed in her white wedding gown. Someone walking by, a stranger no less, found her. The man took her to the nearest hospital, the same hospital where she worked as a nurse. She was well known and loved there. Later that night in the hospital emergency room, she developed a high fever. It did not break, and because of the fever, she died the following night.

I regret to be the one to write to you Rosa, and I realize you might already know this. But as I was close to Manuela, I felt it was my obligation to inform you.

My deepest condolences,
Your cousin, Liberto.

Tears do not fall. I expect to weep, but I do not cry. I love my little sister, I always have, and it is not due to a lack of love that I do not cry for her. It is my own insecurities and anxiety that causes me to be so cold. After losing Tavina, then my father, and now my little sister, I become hardened in a way.

"Obrigado, Eleuterio." *Thank you, Leo.* "Thank you for being so understanding of my situation."

"Rosa, she was your sister, we must go, so of course, I understand."

"We shall return as soon as possible."

The same night I receive the letter, we pack our bags to go to Benguela for the funeral to wish my dear sister a farewell.

The funeral is large, and I have never seen so many people gathered in one place. There are many nurses and doctors from the hospital where Manuela worked. Liberto was right, she was well loved. The service is full of beautiful stories about Manuela growing up, and voices fill the church with the wonderful songs she loved to listen to. The ceremony reflects the person my sister was.

CHAPTER 39

1956

AFTER THE FUNERAL, I am hit with sorrow so deep I cannot shake it. I do not want to talk to or see anyone, and I do not eat a thing all day. I shut down mentally and emotionally. I am slowly slipping back into the abyss that took me once already. My rational state of mind fights to resurface, to take back control of my life, but the sorrow defeats the rational part of my brain. My thoughts, my voice of reason, and my emotions are no longer in my control.

The crowd is disappearing, and people leave to go back to their homes. My brother Julio notices my mood change and tries to talk to me. I refuse to talk, but he does not give up.

"Rosa, you must listen to me, please."

I look away, I do not want him to stare into my eyes or he might see the truth behind them. "I will be all right. I only need a little time to process things."

"What things?"

"Nothing specific. Life."

My answers do not suffice, so Julio's questions persist. "Rosa, why don't you and the children come to Nova Lisboa with Beatriz and me for a while?"

Beatriz is my sister-in-law.

"I cannot leave Leo."

"It's only for a few days, and the time away will do you good."

"Okay, for a few days only," I say. "But I must talk to Leo first."

"Let me talk to him for you," he says.

Julio discusses this with Leo and explains it is not personal. He tells him a few days from the daily life and stress of Lobito is what I need for my mental health and recovery. Leo hesitates at first but eventually agrees to the plan. He returns to Lobito alone, and the children and I go to Nova Lisboa with Julio and Beatriz.

Julio works for the Benguela Railway Company, travelling often from city to city. He has been stationed in Nova Lisboa now for a few months. His company has excellent health benefits, so he arranges to have the benefits cover my treatment. I try to convince him I do not need medical intervention, but he disagrees and pushes harder.

"I buried one sister, and I do not want to bury another," he says while he tries to embrace me, but I do not reciprocate. "Please Rosa, do this for me and for your children."

"All right, I will do whatever you think I need to do."

Julio gets to work right away, searching for a therapist so I can start treatment for the depression that plagues me. By the end of the week, I begin therapy.

I see the therapist twice a week, and I have been taking medication to help me with my moods. During these sessions, we talk about my feelings, and the therapist offers strategies to help me cope. He suggests I eat healthily, exercise often, drink lots of water and practice deep breathing. He tells me to focus on my thoughts, and when I have a negative thought, I am to push it aside and replace it with a positive one. This is easier said than done, and so for the first two months, I do none of it. Beatriz is the one taking care of my children — I cannot even take care of myself, so I cannot take care of them.

After three months, I open up a little, and I even learn how to push away the negative thoughts. I am now eating regular meals, exercising, and taking care of myself. I improve with each day and become myself again. Therapy continues for four more weeks to ensure my wellbeing. After that, I am ready to leave. I have now mastered all the coping skills the therapist introduced. My heart and head are more at ease, and I no longer have the painful struggle with the unstable thoughts running through my mind. I learn somehow to control them, at least a little at a time. The few days I planned on staying turn into four lonely months without Leo.

I miss Leo and our home, and I miss us being a family. But, I am now mentally and emotionally ready to be a mother to my children once again, so we will be a family again soon.

When we return home, the children jump into Leo's arms. Carlos clings to his father the longest. Leo is missed the most by him. Once he puts Carlos down, Leo hugs me and kisses my forehead. "I am so glad you are home, I have missed you so much."

"Leo, I am sorry I had to stay away for so long ...." I do not get to finish my apology; because Leo places his fingers over my lips to silence me.

"It is over now. You are home and that is all that matters. Besides, I have a big surprise for you."

"Oh, when do I get it?" I ask.

"Not yet, I need a few days. I need to wait until the timing is right. You will love it."

Leo has never been good at keeping surprises or secrets, so this has me intrigued. He has done a wonderful job of taking care of things around the house and running the household while I was away. I am lucky to have him in my life.

My first night back, I have another nightmare and this time it is about war. Bella, João, and Carlos are older in the dream. There is a baby, and she clings to me for dear life. I wake up to a sudden crashing sound that has me bolt up in bed, and as I look around I do not see anything broken. What an odd dream, and I do not understand whose baby I was dreaming of.

CHAPTER 40

1956

TWO DAYS LATER, Leo charges through the door of our little house. It is early afternoon, so I assume he is here for lunch, but no, I soon discover he has other plans. Today is the day he wants to give me the surprise he told me about on my first day back. He is beaming from ear to ear and cannot contain his excitement any longer.

"Rosa, gather the children, we are going for a drive," he says, as he continues to smile and bends down to put Carlos' shoes on.

Leo has many different jobs over the years; the most recent is in construction. He likes to try his hands at different things; he does not like jobs tying him down. He likes to spread things around, explore different options and have choices. He also gets bored often, so moving about keeps him entertained.

The construction company provides a vehicle to use for personal use as well as for work purposes. It is not fancy, a work truck, but we are happy to have a vehicle we can use as a family.

I get Bella and Mina ready, while João is still asleep from his afternoon nap. "Can we wait until João wakes up?" I ask, as I peek into the bassinet confirming he is still sleeping.

Leo is getting Carlos ready. "We have no time to waste, we must go now."

"What is the hurry?"

"My excitement is the hurry. Also, you will love what I am about to show you."

"Show me? I thought you are giving me something?"

"You are so literal Rosa, first I must show you, and then I can give it to you. Trust me, will you?"

I glance back at the sleeping baby and decide it will not hurt to wake him up early. "All right, give me a minute," I say.

Leo takes Bella's hand and walks out to the vehicle with Mina and Carlos at his side. He helps them into the tuck as it is too high and they have difficulty climbing in. I stay behind to tend to João, he needs a diaper change before we go anywhere. After five minutes, I join the others and climb into the vehicle myself, João in my arms. "Okay, now you must tell me where we are going."

Leo smiles and looks at me before responding. "You will love my surprise."

He turns on the ignition and puts the car into drive and speeds off. We are on the road for ten minutes before approaching the base of a hill. This hill is so high it appears to be a small mountain. Not stopping, we drive up the side of the hill so close to the edge I fear we will fall into the ocean. As we climb higher we approach a large clearing, a patch of land containing a small structure. "What is this place?" I ask.

"This, Rosa, is our new home," he says, as he brings the car to a complete stop and climbs out. He rushes over to the passenger side, opens my door, and offers me his hand. "Come, I will show you."

I accept his hand and climb out. "I am not sure I understand what I am looking at," I say, as we walk away from the vehicle towards the structure, hands linked. We leave the children in the back seat, other than João as he is with me still.

"Let me explain," says Leo, as he continues to lead me.

"Mama, Mama," says Bella as she notices us leaving.

Leo brings us to a neighbourhood called Morro da Radio. This is a poor neighbourhood, so I do not know why we are here. Leo runs back to the vehicle, opens the back door, and leans his head in towards the back seat. "Bella, your mother and I will be right back. We are only around the corner, so we are not far. You can see us from the window."

"Okay," says Bella, as she continues to frown.

Leo spreads his arms wide. "This is our new home. I built this with my own hands for our family. I know it's small now, but we can add more rooms later."

I shake my head to clear anything that might be obstructing my ears and affecting my hearing. Leo and I walk a few feet past some trees to take a better look at what he says is our new home. It looks too small to be a house, but I do not want to appear ungrateful.

"When did you build this house?"

"While you were away, in Nova Lisboa, with your brother."

This can't be our new home; it does not seem big enough. I look around the premises hoping I missed a building somewhere, hiding behind trees. But there is no other building in sight, and there is only this tiny house Leo built for me, for our family. I am so focused on the house, so I do not notice the spectacular views of the entire city and the bay, until Leo nudges me. The views here on this hill are breathtakingly beautiful. Boats tied to the dock wait for the raising of their sails, palm trees line the welcoming shores, and big waves crash into land. It is a view I can get used to looking at each morning while having my coffee. The poor neighbourhood no longer matters.

Leo takes a few steps away from me and moves closer to the house. He lifts his arms up in a welcoming gesture. "I built us this house, on this land, on this foundation. We can expand this house when we are ready, this is ours now. I drove up here for several weeks, and this land is unclaimed. The foundation has not had any further work done in a long time. I am yet to see anyone on this land in the time I inspected."

I take a few steps closer, tripping over a twig and luckily I am close enough that Leo catches me. "Who helped you build this house?"

"Rosa, my darling, do you not have any faith in me?"

I look up at his face and know he is serious. "Yes, of course, I trust you," I say, as I turn around to see Carlos climbing out of the vehicle's window. I run back to the vehicle with João still in my arms, ready to deal with Carlos. I leave Leo at the site of our new home, alone. I worry about what he might already be planning without me.

Our new home is small, consisting of three rooms, but it is still a house, so we move into our new tiny home two days later.

We do not have a permit as we do not know whom the land belonged to before we claimed it, but we are not worried. This is how things are done. You find land and wait to see if anyone claims it, then you claim the land yourself.

⌀

Leo never thought this would be a problem, not ever. He is too optimistic to think it might be an issue. A few days after we move in, a city official knocks on our front door, the only door in and out of the house. He demands to see the permit, and when I cannot produce one, he warns me that we have fifteen days to demolish the house.

Leo storms into the room upon hearing this threat, hands raised high in the air.

"This is outrageous," he says to the man. "You cannot throw a family with four children out in the street. Where are we to go?"

"Sir, you need to calm yourself."

"I will not have anyone tell me to leave my own home."

"That is not my problem sir, I am only here to deliver the message."

I leave to tend to the children as they are scared because their father is yelling at a stranger at the door, and they don't know why. I bend to pick up João and pat Bella and Mina on the head. "It is okay children, your father is not angry with you."

Since the house is small, Leo's voice carries as he yells at the city official. He continues to yell while I try to calm the children. We do not resolve anything today, and the city official repeats that he expects us to demolish the house in fifteen days. Leo slams the door in the man's face.

He turns around to look at me, and this is the first time there is worry in his eyes. Leo is not the worrying type. I walk over to him and ask, "What are we going to do?"

"I don't know yet, give me a minute to think."

We both remain still and with shock written on our faces. "I am afraid to think about what we are to do and where we will live," I say, as I look over to the children who are counting on us to take care of them. All four of them depend on us.

CHAPTER 41

1956

THE FOLLOWING MORNING, there is another knock. Afraid to open the door, I look to Leo for guidance and support. It must be the city official back to tell us that we must tear down our house. Leo's eyebrows join, and he walks to the door and opens it. It is not the city official, but rather a woman, one neither of us knows. She introduces herself as Laura and announces that she works for the City, but under a different capacity than the man who visited the evening before. Laura says she is here to help with our dilemma. We welcome her into our home, and she explains she is an advocate for families like ours. Leo jumps in and admits we do not have money to pay for her services, but Laura promises she does not expect payment. I search her face for signs that she is lying. She makes eye contact with me, and I look to see if she is fidgeting or sweating, she appears calm.

"Leo, can I have a word?" I say before he jumps with excitement. I grab his arm and lead him outside because there is no space in the house we can have a private conversation. The house is too small, and every word exchanged will reach Laura's ears.

"Rosa, this is fabulous news," he says the moment we close the door behind us.

"We need to consider this woman might be fake," I whisper, not wanting her to overhear our conversation.

"What if she is? What difference does it make to us? You heard her, she is not expecting to get paid, so we have nothing to lose."

"We should ask around, see if anyone knows who she is before we agree to anything."

"Rosa my darling, you are too uptight. We are in no position to question her motives; she is all we have, so we must accept her offer."

Leo walks back in the house, not allowing me an opportunity to respond. I follow him back in with a lump in my throat. Leo tells Laura we are happy to accept her offer for assistance. Although I do not have much faith in this woman, we do not demolish the house yet because we have no other place to go. Our last house is already rented to another family, and it was all we can afford since the house belongs to a family friend. We have little money saved, and Leo's income is not enough to cover rent anywhere else. So, Leo is right, we have more to lose by not accepting Laura's offer, and so we do.

A week passes before there is another knock. Leo answers, from the kitchen, I listen.

"Good day, Madame," says Leo to someone, but I do not know to whom he speaks.

I dry my wet hands with the dishcloth and find Laura sitting on our couch. I take a seat next to her.

"I bring good news today," she says.

She tells us she accomplished what she hoped, so we can stay in this house. I jump off the couch and into Leo's arms. This means we will not be homeless and our children still have a bed and roof, albeit a small one, over their heads.

We celebrate with the children and feed them baked sweet bread while Leo and I indulge in a glass of red wine. There is laughter, chatter, and even dancing tonight as we plan for expansion.

The house only has three rooms. Two of the rooms are bedrooms, one for Leo and myself, and the other for the children. The last room we use as a kitchen and living room combined. Now that we can keep the house we plan to expand, because with four growing children, we need more space. We need to build another bedroom — four bedrooms are ideal. We need a proper kitchen with a sink, and a washroom. Waking up through the night to go outside to pee is difficult with my bladder. I would also love a patio or an area to sit outside and enjoy the view from the backyard.

Leo wastes no time and is soon working on the house every week-end. Once we get close to completion, he takes a few days off work to finish the final tasks. The addition takes a long time to complete, but once finished it is the home of my dreams.

The front door leads to a narrow hallway: to the left is the girls' bed-room, and to the right is mine and Leo's room. Down the small hall is a door that leads to the dining room, and it is big enough to feed all the children at once. To the left of the dining room is the boys' bedroom, and to the right are two more doors: one leads to the kitchen, and the other to a full bathroom. At the end of the dining room is another set of doors leading outside to the large backyard. The house has electricity running throughout each room, so I do not need oil lamps any longer.

Leo builds the house out of cement blocks, but he leaves the exterior unpainted. I beg Leo to paint the outside, he says he will, but he never gets around to it. After a few weeks, he admits it is good enough the way it is, so I need to learn to be content with the unpainted exterior as well. I remind myself that Leo has a habit of starting but not finishing things, so it is a miracle he even finishes the house. To compensate for the unpainted exterior, Leo builds a veranda out back and it is here we sit and watch the boats come in.

The décor inside is simple because we do not have much money left to decorate. Once we finish the house, we cannot be more pleased with the results. It is everything I want in my life, other than the exterior painted, but I must get over that. A permanent home of my own, a family and a loving husband are what I want, what I need. I have come a long way, I am lucky to be here.

Things remain quiet for a few weeks until we receive another visitor. It is the inspector once again. I do not know what he is doing here, and I cross my arms in front of my chest waiting for him to speak.

"Good day Madame, I see you not only failed to demolish the house but instead, you expanded," he says, as he opens his arms wide.

Oh no, where is Leo when I need him? "We have permission to keep the house and the land is now registered in our name," I say with my arms still crossed.

The inspector insists we pay for the addition. The fee is not cheap, and it is more than we have saved. In fact, it is more than we could ever have. Leo is not home, and I must deal with this on my own, but Leo is the negotiator, not me. I try to negotiate a monthly payment plan, but I am not a strong enough negotiator to convince him to agree.

My shoulders are slumped as I sit on the floor with my back to the door. This cannot be happening again. We poured everything into this home: savings, precious time, and hard work, but the reality is we cannot pay the fee. When Leo gets home, I run into his arms and weep. I tell him about the inspector's visit. Leo throws his shoe across the room in fury.

"Two days is all we have?" he asks.

"That is what he said. The City will auction it off if we cannot pay the full sum by then."

Leo storms out of the house, leaving me alone with the children.

My spirits sink. I do not want to leave, but I pack what little belongings we have as I know we must abandon this home.

The next day, Leo leaves for work before I see him. I spend the day moping, and with little energy for mundane tasks. Picking up toys off the floor takes more effort than I can afford to give. Tomorrow is the day, and if we do not raise the money by tomorrow, the house will go up for auction. I throw the last belongings scattered throughout into boxes, and I try to prepare myself for the inevitable. My strong belief in

God tells me sometimes God interferes when needed the most. "God, I need you now more than ever." I pray out loud.

As expected, the house goes up for auction for forty-eight hours, during which time I do not eat, save for a small piece of bread. We wait for someone to tell us we must leave. I have already packed our personal belongings, so it is only the larger furniture that remains. I do not know what we will do with it, we do not have another home to go to, never mind a place for the furniture. I conclude God is punishing me for living with Leo unwed.

After forty-eight hours, we do not receive any news, so we wait. On the third day, Laura returns, and the moment I open the door and see her standing there, I know what she has come to say.

"Miss. Soares, I am glad I caught you at home," she says.

"Oh, please call me Rosa," I say.

"Fine, Rosa. May I come in?"

I hold the door open to allow her to enter. She sits on the same side of the couch she sat on during her first visit. "I bring news, good news in fact. Nobody bought the house as there were no offers on the table."

"Does this mean the City is demolishing the house?"

"No, this means you and your family can stay."

Leo is at work and not here for me to hug, so I hug Laura instead. She stumbles as I crash into her, but she laughs and wraps her arms around me.

For the rest of the day, I sit out front waiting anxiously for Leo to give him the news. This is a miracle, and it is either God's doing, or the entire town feels sorry for us so they do not bid on the house for that reason. Whichever the reason, God or the townspeople, I am forever grateful. The City decides we can keep the house as Laura promised, but we still must pay for the addition, and the City agrees to the payment plan this time. We save all the money we make, other than money needed for food, and when we have enough we pay the balance of the debt.

At this point we decide it is best to obtain legal advice, so we do not find ourselves in this predicament again. To get a deed for the house, we must have plans for the construction which we do not have. So, Leo searches and finds an architect willing to draw the plans for a minimal fee. The City approves the plans, and within a few weeks we are the proud owners of the home we build together.

Leo and I sit outside on our new veranda, and it is now late evening and the sun is setting. He opens a bottle of wine so we can toast to our new home. This is our first family home, the first house we own together. We sit out for hours, admiring the beauty of the city and the big ships coming in from Portugal and other European countries that have trade with Africa. The sun is orange tonight, and the sun's rays peek from behind the marina as it sets into the earth. This is a view I will never forget.

The following year, a house is constructed to the right of us, and a few months later, another house to the left goes up. I introduce myself to the neighbour on the right, Celeste, and I watch her work out in her large, beautiful gardens. Celeste is married and has two girls, they are five and seven. Celeste and I soon become close friends; however, the neighbour to my left is another story.

CHAPTER 42

1957

OUR FAMILY CONTINUES to grow, and I am again with child. It is early in my pregnancy, so I have not yet begun to show. I long for a girl next; is it selfish of me to want a girl and not another boy? If we have another boy I fear he, too, will be rambunctious. A girl is safer.

Leo rubs my swollen feet with one hand and removes a stray strand of hair off my face with the other. "It is not all bad, Rosa, you shall see, within time, Carlos will calm down. This is a disruptive time for a five-year-old child."

"Let's hope and pray you are right." I am losing my mind with the silly things Carlos does day after day.

One afternoon as I prepare lunch, the neighbour to my left, Irene, is at my door. She is a quiet woman who does not talk much and prefers the isolation of her yard. She has a husband, but I am yet to see any children around. We seldom exchange pleasantries because our paths do not cross often. So, for her to be here this afternoon raises my suspicions and I fear something is wrong. I open the door to find her standing with her hands on her hips and a frown on her face. Oh no, she is not pleased. Her lips curl, and she stares at me with squinted eyes. "I knew your child was trouble from the day I laid eyes on him," she says.

There is no need to guess which child she speaks of. "What can I do for you?" I ask, trying to sound confident. My heart is racing, and I know at once Carlos must have done something to upset her.

"It is your son again, it is always your son," she says, as she stands to hold open the door with her hip.

"What about my son?" I ask with a hint of protectiveness, although I know too well Carlos is not innocent.

She narrows her eyes. "He urinated in my gardens. Yes, he did. I saw him with my own eyes from my living room window. I am old, but I have good eyesight."

"He did what?" I say putting my hands to my head.

"You heard me. He saw me watching him, and he laughed as I stood at my window waving the broom at him trying to shoo him away. But he did not leave, NO. Do you want to know what he did instead? Do you?" she prompts me to answer.

"Um, what did he do then?" I ask, but afraid to know the details.

"Well, let me tell you what your son did. He came to my porch and urinated in front of my window. I was beside myself, and afraid to open the door. I feared I would get urine on me, or worse, in my house! That is how far the urine shot out of him! One would swear the boy had an entire gallon to drink this morning to be able to produce so much urine."

"Oh dear," I say, as I remain calm inside the entrance of the room.

What on Earth can I say to this irate and unreasonable woman to make the situation right? I am lost for words today. I suspected Carlos was up to no good, but never in my wildest imagination did I fore-see this.

I brace myself before speaking again. "I am so sorry for my son's behavior. I shall speak to him at once, and I will reprimand him, of course."

I invite her in since she is still standing in the doorway, but she looks at me with a confused expression, placing both her hands on her hips. "Hmm."

"Please, come in, I can make a pot of tea or coffee."

"I do not have time to visit and have tea; I must go wash the porch and window before the smell of urine sets into the wood and becomes ingrained."

She turns on her heel, letting the door slam, and walks down the step and back to her property. I lock the door behind me, afraid she might return, and I let my head rest in my hands for longer than I should.

"CARLOS," I yell, "Get over here right this instant!"

He is not here, so he must be hiding and knows he is in trouble. I yell again, "Wait until your father gets home. I will have him deal with you," I say, but more to the wind because he is not here to listen to me yell.

Things between Irene and I deteriorate even more after this. If we run into each other outside, she turns her head the other way and makes that same sound, "Hmm." Things could be worse, it is only urine after all, and a little urine has never killed anyone. The only exception to the life and death rule are the plants in Irene's garden, they wilt away into the unknown.

⌒⚭⌒

The next day, I plan to take flowers to Irene as an apology. The flowers, however, do not make it to Irene's house as planned. Carlos continues to do things I cannot cope with. He keeps me busy running after him and keeping him from harm, and by the end of the day, I forget about the nice gesture I had planned.

⌒⚭⌒

My son has a fascination for bumble bees and likes to tease them. I tell him often if he gets stung, it will hurt, but he does not care to listen, my words are lost to him.

One day, Celeste comes running across the yard, arms flapping in the air, screaming. From my window, I watch her as she runs straight for my house. She barges through the door without knocking.

"Rosa, come quick, I saw Carlos from my kitchen window trying to knock down a beehive in the woods."

I sink into the chair behind me and let my head rest for a few seconds before getting up. We hike to where Carlos is, and I am startled to see him shaking the branch with force. I approach him, but his last attempt at breaking the branch is successful, and the beehive crashes to the ground. Hundreds, possibly thousands of bumblebees swarm and attack Carlos who stands in the bees' path. He screams so loud it hurts my ears. I stand not ten feet away watching and fearing for my child. Celeste is beside me, and her hands are on her head as she yells, "Santo Deus ajuda-nos," *Dear God, help us.*

I try to get close enough to help him, but I cannot; the closer I get the more I am attacked by the bees. So, I yell from under a tree that provides shelter and safety from the angry, disturbed bees. "Carlos, run," I say loud enough for him to hear. He runs in the opposite direction, and the bees follow. As he runs, he kicks and swats the bees away. He places both hands over his face for protection, so he cannot see and stumbles into a pond. While in the water he looks around, and his shoulders relax when he no longer has bumblebees attacking him. He submerges himself under the water, covering his entire body.

"What is he doing?" Celeste asks me.

"Hiding from the bumblebees."

I walk away from Celeste and head toward my son, swatting away several bees myself. Celeste does not follow, she remains under the tree. As I approach the pond, there are fewer bees here, and Carlos is floating on his back. I wade into the deeper end of the pond; it is warm, but muddy and not suitable for swimming. When I reach Carlos, I grab him by the first body part I touch, his right arm. I pull him out of the water, and I gasp — bee stings cover his entire body. He can touch the bottom, and he stands before me with a smile, hair dripping wet. "Let's go," I say, as I pull him out of the pond. We do not speak as we walk.

Celeste walks with us. When I get to my house, Irene is standing in my driveway. She must have come out when she heard the screaming. Her right hand rests on her waist, and she wears the same pouted mouth and pointy eyes.

She lifts her left hand, points a finger at me, and says, "That child needs discipline. I was trying to sleep, but there is too much yelling."

She now points her finger at Carlos, and he grins back. "Hmm," she says and turns on her heel, heading home.

"She is not a happy woman," says Celeste.

I shrug my shoulders, take a deep breath, and walk up the step to my own home. It could be worse, yes, it could be much worse.

CHAPTER 43

1957

LEO BRINGS HOME a pet monkey, Charley, and he is the sweetest, kindest little animal. He loves everyone in the family, everyone except Carlos. For some reason, Charley is mean to Carlos. He often whips rocks at him so hard and Carlos ends up with a bleeding nose or a bruise. I do not understand Charley's dislike toward my son.

One afternoon, Carlos runs into the kitchen holding his head. I am busy preparing lunch, moving from stove to counter and chopping vegetables, so I do not notice blood dripping from his head. I turn and place more vegetables into the simmering pot when I notice the red blotches on my son's hands.

"Carlos, you are bleeding," I say, as I grab a cloth to wipe his face and hands. "What happened now? Have you and Charley gotten into another fight?"

"Charley is throwing rocks at my head," he says.

"Why on Earth would he do this again? I do not understand why he is only mean to you."

Carlos gives me an innocent look with his brown eyes and confesses. "I feed the monkey, and he loves bananas."

"Yes, I know, but that does not explain his behaviour."

"Well …."

"Well, what? Spit it out."

"I peel back the skin and fill it back up with rocks."

Upon hearing this, my hands go to my hips. "And you feed the rocks to Charley?"

He is now giggling, and this makes my blood boil.

"Yes, but first I use some of your knitting yarn to close the opening, so the rocks do not fall out. Then I give it to him." He grins, and his teeth show. "It is so funny to watch him, Mama. He bites into the banana, realizes it is no banana and gets angry, so he throws the rocks at me."

I shake my head. "Carlos, you cannot do such things. Poor Charley, no wonder he is not nice to you."

"Why can't I feed him rocks anymore?"

"Because monkeys do not eat rocks! I do not want you feeding rocks to the monkey again."

"But it is so funny." He now laughs so hard his arms are around his belly.

"I do not care how funny you think it is. Will you find it funny when I ground you in your room?"

"But what do I do when he is hungry?" he asks, raising his eyebrows showing confusion. The bleeding stops, and I walk to the sink to place the blood-filled cloth into the tub of water.

"You feed him real bananas Carlos, not rock filled bananas!"

"That's not fun," he says, as he gets up off his chair and walks out the door, leaving me wondering where this kid gets his sense of humour from. As I contemplate this, I remember the stew I am preparing. Not reaching it in time, it boils over and spills over the stove and onto the floor. "Oh, for goodness sake," I say, as I grab the same cloth I used to wipe blood and mop up the floor. As I clean the mess, more screaming comes from the other room. I take a minute to collect myself before turning down the pot of stew and walk out the kitchen, ready and armed to put out the next fire.

CHAPTER 44

1957 - 1959

APRIL THIS YEAR brings warmer weather than most years. We get lots of hot weather from February to April, but the soaring temperatures this summer bring a new challenge for many outdoor workers. Even Celeste stops working as much in her gardens. The heat is too much midday, so she goes out in the morning and night when the sun sets. Irene is still cold, isolated, and avoids me like the black plague, I cannot blame her.

The heat affects me most, as I am seven months pregnant and ready to give birth soon. This pregnancy is different from the others; over the last few months, I continue to menstruate.

Two months later, the day I go into labour, I bleed a lot, but this is not the bloody show that accompanies most births. This is different, and I lose a lot of blood. I do not know at first if I am in labour because there is no pain, but Leo encourages me to lie down and rest. He stays home from work today to look after me. After hours of bleeding, Leo calls for the doctor, and he comes to the house to examine me. He confirms I am in labour and suggests we go to the hospital in Benguela.

He grows concerned about me delivering this baby at home. Once the doctor leaves, I pack my bag and it is then the pain starts. After a few minutes, the pain grows strong and hits me hard in the centre of my core, causing me to stop breathing. I have not experienced labour pain like this before. A gripping gut-wrenching pain knocks my breath away. Leo wipes my forehead with a damp cloth and tries to ease my discomfort, but there is no relief from this torture. "I cannot do this anymore. It hurts too much. The pain is ripping my stomach apart," I say pushing away the wet cloth as it is more annoying having him fuss over me.

Leo ignores me and kneels on the floor beside the bed wiping my face with the cloth. Sweat, and not the damp cloth, drenches my hair. "It will be over soon my darling, but you must be strong," he says.

He places the cloth back into the basin to collect more water as it dries out. "We should go. We need to get to the hospital."

I grip my stomach as the next wave of pain hits. "I cannot move."

"You have to try."

I speak to God now and beg him to take me away from here. I am ready to die, and I tell Him if He takes me now, I will not fight to live. Death is the better option, a welcoming sorrow.

Leo leaves me for a few minutes and says he is going to call for a taxi — the company vehicle is in for repairs. We do not own a telephone, so he walks to the store, a five-minute walk from our house. When he returns, Celeste is with him and she offers to watch over the children.

When the taxi arrives, Leo helps me get inside. Halfway to the hospital, there are clanking noises coming from the vehicle, but I am in too much pain to worry about it. The vehicle comes to a stop, and the driver says the vehicle has problems. Leo gets out of the vehicle, but I beg him to not leave me inside alone. I am certain I am dying from the pain, and I do not want to die alone. He assures me he is only going to check on the situation and will be back in a minute. Moments later, he returns with a frown.

"There is something wrong and we need another taxi," he says.

The driver has already set out on foot to call for another vehicle. I am bleeding through the rags and screaming in the back seat, certain my life is ending. My insides are ripping me apart, and I throw up over myself and the grey seats.

When the replacement vehicle arrives, Leo transfers me to it, and soon the car moves once again. "Almost there," says Leo. I distract myself from the pain and focus out the window. The vehicle stops again. I lift my head, so I can see over the dash and there are train tracks. The roaring engine of the train fills my ears long before the train comes into view. I am having this baby in the car, it is inevitable. I have the desire to push, and Leo tells me to fight it off. I hope this is not a long train, but if so, I will bleed to death. Leo is rubbing my back, and his hands shake as they connect with my skin. He tries his best to calm me, using reassuring words, pats my arm and strokes my hair, but it is no use. The sensation of his touch prickles my skin. I welcome death more than I have in the past. At least if I die, I will be with Tavina. We sit in the vehicle, waiting for the train for almost ten minutes. It is past midnight, and a full moon lurks ahead.

Hours later, at approximately four o'clock in the morning, I am dilated and urged to push by doctors. I now have a team of medical professionals surrounding me and helping. I am weak and lose even more blood. By seven o'clock, I gather enough strength for one last, much-needed push. I have no energy left, but I know I need to push this baby out of me before I die. So, I push with all the strength I can muster, and I deliver another boy. It is not until much later when I hold my baby in my arms I realize that I lived through this ordeal.

The nurse sponge-washes my baby, wraps him in a blue blanket, and places him in my arms. I am weak, tired, and desire sleep. With one eye half open, I hold my baby as Leo talks to him, and this wakes me.

"Do not take him," I say, looking into the most precious set of eyes of the one that almost killed me tonight. "Okay, here, you can hold him a little longer. I only wanted you to sleep. What do you want to name him?" he asks.

"Armando," I say without hesitation.

Leo goes home to check on the other children and relieve Celeste of her duties. Back at the hospital, Armando cries much more than the other babies. As I hold Armando in my weak arms, I think of Tavina again. My mind often drifts to her after holding one of my newborn babies. Tavina, my sweet baby that I miss so much. Tavina, the baby girl I lost all those years ago, lost but never forgot. "You will never know your brothers and sister," I say to her, hoping she is listening. I imagine how old she would be, and how much she would love her siblings and cousin Mina. Tears accumulate at my chin, and I wipe one before it falls onto the baby. I need to focus because I have Armando now. He is still crying and has not yet settled. "I do not know what he wants," I say into the empty room, as I try to comfort him.

Armando is going to be the fussy one; I realize this on day one. Over the next few weeks, he cries a lot, there is no soothing him and nothing brings him comfort. I try everything I know, I rock him, I keep his diapers clean, I put him on my breast often, and I sing to him. I am desperate and feel like an unworthy mother. What am I doing wrong this time? This should be easy by now.

As time passes, I do not notice anything out of the ordinary or unusual about my baby. He has all his toes and fingers. He looks normal other than the constant crying, which everyone seems to attribute to colic syndrome. I try the usual tea remedies, nothing helps.

But over the years, as Armando grows older, his development suffers. There are certain things he should do by now that he cannot do on his own. He does not eat by himself, he still wears a diaper when he goes to school, and he has delayed speech. I mention this to our doctor, only to have him tell me every child develops at a different rate and not to concern myself. So, I try to go about my days as usual and not worry as much; although deep down, I know my little boy has many problems we are yet to face.

⁂

By 1959, we fall into a comfortable routine. We finish the house, but Leo does not get around to painting the outside. This bothers me, but I stop bugging Leo about it because when I do, he reminds me that he built a veranda instead.

We are comfortable, so we decide as a family to get a cat. The cat is useful to keep mice out of the house. Bella does not like cats; she has a great dislike for them in fact.

When the decision is made, Bella decides to be bad-mannered about it. "I do not want a cat in this house," she says, as she finishes up her breakfast.

"Your brothers want the cat and you are not the only member of this family," I say to her.

"The cat better not come near me," she warns. She tosses her dishes into the sink so hard they shatter.

Leo reached across the table to grab the jug of milk. "Bella, a cat can keep you company," he says. "Give the cat a chance; you might grow to like him."

He takes a sip of his coffee as Bella storms off into her room and slams the door behind her.

That night, Leo comes home with a cat. Bella disappears in her room, mumbling to herself as she walks away. "What a stupid cat," she says, as she slams her bedroom room again. Oh boy, this going to be like Carlos and the monkey, all over again.

The cat is in our family for one week and immediately senses Bella's dislike for him. She avoids him at all costs. Nobody comes up with a good name for him, so we call him, "O Gato," *The Cat*, and this becomes his name. One morning, I am putting away laundry, while The Cat sleeps outside Bella's bedroom. This is his favourite place to sit both day and night. Of all places, he chooses Bella's and Mina's room to sleep next to. Bella walks out, and upon seeing The Cat, she slams the door. The Cat's tail gets caught between the door jam. He springs up, meows, heaves, and hisses. I am down the hall, arms full of clothes as I watch the scene unfold. Bella stands a little too close to the animal, so he attacks her and wraps himself around her leg. Bella screams. "Stupid cat, get him off me!"

She tries to swat The Cat away with a book she carries, but this makes The Cat even angrier. I do not realize the severity of the situation until blood trickles down Bella's leg. "Oh, dear," I say, running to the bedroom and dropping the pile of clothes on Mina's bed. I bend down, grab The Cat, but he will not let go. "Bella, help me, push him off you."

"I can't, Mother, I am trying. Get him off me," she says, as she continues to try to swat the cat with the book.

After a few attempts, I manage to pry The Cat off her bleeding leg. I toss him down the other end of the hall and tell Bella to sit on her bed, so I can inspect her wounds. They are deep, but I can patch them up without having to call for a doctor. "What were you thinking?" I say, as I wrap her leg in a cloth. Her legs are so skinny, and I realize this only now.

"I did not know he was there, I didn't mean to hurt him."

"I see," I say, as I wonder if this is true.

That night, I open the front door, let The Cat out and decide it is best he lives outside. The Cat meows as I let him out. I am not sure if he is happy or complaining. "Go, shoo," I say, encouraging him to leave.

He hops over to Irene's property and urinates in her gardens. The next day when I run into Irene outside, I pretend I do not know whom the cat belongs to when she asks me about him.

CHAPTER 45

1959

TODAY I RECEIVE an unexpected visit from Antonietta. This is the first time she visits our new home. Once again, she does not come empty-handed. Her arms are full of toys, clothes, and food. We are sitting at the kitchen table talking over tea when Bella enters the room. She stops to look at us and tries to understand who the visitor is. The look on her face tells me she does not remember her grandmother. Antonietta also looks at Bella twice to be sure it is her. Bella has grown so much since Antonietta saw her last.

My mother gasps when she realizes who she is. "Bella, you are a beautiful young girl. Look at that long, shiny, wavy hair, and super high cheekbones, you could be a model."

Bella does not respond.

"Bella, this is your grandmother, do you remember her? Do not be rude, come say hello," I say to Bella while placing my hot tea mug on the table.

Bella is more interested in the bag of toys. "Ohhh, are those for me?" she asks, as she pulls the toys out of the bag.

"Well, I can see nothing changed," says Antonietta, as she helps Bella sort toys. "Some of these are for your brothers, so go find them, will you, dear?" she asks.

Bella runs off to find her brothers.

Antonietta offers to watch the children tonight so Leo and I can go to the cinema. The cinema is a favourite event of ours, and we go every opportunity we get. These days, however, the cinema visits are few and far between with a house full of kids. Sometimes we ask Celeste to watch the children, or if Leo has made extra deliveries that week, we hire a nanny. It is worth the money. It is our only date night, time to reflect on each other and talk about something other than the children. I love dressing up, fixing my hair and applying a little lipstick, so going to the cinema provides this opportunity. I always leave the house well put together, it's my nature. The children get upset when we leave, so Leo brings them each candy from the cinema and they soon forgot about our absence.

Today I accept my mother's offer to watch the children and doll myself up. At the cinema, I lean my head in close to Leo's ear, so he does not have trouble hearing me. "Oh, to be beautiful like these females on the big screen," I say. Leo does not respond, but he touches my cheek with his hand, and that small gesture tells me what he does not say in words. He often tells me I am the most beautiful woman he has seen, and I blush every time he speaks these words.

CHAPTER 46
February 4, 1961

I T IS EARLY evening and the kids sit at the kitchen table, waiting for supper. I am stirring the stew that boils when Leo walks into the room. His hair is a mess, so I know he ran his hands through it, something he does when under stress. "Rosa, do you have the radio on?"

I glance at the large, brown, square radio we keep in our kitchen. "No, why?"

"I heard some bad news."

He walks past the kitchen table, flips on the switch, and turns up the volume.

I freeze, place the wooden ladle on the countertop and turn to look into his sad eyes. "Leo, what happened?" I ask, as I try to listen to the radio broadcast coming through the small speakers.

He takes my hand in his and leads me to the table where the kids are waiting for their supper. "We are at war," he says.

"War?" I say wiping my hands on my apron and refusing to believe the words he speaks.

"It is true. Listen to the radio."

Today is February 4, 1961, and Angola has entered the War of Independence. I look at my children, Carlos, and Mina who are both ten, Bella who is eight, João six, and Armando who is only four. My immediate thoughts are of how I am going to protect my family during a war. I scan each face searching for signs of worry, but I find only innocence amongst them. Their age shelters them from the horrific news; they are too young to comprehend the meaning of war. As if he can read my mind, Leo places his hands on my face and turns my head so I face him. Our eyes lock. "Rosa, I will protect us," he says, as he pulls me into an embrace.

At night during tea time, we talk of nothing but the war and our impending future.

CHAPTER 47

1961

OUR COUNTRY IS growing impatient with the continued forced cotton cultivation rules embargoed upon us. As a result, uprisings form, and soon there are different groups wanting to control the colony. This war is part of the Portuguese Colonial War. There are many other Portuguese colonies in Africa, such as Cape Verde and Mozambique, that also seek independence from Portugal. The Portuguese Colonial War soon becomes a struggle for control.

Three major nationalist movements and one separatist movement emerge, and they fight the Portuguese military.

The first year of the War of Independence brings doubt, fear, and insecurities about our future. We keep one eye open always, and ears well-tuned in case of raids, bombings, or other threats.

The houses in the nearby town gather one afternoon to form a plan for a safe meeting place should there be any threats. In case of a threat, we decide to meet at Miss. Delfina's house. Miss. Delfina has a big barn, and it is large enough to accommodate a lot of people. We hope and pray we do not need to execute this plan, but during times of war, it is best to not take things lightly.

Things change as time passes. We now watch the amount of food we eat so we can preserve some for darker days. We no longer go to the cinema as often. So far, we are lucky and have not encountered any battles. Up until now, most of the fighting is in the jungles, away from towns.

In August, I discover I am carrying another child. My calculations tell me I am to deliver the following April. I need to prepare for this physically and mentally once again. I am not sure I am ready to go through what I went through with Armando, because that labour almost killed me.

⁓

I am seven months pregnant when my brother Manecas arrives at our door one morning, looking frantic. His shirt hangs over his pants, and his hair covers his eyes. "Rosa, you must get the children and come with me at once," he says. "Where is Leo?"

"Leo is at work, what happened?" I ask.

He scans the room, looking for something, but I do not know what. "There is a threat. I am not sure of the details, but it is probably a raid. We need to hurry and get you and the children to safety."

He moves fast and helps me get the children together. "Bring only what you can carry, and head straight to Miss. Delfina's barn. I will get Leo and tell him to meet you there."

Leo rushes through the door one minute later. He has heard of the threat.

"Rosa!"

"Yes Leo, I know, my brother is here," I say, as I pick up a screaming Armando in my arms and try to soothe him.

"We need to get to the barn," he says.

"Thank God you are here, I was about to come for you. I was not sure if you knew," says Manecas.

"I left the moment I heard, and I came as fast as I could," says Leo.

João's body shakes uncontrollably. This event affects him the most of all the children. He clings to my skirt, and this prevents me from moving fast.

"Mama," he says. He holds up his arms and waits for me to lift him. But my arms are already full as I hold his little brother Armando.

"João, you must be a big boy for Mama. We need to move fast and get to Miss. Delfina's barn. Hold Carlos' hand," I say. I motion to Carlos to come here. "Carlos, take your brother, your cousin, your sister and stay close. All of you, link hands."

Leo leads us out, and Manecas follows closely behind. There is chaos everywhere. Everyone is screaming, running, and fearing for their lives. Women carry their babies in one arm and loaves of bread in the other. Men carry blankets and barrels of food. We join Celeste and her family and run down the hill together to the predetermined meeting place. By the time we arrive, crying children and panicked parents fill the barn. There is no organization whatsoever. We enter, and Leo closes the large barn doors behind us. The room smells repulsive; a mixture of sweat, manure, and fear hangs in the air. We make our way through the crowds to the back of the three-hundred-and fifty square foot barn and find an empty spot. Leo tries to find a place away from windows, "Just in case," he says.

We sit the children on the dirty floor, Leo and I stand next to them. We wait for hours, but each minute feels more like an eternity. I search the crowd for Manecas, I lost sight of him. He must be with his own family now.

"Leo, what do we do now?"

"We wait."

We wait for many things in our lives, some happy, some sad. But to wait for your impending death as we are is a different kind of waiting. This type of waiting brings the darkest fears and the brightest memories to the forefront at once. My mind goes to Tavina again. One reassuring thought is that she does not have to face what the rest of us are facing today. A tiny voice coming from behind me interrupts my thoughts. At first, I think it is Tavina, and then I am reminded she is not here. She is still gone. The voice belongs to one of my other children.

"Mãe, eu tenho que fazer xixi," *Mama, I have to pee,* says João.

He places his hands between his legs and rocks back and forth. At hearing his voice again, I pull myself out of my deep trance and bend down on my knee to be at height level with him. He sits in the middle of a pile of hay.

"João, we cannot go outside, you have to hold your pee," I say, not looking at him.

I do not want to give away the worry on my face. Instead, I focus on the hay bales to his right.

"Mama, I am hungry," says Carlos, as he shifts closer to João.

"I am cold," says Bella.

I take a deep lungful and concentrate on breathing as I exhale out. So, it is time for the complaining to start, they have been patient long enough. The only child who does not complain is Mina. She remains silent in her own little world with her hands covering her ears.

We stay inside the barn for hours, waiting, hoping, and praying. During the waiting period we cannot go to the bathroom, and we do not eat, save for some bread I brought. The bread, however, is long gone now. I look down at João and his pants are wet, he has gone to the washroom where he sits. He held his pee as long as he could, poor child. My thoughts again go to Tavina then to the child in my womb who is growing and waiting for his or her chance at life. Will this baby have an opportunity coming into this world during a war?

It is approaching midnight when another neighbour comes to notify us that the threat is over. They bring news that the radio announces the enemies have retreated. We are safe, at least for tonight. I manage to take my first full breath at that moment. It is after midnight when we leave the barn and take the chance to walk back to our own homes.

Once back home, I lay the children in their beds and thank God for His protection today. As I rub my growing belly, I think of the child inside me and speak softly. "I am sorry for bringing you into this world at this time."

I give birth to Rosa Natércia in April, the year of the bomb threat. She is born in the hospital in Benguela like Armando was. Benguela is still the only nearby city that has a maternity ward. We name her after me, of course, but to avoid confusion, we call her by her middle name, Natércia.

CHAPTER 48

1962

IF DEALING WITH a new-born baby is not enough, a few weeks after Natércia's birth, everyone develops measles. João has it worst. When he first develops the bumps, I assume it is an average case, like the others. But after a week he is still plagued with high fever and is bed-ridden. He is lethargic, does not eat or drink anything. I do not know what to do, and each day he appears thinner. I try to feed him soup, but he cannot swallow. I abandon the soup and give him water with a spoon. His body accepts the water in small quantities and this keeps him alive. I wish my mother was here, I need her now more than ever. It has been months since she visited last. So, instead I do what I must do, and I manage things myself. Leo works long hours to earn extra money so we have something to fall back on should the war take a turn for the worst. Each day we wait for the next bomb threat and open fire to break.

Towards the end of the week, I am certain my son will die. Celeste comes and we both sit in silence on the edge of João's bed, praying. She holds a wet cloth to my son's forehead while I feed him water with a spoon.

"I fear for his life. How long can he last with no food and such little water," I say, as I choke back tears, and try to appear stronger than I am.

"Rosa, my friend, there is a healing herb you can use to make tea. It's called lemongrass. I understand it is beneficial and useful in many ailments and can cure fever. I do not know for sure if it will help, but if you can find this herb, it might be worthwhile to try," she says, as she continues to pat João's forehead.

This has my interest, as I am desperate and willing to try anything to save my son.

"Where can I get this herb? I must find some right away."

I get up off the bed and pace the room. As far as I know, I have no access to this herb. I do not grow it in my gardens, and I do not know anyone who does. I am annoyed at myself, as if I failed some test to prove I am a good mother. If this herb has the healing powers Celeste claims it does, then why do I not have it growing in abundance in my own yard?

Still carrying the wet rag, Celeste walks over to me and water drips on the floor.

"Rosa, there is a house owned by a single woman who has the herb growing in her garden. She lives some ways away, within walking distance. I am sure if you go to her and explain the situation, she will part with some of the herbs."

My eyes light up. "Do you think so?"

She sighs, "It's worth a try."

Celeste offers to watch the children as I go in search of the lemongrass. I am hopeful this is the remedy needed to save my son. It is a longer walk than I expected, and my legs are sore when I arrive. I am not used to walking much these days, since the start of the war we stay indoors to avoid trouble. As I approach the house, I turn to my other loyal friend, God, and I beg Him to once again to be by my side.

A lady emerges from around the side of the house, and she looks native with her dark skin. She appears like a free spirit, bandana around her head. The ends hang loose and fall over her right shoulder. She wears a long, floral, flowy dress that covers her ankles, and she has a smile that can brighten the sun. I tread lightly up the side of her house not knowing what to expect, but she seems friendly as she greets me. I introduce myself and explain the situation with my son. I convey the symptoms and what Celeste suggested I ask for. She looks at the gate that leads to her backyard and glances up and down a few times. She shifts her weight from her left foot onto her right before she speaks. "I see. Yes, I can help you, come with me," she says.

She leads me through the gate into her impressive, large garden. The smell is extraordinary and scents I have never smelled before fill the air.

The mysterious woman, who never gives me her name, pulls two lemongrass stalks out of the ground and hands them to me. Still wearing a happy smile, she says, "Take these."

As she passes me the lemongrass stalks, our hands touch and I get an electric shock.

"Cut off the root at the end of the lemongrass stalks and remove any dry leaves on the outside. Then, tie the lemongrass into a tight knot so it does not come undone. Place it in a cup with cinnamon and some sugar, preferably from a sugar cane if you have it. It is easier to digest if sweetened. Pour the boiling water into the same cup, but make sure it comes to a full boil for maximum benefits."

I listen to her intently, and accept the lemongrass stalks, committing the instructions to memory. "I cannot thank you enough," I say, as I hurry out of the yard, and back home to my dying son.

"Save João," she yells behind me as I run off.

I do not know who this woman is, but I do know she gave me an opportunity I did not have this morning. I have positive thoughts as I make my way home in half the time it took me to get there. I repeat her last words spoken, "Save João." How did she know his name? I do not remember telling her his name, but I must have.

"Celeste, I got it!" I say running through the door, and straight into the kitchen to set the water boiling on the stove. Celeste stays with me through the evening until Leo comes home. I tell him about my day and about the tea I am successful in getting João to swallow by spoon feeding him.

Leo seems skeptic. "Are you sure this is safe?" he asks, as he takes off his work boots and sets them in the nook by the door. "We do not even know who this woman is. What is her name?"

"I do not know," I say.

I go to Leo pleading with my eyes and tell him it is the last chance we have, so we must try to save him. I do not think Leo realizes how close to death João is. The tables have turned as it is I who am the cautious one, not Leo.

Twenty-four hours later, a miracle occurs; the fever reduces, and my son's forehead feels cool to the touch. His clothes are drenched in sweat. João finally opens his eyes; he is coherent and moves around. The mysterious woman saved my son's life. I run next door with Natércia in my arms, excited to give Celeste the news.

A few weeks later, Celeste is over for tea and offers to watch the children so I can go to the mysterious woman's house to thank her. Once again, I make the long walk and my feet are as sore as before.

As I approach, I look for her, but she is not outside to greet me like last time. She must be in the backyard, but I do not want to trespass, so I knock on the door instead. When my knocks go unanswered, I sneak around back and peek into the backyard, but there is no sign of life. The plants are still there, but they are lifeless and dried up. The inviting scents from before, are no more. I peek into the front window, and there is no sign of life inside either, as the house is empty. She must have moved right after my visit, how ironic.

How lucky am I that she was here at the exact time I needed her? If João had gotten sick only two weeks later, then I would not have the herb to save him. As I leave the abandoned property, I look up to the blue, vibrant sky and tell God I understand. The mysterious woman is no ordinary woman, she is an angel sent from Heaven, to help me.

CHAPTER 49

1965

WHEN A WOMAN becomes a mother, she never stops worrying, at least I don't. Over the years, we go from one emergency to another, and each time I hope this will be the last. Although, I know it is only the beginning and the next emergency silently waits to explode.

The war between the natives and Portugal continues, but we are lucky thus far because we are outside of fire zones. We have our share of threats and scares, but we are not caught in any crossfire, and this is one thing to be thankful for. Ongoing since 1961, Portugal sends a record number of military troops to defend its territory, so we are safe for now with many Portuguese soldiers protecting our streets.

Bella sees more of hospitals this year than any other. She is twelve years old and growing into a beautiful young lady. With her silky, chestnut hair, slender figure, and well-sculpted high cheekbones, she could be a model. Many modelling professionals have wanted to photograph her already. Her skin is fairer than mine; she takes after Leo in skin tone. Her beauty marks her in a way, and everyone knows Bella to be beautiful. So, it is a shock when she wakes to find her body covered in sores. I am preparing breakfast when she yells from the bedroom. I run to her room not knowing what to expect, and I am stunned at how she looks. Her beautiful glowing and cream-coloured skin is no more and large, red, pussy, blisters take its place. It does not stop on her face though; it extends to her neck, arms, legs, even her belly. The eruptions are everywhere, not an inch of normal skin remains. I freeze at the doorway as she sits up in bed, frantically scratching.

"Mama, what are these bumps on my arms and legs? Is it on my face? Please tell me it is not on my face."

I do not want to worry or frighten her, so I lie. "No, it is not on your face."

"So, it is not too bad then?" she asks, still scratching.

"No, it is not bad." I lie again.

"Am I still pretty?" she asks.

"The prettiest," I say not looking at her.

We only have one mirror in the house, and I decide I will not give it to her. I do not want her to see how horrible she looks. I run next door to get Celeste, she will know what to do. Celeste suggests we go to the hospital, so when Leo gets home from work, he drives us. The hospital in Lobito is not as big as the one in Benguela where Armando and Natércia are born, but it will do. The doctor prescribes antibiotics and stresses the importance of not scratching to avoid scarring. My daughter finds a mirror, and when she brings the mirror up to her face she screams after looking at the reflection staring back at her.

She has hopes of someday becoming a model, and it is Leo's reservations that keep her from this dream. Leo does not want her exposed for her beauty, so he forbids photography.

The doctor says to give it a few days before the sores disappear. He says within a week she should be back to normal, if she does not scratch. Bella remains hopeful, and after a week her beauty returns. Her dreams of becoming a model have not shattered after all.

⁓⁓

One week later, Bella sits in the living room with Mina and me, knitting blankets for Christmas. Natércia jumps onto her big sister's lap, causing Bella to poke herself in the mouth with the needle. The needle is not clean since we use it every day for knitting and leave it in the sewing kit, unwrapped. What seems to be an insignificant prick in the mouth results in another hospital visit. Bella gets an infection that festers. She develops a rash in her mouth, and then a fever. My thoughts drift to João and the time he had the fever that almost killed him.

We have a little more money saved up. We are prudent with our money because of the war, so we save as much as we can. For the second time this month, we take Bella to the hospital. The same doctor that treated the boils is here, he recognizes Leo and I, but not Bella. Her face looked different then. After a brief examination, the doctor confirms Bella has an infection from the contaminated needle. We leave with a prescription for penicillin this time.

⌒∞⌒

We try to live as normal as possible during these years. Each day we have lunch together as a family at noon until two. It is a tradition, and no matter where everyone is, work or other social engagements, no one misses lunchtime. Stores, banks, offices, and factories shut down between the hours of noon and two.

The house on the hill is our anchorage, our own slice of Heaven. We have a big garden in the backyard full of vegetables I use in the soups and stews. We also have a large pond on the property where the kids splash around, getting some relief from the scorching heat. This is the pond Carlos fell into during the bee attack. We often find many ducks and flamingos wading in the pond. Throughout the yard are many chickens, approximately thirty, roaming the grounds. It is from these chickens we get our eggs for breakfast. We also have a few pigeons, and each time a new baby pigeon is born, Leo takes it to the market to sell. We use this extra income to buy things such as school uniforms, books, and soap to bathe with. Every so often, I buy a new, used book for myself. I look forward to the nights when I sit in my comfortable chair absorbed in a book. With a large family like mine, these moments are rare. We have a big tub we use for bathing, and each family member has a specific day to bathe. Since we live on top of a steep hill, getting water to the house is a challenge so we have water tanks. All in all, we manage as best we can, and better than most families. I try to take on extra sewing for people in the village, but work is scarce, everyone is afraid to spend money.

The kids are still in school, but soon the expense of buying supplies becomes a burden. Leo is adamant in keeping the children in school, so we use some of the money from the sale of the pigeons and some of Leo's salary to pay for school supplies.

While the girls, Bella, Mina, and Natércia, often splash in the pond to fill the days, the boys, Carlos, and João, have other interests. Armando mostly stays home with me, he does not like the outdoors. The other boys often go off on "adventures" as they like to call them.

CHAPTER 50

1965

JOÃO AND CARLOS wake up early this morning and announce they are off for the day. They do not tell me what they are up to or where they are going, so I assume they are off on one of their adventures. When the boys do not show up for dinner, I grow worried and pace, so Leo goes out to search for them. I sit at home, waiting. Much later, I am greeted at my door by a tall man I have not seen before. He stands with his hands crossed and a stern look. "Oh no, what now," I say out loud.

The stranger yells and demands money from me, but he speaks loud and fast, so I have a difficult time comprehending him. I hold the door open while looking over the man's shoulder; my boys stand a few feet away. They hide behind a bush and their faces are pale. I understand now, they got themselves into trouble again and that is why this man is here. I open the door wide and gesture to the man to enter. "Please sir, won't you come in? I am sure we can talk about whatever it is that upsets you," I say, as I close the door behind him.

"Are those your children?" he asks and points to the window.

I want to say no. "Sim." *Yes.*

"They are my problem," he says.

Yes, of course they are, I already guessed. Realizing I left the boys outside, I reopen the door to let them in. "You two, in here. Now."

I slap them on the back of their heads as they walk through the door.

"Ouch," they both say.

The man pants and my imagination runs wild. He introduces himself to me as Antonio. I hold my breath; he smells of wine and stale cigarettes.

"I am Rosa, these are my boys. I am sorry for any trouble they caused you, but I am sure we can sort it out."

Antonio has an axe, and he swings it in his left hand. How did I not see the axe before now? I welcomed a stranger into my home, but not just any stranger, one the boys upset no less. When Leo returns, he will be unhappy at my judgement tonight.

Antonio paces the family room, and his left hand swings the axe while his right hand rests inside his loose, dirty overalls. What else is he hiding under there?

"Your children broke into my boss' sugar plantation farm and stole sugar canes from under my nose. I saw them with my own eyes. There is no denying this. These two, they are the kids," he says pointing at the boys. "There was one more, but he ran faster, so he got away. Lucky for me your two are much slower, and I was able to catch up to them."

Carlos comes closer. "Mama, that is not true."

"Liar! My eyes do not deceive me. I know what I saw," says Antonio.

João comes to his brother's defense. "We did not steal anything, and we only looked around." I hide my smile because no matter what the situation, the boys are bonding and that brightens this dark day.

I know I must reprimand the boys, even if only to prove to Antonio that I am in control. So, I say, "Quiet, both of you. I heard enough. You two go to your room at once so I can settle this with Mr. Antonio."

I point my index finger at them and give them a deep stare in an attempt to convey that I am serious. I need to be in charge and show them I am in control.

After the boys go to their room, Mr. Antonio and I continue our discussion. He no longer yells, but still paces while swinging the axe and inhaling heavily. I back up from him a few steps to allow more space between us.

"Your boys stole the sugar canes. I know what I saw," he repeats.

"Okay, I understand, and I am sorry. How can I make this right?"

A smile forms on his lips and he stands still for the first time since entering my house.

"Well let's see, we can settle this for $1000 escudos, and I will not go to the authorities. That is what it will take to 'make it right' as you put it, Madame."

$1000 escudos is a lot of money, money we do not have. Yes, we have been saving, but this is too much to spare. I am not sure how to bargain with this man. Leo is the negotiator not me, and if he were here, he would know what to do.

Antonio swings the axe again. "Well, what will it be? If you do not pay, I am going to the authorities and the boys will have to attend court. If that happens, you will pay more than I am demanding."

I ponder his threat and decide he is right — I do not have a choice. Living with Leo these years must have left an impression on me and I do something out of character, something I have not done before. I bargain with Antonio and manage to settle on $500 escudos as payment, in addition to proving information on the other boy. This way, Antonio can collect the same payment from the other family. This relieves the burden off my shoulders by $500 escudos. Is it a moral thing to do? Well, it is fair, after all, my boys are not the only two involved in this mess. My family should not be the only one to suffer the consequences. I know who the other boy is, so I give Antonio the address.

I instruct Antonio to wait in the family room while I go to my bedroom to get the only money we have, hidden in my mattress. I unwillingly hand it over, and he snatches the money out of my hand and puts it in his pockets. He leaves my house grinning.

Later at night, I lecture the boys about what they did and the financial burden they placed on this family. They are not attentive and seem distracted as they look out the window. When I finish my talk, they tell me they put the sugar canes in our front garden. At hearing these words, my mouth waters. It has been so long since I ate a sugar cane, so the three of us go outside to retrieve them. We sit at our kitchen table enjoying the delicious sweetness of the sugar canes when Leo walks in.

"Good, you found the boys."

The three of us look at him with mouths full and sugar canes dangle from our lips. Leo crunches up his nose, confused by what he sees. "Where did you get the sugar canes?"

He places the keys on the table and sits to join us.

"Oh Leo, before I tell you the story, you better sit and have one yourself, it will make what I am about to tell you worth it," I say, as I lick my lips.

I worry about what to say to the other boy's mother when I run into her in town. Surely, she will know it was me who gave Antonio their address. I decide to wait until our paths cross, and not worry about it until then.

It only takes two days before she and I run into one another. I act innocent and greet her like I always do and she does not bring up the subject either. She must be as embarrassed about the situation as I am.

The War of Independence is now into its fifth year. Most battles occur in Eastern Angola, in the jungles and out of the cities far from where we live. In 1966 one of the separatist forces, UNITA, has its base in the south east, and they carry out an attack on December twenty-fifth, Christmas Day. We are huddled in our kitchen enjoying a Christmas breakfast when the news blasts through the radio. It is said they prevent trains from passing through Benguela, and they derail the trains. When I hear this, I run to shut off the radio, today is not a day I want to bring sorrow into our house, even if we do live in a colony that is at war. I want one day of peace, and Christmas Day is my chosen day.

In 1968 there are more attacks, this time by the FNLA separatist group. Once again, we learn of these attacks through radio broadcasts. The FNLA troops enter eastern Angola and carry out violent attacks against many locals. I thank God we are not involved so far, not since that bomb threat a few years ago. We are able for the most part, to go about life as we have before. But are we next? War is like a bow and arrow, always moving and looking for its next target.

CHAPTER 51

1968

A S THE BOYS grow older, they settle. They now spend plenty of time with Natércia and try to teach her how to ride a bike. We own one bicycle the boys share, and they often fight over who gets to use it first.

I am in the garden, Armando at my side; he is eleven years old but still prefers the company of adults over his brothers. We are picking potatoes for tonight's soup when the boys come riding down the street, both on the same bike.

Carlos peddles too fast, and João hangs like a monkey, upside down on the handlebars. I squint for a closer look at the bicycle; this is not their bicycle, this is a different bicycle. The thought crosses my mind that they stole it. These boys better not have stolen it — I do not have any backup money left to bail them out of more trouble. They ride the bicycle up the road with ease, despite the uphill slope. Carlos screams, a cheerful scream, while João holds both arms to the side and tries to catch the wind.

"Whoo hoot," says Carlos.

"Go faster," says João.

It does not appear the bike has brakes, or perhaps they do not know how to use them. They speed past me and head straight for a banana tree. I shut my eyes just before impact, afraid of the damage they will inflict on themselves. Upon hearing the bicycle crash, I open my eyes and find them face down on the grass. They move, so I allow myself to breathe.

"Are either of you hurt?"

"No Mama, we jumped off before we hit the tree," says Carlos, proud of himself.

I raise my eyebrows. "Where did you get the bicycle?"

"Mama, we did not steal it. We promise," says João, as he lies on his back.

"I did not imply you did. I asked where you got it."

"We found it," they both say in unison. Hmm, their reply sounds practiced.

I tower over them with arms crossed and try to look stern but also push back a laugh. "I am sure you did," I say.

I walk back to the house with the basket full of potatoes, ready to boil water for the soup. "Armando, come along." Armando follows, oblivious to his two rambunctious brothers.

Natércia is eager to learn how to ride the bike and asks her brothers every day to teach her. She has no balance, so this task is difficult. She is a determined little girl who does not give up easily. Her brothers try to teach her every day for weeks resulting in scrapes, scratches, and bumps on the head, but the effort is to no avail. Natércia does not possess the skills necessary to learn how to ride. Her brothers soon give up, regardless of her determination. I am so proud of them for showing love and support, and for taking time out of their many adventures to try to teach their little sister.

❧

Shortly after the stolen bike incident, Carlos gets a job as a mechanic at a garage in town. This means extra income for the family and less time out on adventures.

Leo and I also finally get married this year. Five children and many homes later, we become husband and wife. I received word years ago from Julio that our lawyer had the necessary paperwork, but over the years, we became consumed with everyday life and we forgot about marriage. I was troubled at the start of our relationship with the arrangement, but as time passed I grew more comfortable, but at heart I hoped we would be married soon. Leo was never bothered by the fact that we were not married. His skin is like a carapace, refusing to allow vulnerability to penetrate. I, unfortunately, am not as strong.

Leo and I have a small ceremony at City Hall consisting of only us, our children, and Celeste. It is an intimate, small ceremony, but this day means the world to me. I always considered myself Leo's wife for all intents and purposes, but now I change my surname to Carvalho, and for the first time we are a real family.

There is no reception, but to celebrate Leo gets a bottle of wine from the pantry, a bottle he saved. We open it and toast to many more years ahead, together. Not once tonight do we turn on the radio for fear that negative words might seep through the speakers and cast a shadow on our day. This is the second night of the year when I want peace and harmony; I deserve this much in a world clouded with darkness.

CHAPTER 52

1969

W HEN A CHILD enters this world with difficulties, a mother never stops worrying, at least I don't. I have known since Armando was little that something is wrong. Back then, and even now, I attribute his difficulties to the arduous labour I had. People look at him in a different light than other children his age. He does not make eye contact; he is not social and prefers to be alone. Because of Armando's delays, school is a challenge. He cannot concentrate on simple tasks and becomes overwhelmed with too many choices, resulting in meltdowns. As he grows older, he becomes more withdrawn and even more antisocial. Now at the age of twelve, he deteriorates further physically. Within a short period, he loses too much weight and his cheeks draw into his jaw.

Tonight, I wake up to a scream from the boys' room, the voice belongs to João. I jump out of bed and startle Leo awake. Most nights he sleeps through all sounds, so he does not hear the scream until I wake him. He races to the boys' bedroom. By the time I get there, Armando is shaking violently. I watch as he foams at the mouth and wets himself.

Leo shakes him and calls his name in an attempt to wake him. I stand three feet away, unable to move and do not know what to do. What is happening with my son? Is death here to take him? Is he possessed? After seconds of agony, I form the words, "What should I do?"

Leo ignores my question and continues with an effort to wake Armando. Carlos and João sit on the bed they share and stare at the scene before them with horror in their eyes.

"Boys, your brother will be fine," I say unconvinced.

"Rosa, get some water, now," says Leo.

I hurry off, and when I return Armando has come to. He now sits up with his back against the bed. Leo is beside him and sweat drenches his clothes. I pass the water to Leo who then puts it up to Armando's mouth and encourages small sips. Armando has no recollection of what happened or what he went through tonight. The three girls are now awake due to the commotion. Each of them stands in the doorway asking questions. They want to come into the room to see what the fuss is, but I tell them to stay outside.

"Get the girls back to bed, I will stay to make sure Armando is all right," says Leo.

"Okay," I say, as I direct the girls back to their own room.

Later at night we bring Armando's mattress into our room and set it beside our bed. Leo and I decide together this is best for now, or at least until we can get him to a doctor. From this night forward, Armando sleeps in our bedroom for safety.

We do not call for the doctor right away since the imminent danger is over, instead we wait until the weekend to go to the hospital. Armando goes through a series of tests, and we receive a diagnosis of epilepsy. Days turn to weeks, weeks to months, and Armando continues to sleep in our bedroom. The medication does not help, so after a few months I decide to get a second opinion. Armando and I go to a clinic in Lobito, as I am told they have more specialized medical professionals. At this clinic, they confirm the diagnosis of epilepsy, but they also prescribe a new medication they believe is more effective. This medication is more expensive than the last, so I do not fill the prescription right away due to lack of funds. Later at night, Carlos is home from work and hears of the troubles and offers to pay for the prescription. The next day, I go back to the clinic to fill the prescription.

The new medication proves to be more effective than the last, and the seizures, while they do not stop, are less frequent. Rather than a few seizures a week, Armando now only has a few a month. It is then we move Armando's mattress out of our bedroom and back into the boys' room. The first night, I do not sleep. I keep waking to check on my son. The second night, I manage two hours of sleep, and by the end of the week, I am only getting up to check on him once. I cannot keep him tied to my skirts forever. A mother needs to know when to let go, or at least loosen the grip of a tightly formed knot.

CHAPTER 53

1969

A S OF LATE, I have let go a lot and this is hard for a mother. When will this feeling of loss end? It is nighttime, the children are settled in their beds, and I sit in the living room reading a book. Leo sits across from me reading the newspaper when Mina comes in. She walks into the living room with a frown. She does not smile, nor does she make eye contact. She heads over to me and kneels.

"Mina, why are you not asleep? Is there something wrong?" I ask, as I set my book down.

Mina reaches out to take my hand and brings it to her lips. "Aunt Rosa, I cannot tell you how much you mean to me. I appreciate everything you have done all these years. You are a mother to me, and I will never forget the encouragement and love you show me."

I do not like the sound of this, so I brace myself for whatever else she has to say. "You sound serious. Is something wrong?"

"I am serious." Tears pour down her face.

"Are you leaving us?"

"Yes, I am afraid so."

"I understand. I felt this was coming," I say.

"I am sorry."

"Have you been in contact with your father?"

"Yes, he made arrangements for me."

"Will you promise to write?"

"Of course. I will write to you every week."

Mina has been in our family since she was five years old and I raised her like one of my own. She is a daughter to Leo and I and a sister to my children, so when I lose Mina, I lose a daughter for the second time in my life. Mina is a hardworking, caring human being, and when she leaves our home at the age of eighteen, she leaves a void that could not be any larger, had she been one of my own. Within a month, Mina moves to Lisbon to be with her father, my brother Eduardo.

My sweet niece is gone three months now, and I suffer her absence every day. I receive a weekly letter from her as promised. She is well and working hard. She has always been ambitious and responsible, and I am so proud of the young lady she becomes. I am happy for her, but my heart still aches to see her glowing face. I miss her, so I remind myself about loosening the grip, but the knots get tighter with each sacrifice I make.

CHAPTER 54

1973

AS I SIT in my favourite chair and reply to Mina's last letter, the door bursts open. I stop writing mid-sentence, put the pen down, and look up to see who my visitor is. "Natércia, it's you. What are you wearing? Those are not your clothes," I say.

In her arms, she carries her clothes, wrapped in a bundle and dripping.

"Why are your clothes wet?"

She sniffles as she speaks. "I fell into the river."

"What? How?"

I grab a bag from the linen closet to place her wet clothes into. Half a minute later, a woman enters and introduces herself as Paula's mother. Paula is a friend of Natércia's. I lead Natércia into the kitchen and offer my visitor tea, still unsure why she is here and why Natércia is not wearing her own clothes.

Natércia sobs as she tells me her story. "I was with Paula when we got out of my tutoring lesson. I was carrying my school books, and, oh Mother, I assure you I was holding the books tight. I understand how expensive they are. We were walking and chatting as we crossed the bridge."

She stops mid-way to wipe her nose. This bridge she speaks of is in between two main buildings. On one side of the bridge is City Hall where Leo and I got married. On the other side is the fire station, the river running between both. A wooden bridge provides access to both sides of the land. It is a pretty view from the bridge, and pedestrians often stop to take in the beauty of the buildings and the waterway that flows rapidly through Lobito.

Natércia puts down the napkin and continues with her story. "As we admired the view, I leaned over the railing, and the books slipped from my arms and tumbled down, making a splash as all four of my books hit the water."

She wipes her nose a second time using the same napkin. "Mother, I was so scared, I did not know what to do. I kept thinking I could not return home without the books."

"So, what in heaven's name did you do?"

"I jumped after the books."

"You did what?"

"I jumped," she says again, thinking I did not hear her.

"You don't know how to swim. What possessed you to jump off a bridge?"

"I did not want to get in trouble," she says. "I tried to save the books."

I am speechless at how foolish my daughter is. Paula comes close so she can give me her account. "The current was strong today, and since Natércia can't swim, she almost drowned. I screamed for help as I watched her hands flailing above the water, and saw her head peek above the water, searching for air. I thought she was going to die, but a pedestrian walking across the bridge heard my screams and saw Natércia in the water, drowning. Luckily this girl, who appeared to be about fifteen, jumped off the bridge and pulled Natércia to shore."

"It is true Mother, I was on my last breath," says Natércia.

I am shocked beyond belief. I cannot imagine the scene, I want to ground her for life over her foolishness, but I am relieved at the same time. "And you came straight home?"

"No, she came to my house," says Paula's mother. "The girls were upset, and we live only a few blocks away, so they came and told me the story. I offered some of Paula's clothes to keep Natércia dry and drove her here. I wanted to come in case you had questions about what happened, since I heard the account first hand from Paula."

I turn to Natércia, whose face is still covered with tears. "Who was the girl that saved you?"

"I do not know, Mother, I have never seen her before."

Paula's mother jumps in. "Paula says she left right after she pulled Natércia out, so neither girl had the opportunity to get her name or thank her."

"So, I will never know who saved my daughter's life?"

"No, you will not, but thank the Lord she is alive," says Paula's mother.

And so, thank the Lord I do.

The remainder of this year passes with not much incident, that is, until I receive more shocking news. I am sitting in my favourite chair with my feet up and nose buried in my newest romance novel when Bella walks in. She is biting her lip, a sign of nervousness.

"Mother," she says. The girls now call me Mother, they say Mama is a term reserved for children, Mother sounds more sophisticated, more grown up. "We need to talk."

"Yes, Bella."

"I would ask you to sit, but you already are."

"Is something wrong?" I ask, as I flip the end of the page slightly to mark my spot and put the book down.

"I am pregnant."

CHAPTER 55

1973 - 1974

WHEN MY DAUGHTER announces she is pregnant, the words that echo in my head are, "You will be a grandmother." I do not consider myself grandmother material. I am far too young, and I do not look like a grandmother. I have my hands full already, what will I do with a grandchild? But, Bella is expecting, so it is inevitable, this baby is coming whether we want this to happen or not.

As I prepare tea, Bella enlightens me on how this happened. She has a good job working long hours for a customs broker, so she often spends extended amounts of time away. She met someone, and they became involved in the summer of 1973, and by the fall, Bella discovered she was with child. The father was a soldier for the Portuguese army, but he died in battle a few months ago. This means my daughter must raise this child on her own, with my help of course, because she does not know a thing about raising a child on her own.

As Bella and I talk, a loud bang and commotion develops from the boys' bedroom. I jump off the chair, causing a nearby lamp to fly across the room. Bella arrives at the boys' room before I do. It is Armando again, and he is having another seizure.

Armando, Carlos, and João went out earlier to see a movie, and they returned only moments before I settled with my book. They have not been home for more than twenty minutes, and already Armando is foaming and shaking. Bella clears space around Armando and flips him over to his side. Carlos and João both speak at the same time and try to tell me what happened. I calm them enough to get the story out of them while Bella stays with Armando, to comfort him.

"João, what happened?"

"He was wobbling, fell and banged his head on the dresser, but we swear it is not our fault. We did not do anything."

He is afraid I will blame him.

The seizure lasts four minutes; this is the worse one yet. Armando's doctor told me to count how long the seizures last, to get a sense of severity. Most seizures are between one to three minutes, but this one lasts four minutes. Blood spills from my son's mouth; he must have bitten his tongue.

"Bella, go get a wet cloth."

"I am on it."

"Hurry!"

She runs off and meets her father in the kitchen; he arrived from work a few minutes ago. She tells Leo about the seizure, and within thirty seconds Leo is in the room.

"Are you all right?" he asks Armando, as he gives him a hug.

"Yes, Papa, I am fine, but I bit my tongue," says Armando, not making eye contact.

I look at Leo and give him a long stare, raising both my eyebrows. He knows this means I have lots to tell him. Natércia is in bed, asleep. Luckily for her, she missed the action tonight.

Once we get Armando cleaned and settled into bed, Bella sits with her father and me so she can tell him her news. Certainly, I do not want to be the one to break the news to my husband. My daughter got herself into this situation, so she can be the one to tell her father. Years ago,

I would have protected her more, but one thing I learned is, the more you protect children the less they protect themselves. Leo says he had a hard and long day at work and wants nothing more than to sit with his feet up and have a cigarette, a new habit he has formed. He is not in the mood tonight for a discussion such as the one we are about to have.

Bella opens her mouth to speak, and I brace myself for what she says, but then no words come out. She needs prompting. "Bella, do you have something to say to your father?" I ask. She looks at me like I slapped her across the face. I want to get this over with, there is no point in procrastinating.

Leo takes a puff of the cigarette and looks from me to Bella, his eyebrows crease. "I want to relax, but you both have something you want to tell me, so what is it?"

Bella and I exchange glances.

"Are either of you going to tell me?"

Bella sits on the rug next to her father's chair, she places her head on the armrest and reveals her secret.

"Pregnant?" shouts Leo.

"Yes."

"How is this possible?" he asks. "Never mind, do not answer. How are you going to raise a child?" he asks instead.

"I will learn."

"How will you provide for this child?"

"I have a job, and I am saving."

"Who is the father?"

"He died Papa."

Leo gets up from the chair, puts out his cigarette in the ashtray and leaves the room. Bella turns to me for comfort.

I place my arms around her. "Give him time, he will come around."

Bella delivers a baby girl on July 29, 1974, weighing 2.900 kg. This is my first granddaughter. The moment I lay my eyes on her, shivers run through my body. A sense of joy and excitement takes over. My heart melts as I look into her big, brown eyes, and my own personal qualms over becoming a grandmother now seem foolish.

Carlos is the baby's godfather and Mina her godmother; although we do not baptize the baby right away. Carlos names the baby Telma Cristina, and from the moment she comes into this world, this little soul changes the dynamics of our household. Where there is sadness my granddaughter replaces with comfort and a sense of hope.

She loves milk and drinks lots of it. She soon grows into a chubby baby with full thighs and round cheeks Leo loves to pinch. Her hair is light brown and straight. Bella often works during the day, so I become the baby's primary caregiver. The baby and I fall into a smooth routine, washing diapers, feedings, and bathing time. It is I who puts her to sleep every night and I who suffers her colicky cries. I am even the one who gets up through the night to feed her when she whimpers from hunger. Even when Bella is home at night, I do not want to part with the baby. I want to keep holding and coddling her as if she is my own. Over the next few months, I consume myself with taking care of Telminhas, that is her nickname and how we all refer to her.

CHAPTER 56

October 1974

L IFE WITH A newborn is unlike the last few years. My own children are older now, so I must adjust to this new lifestyle again. My days are full, but I love every busy minute of every messy day. Although I do not need more excitement or chaos in my life, I recognize Leo has something to say. During lunch he fidgets with the fork and pushes his food around on the plate, but I do not prompt him into speaking. He will get the words out when he is ready.

Out of the blue, he clears his throat and says, "We are moving."

I drop my fork onto my plate; it makes a clanging sound and causes Telma, who sleeps next to me, to stir. Bella chokes on her food and has a coughing fit as Carlos smacks her on the back.

I narrow my eyebrows at him. "Moving where?"

"To a house on the ocean."

It does not surprise me that Leo wants to move close to the ocean, our family loves the beach. Beach outings have been a weekly event during the summer since the kids were little. Each Sunday we pack a picnic and swimsuits and travel to Restinga beach, twenty minutes away. We spend the entire day soaking under the glory of the warm sun and breathing the salty air. As old as the kids are now, they still love the beach as much as they did when they were little. We often talk about living on the ocean, and as of recently, Leo has brought up the subject frequently. It never occurred to me that he was searching for a house, nor did I know he had acquired one, until now. I should be unhappy about this, I love our house on the hill, but I also am at peace by the water, so I am both sad and thrilled at the same time. I am sad for what I will leave behind, but thrilled at the new opportunity. I tell Leo I am surprised at this news, and he explains he has come across this opportunity rather suddenly.

"Is this not a risky move now, during a war?"

"Rosa you must understand something. Small risks bring small opportunities. Big risks bring opportunities that can make us greater than our current reality. I want to give our family something great. You will love it, I promise."

"I am sure I will," I say.

"Rosa, please be positive about this, it is a good thing for our family. I know what I am doing."

Society and class are important to Leo, so he upgrades our family from what I thought would be our forever home to a better environment. This new house is not any bigger or glamorous, but it is in a more prestigious neighbourhood. The memories we will leave behind are so deeply ingrained into these walls and will eventually fade as they are replaced with newer memories, and this saddens me.

"Okay then," I say.

The rest of the lunch passes without another word from anyone. There is no further talk today of the impending move.

We leave our old furniture behind; Leo wants a brand new start and decides to buy new furniture, with the help of Carlos' and Bella's incomes. When my granddaughter turns three months old, we move from the home we built a life in to an unfamiliar structure. I am hopeful in time that I will grow to love the new house, but right now it feels empty even though new furniture fills the space. We are in the new house for three weeks, and I miss Celeste already; she was more than a neighbour to me, she was a lifeline.

⚮

Today I discover Leo had another motive for moving us away from the hill. On April 25, Portugal granted independence to Angola in the Carnation Revolution, and the country becomes more unstable than it has been since the beginning of the War of Independence, back in 1961. This is thirteen years, two months and three weeks the country has been at war. But since April 25, Angola becomes more of a war zone. As Portuguese troops pull out of Angola, battles rage across the land. The soon-to-be-formed country has many difficulties, including economic and social troubles. These complications create internal power struggles within the country. Angola goes from one war to another, only this time, will we be so lucky?

The new house is on a street called Rua Fragosso de Matos in the 'Compáo' neighbourhood. The house is airy, it contains many large windows, some stretching from floor to ceiling. The builder captured the essence of the sea in the architectural design — it is a beach house you can rent for a vacation. It is a one-story structure, like our old house, and with the same number of rooms. This means Bella and Natércia still share a room as do the three boys. Telminhas, of course, remains with Leo and me in our room. There is a spacious, covered back porch, and this offers us a place to sit outside on rainy days. I love listening to the rain falling on rocks that line the shore. It does not take long for me to find my new favourite reading spot. We even splurge and purchase new decorations, paintings of landscapes for the walls, new rugs, and outdoor chairs for the back patio. There is an unsettling feeling in my stomach over spending so much money, but since there has not been any crisis, I throw caution to the wind. Leo convinces me saying, "We cannot take it with us."

The first few months we live here are typical and nothing out of the ordinary happens. Natércia and Armando still attend school, and João started a new job working as an auto mechanic apprentice. Carlos and Bella still have their same jobs from before. I am busy with the baby and that is my biggest responsibility.

⌒

Telma is not yet baptized and this worries me, so I bring the issue up one day when we are together.

"We need to baptize this child," I say to Leo as he listens to the soccer game on the radio. "We have been negligent in not baptizing her sooner. Leo, are you listening to me?"

"Hmm," he says, as he looks up.

"Telma, baptized? Did you not hear a word I said?"

Again, I am met with silence. The soccer game that blares through the speakers is more interesting than I am today, so I walk away a little hurt.

I am not sure why we have not baptized the child, but I can only speculate it is because Bella is always working, so it is not a priority. I do not like that she is not baptized, but it is not my business to force the issue. Today, however, I make it my business. With the ongoing issues with the war and troubles we keep hearing about, it is time. I need Telma to be a part of God's family, and that means baptism.

I write to my niece Mina since she is the godmother, to inform her of our plans. Mina writes back that she plans to come to Lobito for the ceremony, so we proceed with the arrangements for the baptism. We need to get this planned and done with before anything bad happens. I have a feeling in the pit of my stomach I cannot explain, urgency of a sort, so in a few days, the plans are made.

The ceremony is intimate and takes place at a small Catholic church, Sagrado Coracáo de Jesus, and only the family is present. We have a little party at home after the ceremony with lots of food and treats to celebrate. The moment it is over, I relax, and a burden lifts off me.

⌒

Close to Christmas, things worsen, and our lives begin to change forever.

Each day, there is more news of devastation occurring all around. We hear the news from the radio broadcasts. We keep the radio on now all the time to stay informed.

There are three major liberal movement parties fighting, and so Angola enters a civil war. The three major movements are: The People's Movement for the Liberation of Angola known as MPLA, The National Liberation Front of Angola, knows as the FNLA and The National Union for the Total Independence of Angola known as UNITA. We do not know whom to trust, but Leo and I favour UNITA, and the rest of my family supports MPLA movement. After some time, I switch sides feeling UNITA no longer offers enough protection. This is not about loyalty to our future country, this is now about survival.

Months leading up to Independence Day, battles start to rage across the land. The FNLA sends troops to Luanda to seize the capital before Independence Day, they have high hopes of winning, but they fail in their attempts. Moscow sends ships, tanks, and armies to Luanda in its defense for the MPLA.

War is now all around us, and my family and I are in the middle of the crossfire. We had high hopes for a free, peaceful country after being at war for so long. Instead, what we get in return is more war. Along with control from the different parties, there is now a shortage of food, lost jobs, and more fighting over the next few months. The battles are closer to home than before. I fear for my life, for my children's lives, for my husband, and for the baby. She is only a few months old. This innocent child was born into this world at such a deadly time, it does not seem fair to me. I make it my job to protect her at all costs. I know I will do anything to save her, to protect her from the tragedies of this sad and brutal world.

PART FIVE

1975 – 1976

CHAPTER 57

October 5, 1975
Present Day

O NE YEAR LATER, I am consumed with memories and feel empty inside as I stare out to sea. I am brought back to reality with Leo's voice close to my ear. "We need to leave the country." His voice is shaky. "Are you hearing me? You have been off in your own world now for quite some time. What are you thinking about again? You keep slipping away from me into another world, one without me."

"I am sorry Leo. You're right, I was thinking," I say, as I come to the realization he is speaking to me while I am lost in my own world.

I am disbursed by my thoughts, thinking about my entire life and the events that lead to this day. I look around at my surroundings and realize I am back in the little haven with my family, hiding from the raging battles that stole many lives already.

"What about?" he asks.

"My life. And, it is not an entire world without you, it was only a small part."

We are in our home, trapped due to the battle in town. It is the fifth day we have been unable to leave the house. The news on the radio about the woman who got shot on her balcony blasts through the speaker. Our food storage is now depleted, and everyone's stomachs are empty. Other than the radio, the sound of growling stomachs fills the room. It is quieter today than it has been the last five days and I am hopeful this means peace.

The radio broadcaster announces that the fighting has ceased, and the troops retreated to their camps. This explains why we have not heard shots fired or explosions for a few hours. "Do you think it is safe to go out now?" I ask Leo.

He walks over to the window, uncovers the side, and peeks out. "I think so, it seems quiet out."

We cannot sit here any longer waiting for the unknown, so on the fifth day, we set out late in the afternoon to inspect the town. Leo wants to go on his own, but I do not want to stay behind. The older boys, of course, want to go off on their own. They are old enough, so we cannot stop them. Bella stays at the house with Telminhas, and Armando — Leo does not want the baby to come with us, just in case.

When you go through a difficult time in life, you think you can't handle worse, that is until the next catastrophe and then the rollercoaster repeats. This is how I feel now. I am not sure what I am expecting to see, I suppose I have not given it much thought. I am living in my own world, oblivious to the fact that death is all around me. We are not prepared for the tragedy we see today.

I walk out onto the street, and at first there is nothing of interest, but the raunchy smell is overwhelmingly strong. I gasp, hold my breath, and cover my mouth with my right hand. As I turn another corner, there are dead bodies everywhere. Corpses scattered everywhere, on the roads, lawns of homes, and sidewalks. My left hand holds onto Leo's tightly. Natércia screams and buries her face in her father's chest. The smell is horrific, making each breath we take difficult. The air contains a mixture of decaying bodies, gun powder, and ashes mixed together into a cloud of dust. I cannot believe the scene before me. I must be dreaming again, but as I try to open my eyes wide to force the dream to end, nothing happens, and I remain in this living nightmare.

There is a creek nearby that people throw bodies into to get them off the roads. As the bodies hit the water, they make a splashing sound.

"Leo, oh my God," I cry in disbelief.

Leo, too, is in shock. Neither of us says much as we look around and try to comprehend this horrendous vision before us. A few times Leo tries to speak, but he has lost his words.

I take another look around at the dead bodies lying everywhere. I glance into the creek where bodies float, reminding me this is real. One of them looks right at me, only he is dead, so he cannot see me. But as I look into the dead man's eyes, I stare deep into his soul and shivers cover my skin. I squeeze Leo's hand even tighter, and I throw up on the side of the road. Natércia stands a few feet away, covering her eyes with both hands, screaming.

Leo squeezes my hand back to let me know he is here. "Let's get out of here. It was a mistake to come. I should not have brought you."

I am not sure I hear what he says, as I am hunched over vomiting again. Leo tries to keep my curly hair from falling forward into the vomit.

"Rosa, let's go," he says urgently.

We make our way back, but I stop often to throw up. When we return home, I pick up the baby off the floor and lay her on my bed. I stand over her, watching her nap as I weep for the souls of the dead men, women, and children I left behind.

CHAPTER 58

1975

L EO HOPED THIS house would provide peace and a protected living lifestyle. But this does not turn out to be the case. We are no safer here than we were out in the country. After the battle in the city between UNITA and MPLA, things deteriorate further. We can no longer buy food at the market, and the kids can no longer go to school, it is too dangerous. Food is too scarce, and I am not sure how long we can continue this way, surely we will starve soon or worse, be killed by the enemy in crossfire.

We know we must leave our country and soon, but we procrastinate, we are still hopeful for peace. Most neighbours begin to flee, and we decide we need to evacuate as well.

The next day, Leo goes to the Red Cross centre to get our names on the list. Red Cross is arranging for people to flee with the help of Portugal. He, too, has had enough and says he cannot stay any longer. I agree wholeheartedly. Red Cross informs Leo that we will be on a boat to

Luanda in less than one week. Leo must report back to Red Cross in three days to confirm when the ship will arrive and when we need to be at the dock. When he returns this evening, he gives us the news as we continue to sit in despair over what we saw the day before. I try to soothe my children as best I can, especially the youngest, Natércia and Armando. "We just have to last a few days. It will be all right," I say, unconvinced. A few days are not long, but when you are trying to stay alive, then each day feels like a lifetime.

Bella, who remains the quietest during this time, catches me off guard. "I cannot leave with the family."

I am feeding Telma soup I prepared this morning after making a trip to the market and getting lucky to have found some items. I drop the spoon full of hot soup and it splashes over the table.

"What did you say?"

"Please Mother, do not make this harder for me than it already is. You heard what I said. I need to stay to finish my contract."

"I do not understand you."

"Please try to understand. The government is offering protection, and I want to see this contract that I am bound to through," she says.

I know she has a contract she needs to finish, but I do not understand why she feels it is more important than fleeing with her family. As she tells me about the protection plan, my thoughts go to Telma, and I make mental preparations for her to leave with me. She is not staying behind, that is not a consideration and not up for discussion. Bella never mentions Telma, and I am afraid to ask, afraid of what her answer will be. So, I remain quiet and keep my thoughts to myself.

I plan our next few meals, but I do not know where they will come from. I got lucky this morning at the market, but if I had arrived only a few minutes later, there would be nothing left to purchase. I have saved my entire life, other than the spending spree when we moved into this house. That was not the norm by any means. I try to conserve food, to keep my pantry full of canned vegetables. I am comforted knowing if anything happens I can feed my family at least for a few days. But when a country is at war for so long, the preserved food and the saved money are consumed faster. Money is irrelevant now anyway, what good is money when there is nothing to purchase with it.

We moved into this house ten months ago, and for the first time, I wonder what would have happened if we had stayed at the house on the hill. I think of Celeste and her family, hoping they are all right and wondering if they left. If they are still there, I hope they have enough to eat. The shortage of food supply at the stores is a great concern for everyone. Many crops have been destroyed by the war, adding to the decrease in food supply. I am taking stock of the pantry, of the remaining inventory, when Leo approaches. "How are things looking in here?" he asks, referring to the food supply.

The pantry is dark, and big enough to store our food, but not spacious enough for two people to stand in comfortably. There is no electricity in here either, so I must bring an oil lamp, but still, it is hard to see. "We have enough food for one week. That's it," I say. "After this, the food will be gone, and I do not know what we will do."

Leo comes closer and places his arms around me. Cigarette smoke from his breath fills my nostrils, and together we stand inside the dark, crowded pantry. Neither of us says a word for a long time. I hope if we wait long enough, I will wake up to find this has been nothing more than a dream and the shelves will be full of food. But this is no dream; this is our sad reality, empty shelves and all. This war is consuming me and destroying me one day at a time. Leo breaks the trance we are in.

"How much milk do we have for the baby?"

I wipe a tear from my eye before answering. "Not much, there are four bottles left."

"I do not want you to worry, especially about the baby. I will get more milk, this I promise."

"How?"

"You worry about getting to the market tomorrow to buy what you can, so stand in line as long as you need. Buy whatever is left. Carlos left money on the table for you to use. Leave the milk to me."

⌒

By morning, it is pouring, but I am determined to not let the rain keep me from getting what I need. My plan is to get to the market as early as possible, so I can be first in line. Sometimes, I get to the counter and there is no food left and so the trip is useless. However, the trips must still be made even if the chance of getting food is slim. So, this morning I get up earlier than usual, hoping to beat the crowds. I take the money Carlos left, bundle up the baby, and tell Natércia and Armando to get dressed, they are coming with me. Nobody stays home alone today.

The three of us walk side-by-side, as I hold Telma tight in my arms. As we walk through the sodden streets, I notice neighbours up ahead. I call their names, so they stop, turn, and smile. They wait for us to approach, and we walk the remainder of the long way together in silence. We see many military supporters out today, parading their guns and control. I tell Natércia and Armando both to keep their heads down. "Nao faca contado visual," *Do not make eye contact*, I say.

There is a man protesting on the street, he has a sign and it reads 'Free Angola.' Militants loiter the streets and we ignore them and keep walking.

As soon as we reach the market, the lines are already out the door. I sigh, knowing too well we are not leaving with food today. We stand in the long queue anyway and hope for a miracle. I say a silent prayer while we wait. As we get closer, I notice what others are walking out with. Some carry sugar, others flour, but no one has anything of substance, no meat, and no vegetables.

It is my turn, so I approach the counter where an older woman greets me.

"What can I get you?"

"Do you have any meat left?"

"No."

"None at all?"

She frowns and points to the empty shelves behind the counter. "Does it look like there is any meat?"

"What are my options? I will take whatever you have."

She points to the near-empty shelf, on it sits: sugar, various spices, and coffee. "Well, what will it be?"

"Nothing, thank you," I motion to Armando and Natércia that it is time to leave. We walk away empty-handed and speed home. I want to get off the streets, and back in the safety of our home. I try not to think about what life will look like once we are out of food. The lack of milk I have for the baby consumes me, but right now, I only think about getting home.

When we arrive, Leo is standing in the kitchen, waiting. In his hands are two bottles of milk, and on the counter is a crate containing a few more bottles. I count five bottles in total, and my heart skips a few beats. I look up at him and smile, trying to hold back tears of joy. He touches my chin softly.

"I promised."

"Yes, you did."

Leo is in love with the baby as much as I am. From the moment she came into this world she changed him, and he would never let anything happen to her. He will protect her at all costs, like me. I do not know where or how he gets milk. I do not know what promises he made that we most likely cannot keep. And, I do not know to whom he begged, but I am grateful he did these things.

We try to live as best we can for the next few days, rationing our food and waiting for word from Red Cross about the ship. The days are long and seem to never end. Our plan is to take the boat to Luanda, which is where Portugal sends the displaced families, and from there we hope to book a flight to Lisbon. The Portuguese government, along with other countries, is sending aid to get people out to safety, and this includes the boat we will be on soon.

Some residents leave to go to Portugal, others leave for South Africa, but you must be white, or you are not accepted into South Africa freely. If you are not white, and even if you are of mixed race, they separate you upon arrival. Apartheid is an institutionalized system of racial segregation in South Africa. It started in the late 1940s, therefore, most mixed families choose to leave for Portugal instead, over the fear of separation.

My family plans to go to Portugal, which is our hope. Bella still maintains she is staying behind. She never mentions Telma, and I remain silent on the subject as well. The topic is like dust that you sweep under a mat to avoid dealing with it.

Over the course of the next few days, all around us people pack and leave. We have spent years building a life here, and it is now coming to a devastating end. Should we have left sooner? Have we waited too long? These questions race through my mind now. We tried to hold out as long as possible, hoping and praying the war would end, but it is only getting more dangerous. Days do not pass without me praying for a miracle. Leo checks with Red Cross daily, anxious to receive news. The boat is still on schedule and we will leave in three days. Three more days is a long time to try to stay alive.

CHAPTER 59

1975

TWO DAYS BEFORE we leave, Carlos arrives home covered in blood. He has a broken nose, beat up face, and broken ribs. I am washing the dishes, and I drop a plate, smashing it to pieces. I let out a scream because of the shape he is in. I run over to where he barely stands, as he leans against the wall for support. "What happened?"

I place my left arm under him to support him, and I help him get to the couch. I leave him long enough to get a cloth and a bowl of water. I wipe the blood off his face as he tells me his story.

He closes his eyes as he speaks. "I got captured by one of the activist groups as I was going for a walk on the beach with my friend."

"Oh my God!" I yell too close in his ear, and this causes him to wince.

"We were handled roughly, held at gunpoint in a lineup and taken to the military base. They tortured us there, and I was certain they were going to kill us."

"How did you get away?"

"Well, we got lucky I suppose. I was preparing myself mentally for the end of my life. Our saving grace was that someone from the base recognized me, maybe he knows Father? Anyway, he told the leaders of the group to free us both."

"You did not recognize this man?"

"Not at all. After that, they threw us outside and told us to leave the premises immediately."

"You two were lucky, they could have killed you."

"Yes, I know, it took me a while to get here, I practically had to crawl. I went to the hospital first, but they demanded money, I got scared, so I left, and came home. My friend suffered much the same fate."

I look in the bowl and stare at a pool of red water stained from blood that came off the cloth.

Tonight, our dinner is soup with onions, collard greens, and a few potatoes. Soup goes a long way when you have many mouths to feed. There is neither bread nor wine tonight, just soup. We have not had bread and wine for months, these items are now a luxury. Telma has begun to eat solids, but she still loves her milk. She, too, eats the soup along with a bottle of the milk that her grandfather found. Nobody speaks much during mealtimes anymore. Everyone is lost in their own thoughts. Wondering.

The next day Leo receives news from Red Cross, the ship arrived a day early, and we need to be at the dock tonight if we want to be on board. It is leaving port early the next morning. Leo is already gathering items that he needs to bring. "We need to pack fast, we do not have much time."

I turn to look at him. "So, this is happening?"

"Yes, it's time."

"I thought I would have more time to pack."

"As did I. Get yourself and Telma organized, and I will go tell the others."

Telma. At the thought of her name, my heart almost stops beating. We have not yet settled things with Bella with regards to my granddaughter. There is this unspoken situation that looms over us, but neither of us wants to talk about it. Only now, we have run out of time.

"Leo, what about Bella?"

"Bella can do what she wants. If she decides to stay behind, then fine, she stays, but Telma is coming with us, and that is final."

"Where will we sleep tonight?"

"That my darling, I do not know. Let's get there, and then we can figure it out."

I do not like to figure things out; I am a planner, so this leaves me unsettled. "Okay, when do we need to leave?"

"As soon as we are ready."

MPLA has the support of the Russians, so they have thousands of highly trained Cuban soldiers on our land now. We cannot take any more chances; we need to be on the ship tomorrow morning when it leaves Lobito's dock.

We gather the children to inform them of the impending situation. They remain quiet, all but Bella. Natércia bites her nails to ward off nervousness. She is not quite old enough to grasp the severity of our situation, but not young enough to be naïve.

Bella paces back and forth before she speaks. "I am not going with you. You know I must stay."

Leo bangs his fist on the table. "That is ridiculous!"

"Father, please do not make this harder than it is."

"You want to stay behind? Fine that is your choice, and I cannot make you leave with us, but Telma comes with us." He leaves the room and storms out slamming the door behind him. He leaves before Bella has an opportunity to respond.

She turns to me and says, "Mother, I need to stay. This is important to me. If I finish out my contract, my future in Lisbon is set. I will be able to transfer to another office there, and I am guaranteed a high paying position."

I have butterflies in my stomach. After all this time, we are having the dreaded conversation. My only thought is of the baby. If Bella refuses to flee with us, I cannot, and will not leave her behind.

"Did you hear what I said?"

"Yes. I heard you loud and clear," I say.

There is a noise coming from the bassinet. "Excuse me, I must go tend to Telma, she needs me," I say, as I leave Bella alone.

Once again, I avoid the discussion. I do not have it in me to deal with it right now. After a few minutes Leo returns, he appears calmer. He says he mailed another letter to his family in Canada — he has written several times asking for help. Canada has become a possibility for us, a hope for our future. Leo asks if Bella has said anything more regarding Telma. At the mention of her name, I get a lump in my throat and it is so big it prevents me from breathing. I am sure I am suffocating. I swallow the bile that accumulates in my throat.

"We will not leave Telma behind, I promise," he says. "We will convince Bella to come, and we will leave as a family."

I cannot control my nerves any longer, and I barely hear Leo as I run towards the washroom to throw up.

Leo follows and comforts me. Once again, he pulls back my hair to prevent me from getting sick on it. He understands me.

CHAPTER 60

1975

LEO TELLS ME to pack as light as possible; we can only bring essentials that fit into one small bag each. There is no room for valuables or anything sizeable. That would be foolish anyway; valuables and large objects will make us targets. I pack one change of clothes, and undergarments, that is all there is room for, nothing more. The baby, of course, is the exception; she is not to go without if Leo has his way. I set aside the biggest bag for her and reserve the smaller bags for myself and Leo.

We are in our room. Leo is pacing and watching me pack. "Make sure you have everything she needs, I don't want her to be without anything. If need be, use my bag, fill it with clothes and diapers for her. I don't need anything," he says.

"She is my priority as well," I say, as I stuff as many diapers as we own into her bag. I count fourteen cloth diapers. This is not going to be enough. I go through this many in a day, so where will I wash the soiled diapers if this is all I have? We need more, so I begin to rip shirts to make more cloth diapers.

I share my concerns with Leo, but he only half listens as he too is busy throwing items into his bag. "We will figure things out as we go. Once we get to Luanda, I am sure the government will help."

"I hope so."

Leo looks at the time. "We need to hurry; we are running out of time."

I put the last of the clothes Telma owns into her bag, and struggle to get the zipper to close, it is so full. The zipper finally manages to zip up without breaking. Telminhas has the most belongings packed of all of us. I check if Bella is home, but she is not. After our conversation, she announced that she had to go to work and left. I think she wanted space from me, and she still does not know we are taking her daughter. Once I am satisfied with what I packed for the baby, I look around at my own belongings, and only half satisfied I have what I need, I zip my bag and walk out of my room carrying mine and Telma's bags. I set down the bags in the living room by the front door. Leo has already packed and is now with the boys, making sure they are getting ready.

Loud voices emerge from the boys' room, so I head over to see what the commotion is. Leo's hands are on his head. "Carlos says he is not coming with us."

"What?" I say in frustration. How can this be?

"He has planned with his friend, the one that was with him when he got captured, to leave with him instead. The two decided a few days ago to take another boat, a Russian ship, they are going directly to Lisbon."

If I was not holding the baby, I think I would faint, so instead, I fall to my knees. I am losing my family; my life is falling apart, first my daughter, now my son. Who will be next in this family to decide they are not coming with us? I have been more nauseated in the last month than I was with my pregnancies combined. My body cannot handle any more stress.

Everything is wrong, nothing is right. João is frantic that his older brother is not coming with us. Leo tries to soothe him as I remain frozen on my knees, unable to move. Carlos is asking lots of questions, wanting to know what the plan is. He wants to know when we expect to arrive in Lisbon, and where we will go once we set foot on Portuguese soil. We have no answers; we do not know what our future holds.

I head to the girls' room to see how Natércia is making out with packing. She is contemplating what to bring. She does the same thing I did when I packed Telma's things, trying to overfill the bag. She does not see me enter and she jumps at my voice.

"Remember, you cannot take anything other than a change of clothes and undergarments. We can only bring one bag each."

I am sure she knows this, but I need to remind her.

She looks at me with her dark eyes and sad expression. "Bella has not packed yet, she is not even here."

She goes through her sister's clothes as we speak and separates items for her, she must be worried about her sister.

"I know."

Bella is late, so I wait anxiously for her. She better arrive before we leave. It will break my heart to pieces if she is not here by that time. A few moments later, she arrives. I waste no time and tell her Telma is coming with us. Bella must agree to this, how can she not? She will be working long hours, and there will not be anyone to watch the baby. She must want to see her daughter safe.

She walks over to me and takes Telma from my arms, pressing her tight to her chest. "Take her with you. You need to get out of here, and you need to take her. I want her safe. Her safety is the most important thing, but I need to stay. I need to secure my future, so I can one day take care of my own daughter. I promise I will leave as soon as I can."

"We will keep your daughter safe."

"I know."

She leans in to give me a one-armed hug as she holds her daughter in the other arm; this is her form of goodbye, without speaking the words. After she pulls away, she kisses Telma's cheeks one last time, hesitates, then passes the baby to me. I take a hold of her as if one would grab a boomerang before it changes its mind and swivels the other way.

She then turns and walks away, looking back over her shoulder, at her baby daughter who clings to me.

Leo and I look at each other wide-eyed, mouths open, and relief washes over us.

A half hour later, there is a knock on the door, and I run to answer it still holding the baby in my arms, thinking who it might be.

To my surprise, it is a group of men, going door to door, and they come to warn us of more danger. They say there are rumours of another battle, and we must remain indoors again, so this is it, we must evacuate now, or we will be trapped again and unable to leave.

Leo works quickly loading the bags into the vehicle. We must find a way to fit us all in one trip. There is no time now to make two trips, we are running out of time, fast. We cannot miss this boat, and I need to keep myself together and stay strong to pull us out of this. The boat can only take so many, and we do not know when there will be another boat. I cannot risk my family by becoming trapped here again; we will not survive this time, not without food.

Celeste and her family must be long gone by now I am sure, and I say a prayer for them, hoping one day we can be reunited.

Natércia, João, and Carlos cram into the back seat with some of the bags. The rest of the bags are in the small trunk. Leo hands each of them money and tells them to hide the money in their socks. It is for safety in case we are stopped by the Militants and they search us. He turns to me and does the same. It is best to have the money spread out amongst each of us, rather than with one person. I sit up front with the baby in my lap, and Armando sits quietly in the middle seat. Leo takes a deep breath and puts the vehicle into reverse.

"Let's get out of here."

Before we drive away, I remember something that I need. "Stop the car, I need to go back," I say.

"Não temos tempo," *We don't have time.*

"You must go back. Please. It will only take one minute or less. There is something I forgot."

Leo grunts, but then looks at my pleading eyes, stops the car and puts it back into park mode. "Hurry up; you have sixty seconds to get what you need."

"I will return in fifty."

After opening the door and stepping out, I run across the driveway with Telma in my arms, back into the home that is no longer ours. Where is the blanket? I left it right on top of the couch. When I spot it, I grab it and head back out the door. I return to the vehicle carrying the blanket and Leo looks at me with raised eyebrows.

"What do you need a blanket for; it is nearly one hundred degrees Fahrenheit?"

"You never know."

He shakes his head and drives away from our home for the last time. I don't dare look back, from this day on, I only look forward.

The port is thirty minutes away, and Leo drives fast, faster than I have ever seen him drive before. I bounce Telma on my lap to keep her entertained as we drive through crowded neighbourhoods. People rush to put bags in the car, children frantically run around with no direction, desperation and worry litter the streets.

We are one of the last families to arrive at the dock, even though the boat is not leaving until the next day. It is a good thing we decided to come tonight, they are boarding passengers and allowing us to sleep on board. As we wait to get on, many families crowd the boat, some sleep on benches, some on the floor, and I hope there is still space for us. Leo finds us a spot to wait while he gets us registered. We huddle in a corner next to our bags and wait.

CHAPTER 61

October 11, 1975

"I WILL BE ON the next boat, I promise," Carlos says, as he helps me with my bag while I climb on board.

My family is falling apart, and I am helpless. First, I lose my daughter, and now my son, too. How am I to cope with so much loss in such a short time? Before stepping on board, I hesitate and consider if I am doing the right thing.

Leo encourages me to get on the boat. "Rosa, we don't have a choice."

Carlos drops my bag and waves goodbye as he disappears behind the crowd. On board the ship, passengers search for an empty spot, but there is not much space. The ship is so full that one more body can tip the scale, causing us to dive into the Atlantic Ocean. Families huddle in every corner. All sorts of people are on board, some families with young children, men fleeing solo, even some lone women. Conversations spark around me, and one man speaks of the family he sent to Lisbon weeks ago. The boat is not big; it is a medium-sized cargo ship from Portugal. The boat contains two levels and a deck that wraps the entire boat, allowing views of the water and land from all positions.

Many children fill the space around me. There are kids running, screaming, and some laughing as they play. Most are too young and naïve to understand what is happening around them. Babies cry for their mothers' breasts, and toddlers search for their bottles, including Telma. We spend the night on the boat huddled together in a corner.

Early the next morning, the captain announces that the ship is leaving the dock soon. I watch as the land around me vanishes. The boat ride from Lobito to Luanda is less than three hours but feels longer. Telminhas, unlike the rest of the family, has two bags, and the second bag contains her bottles of milk. Leo comes through once more and obtains a few more bottles for the trip. I am still in the dark about how he finds the milk and he does not tell me. In a corner next to an empty spot are our bags and I keep them close by, always. Bags disappear often, so you can trust no one. I have already witnessed one frantic woman looking for her stolen bag.

Lying on the bench next to me is Telma, crying for her milk. Her mouth is open, and she is reaching her arms out, but there is nothing for her to grab. "Okay, Telminhas, I know what you want." I reach to get a bottle from her bag, and I feel nothing but empty space, the bag is gone. Her cries intensify, and passengers down the hall turn to stare. She wants to eat, and now. "Shit," I say aloud. What am I to do now? Of all the bags to go missing, it had to be hers. My bag is still here, useless on the floor, taunting me. I would give up my bag with the only clothes I have left in the world so Telma can have both of hers. I need to be more careful, more observant. I should have tied the bags together, making it more difficult to steal, but I did not do this, and this is my mistake. I begin to fidget and look around at my surroundings, trying to find the evil person who would do such a thing as steal milk. At that moment I come to reason, the thief is most likely more destitute than us. Otherwise, they would not be as desperate to steal in the first place. They must not have known the bag contains milk for a little girl, how would they, the bag was closed. Understanding this leaves me more at peace with humanity and the world around me.

We have been travelling for over an hour and there is still at least one more hour to go. Leo takes Natércia and João to speak to the officials to try and get information on what is to happen once we dock. He takes it upon himself to attempt to work out a plan since we are now homeless. Armando stays with me, always. Lisbon is where we need to go, where we want to go. Lisbon gives us hope we otherwise do not have.

I try not to let my thoughts drift too much to Bella and Carlos, because if I do, I will break down. I miss them already. Telma is hungry and keeps everyone on the ship awake with her screams. I reach to pick her up and walk up and down the hallway to soothe her. Hunger pains are one of the worse types of pain to experience; hunger pains feel as if your insides are decaying. Moments later, I let out a moan when Leo, Natércia, and João come around the corner. I rush over to them, fighting the crowd; I need to tell Leo about the stolen milk.

"The milk is gone," I say hoping he is close enough to hear me through the mass of people.

The second he hears me, he squares his shoulders. "Where did you put it?"

"I had the bag beside me with the others, but someone stole it."

"No, do not tell me that."

"It is true. It is all gone."

Leo's face changes and resembles a look I have not seen on him before today. His eyes and ears turn fiery red, and his breathing is heavy. "Did you see who took it?"

"No, I did not see anything. One minute it was here, and the next, it was gone."

"Natércia, and João, stay here, help your mother watch the bags. I will be back in a few minutes."

Within seconds, he is off and running through the crowds before I have an opportunity to ask where he is going. Telma's desperate cries are out of control, and strangers ask me if I can quiet her. Do they not think if I could settle her, I would have by now? Do they think I enjoy listening to the devastation in her voice? People can be so rude and inappropriate at times, so I ignore them and shake my head. Instead, I focus my energy on the baby and try to rock her in my arms, but this gesture only makes her angrier. There is no comforting her now, and the only thing she wants is her bottle. Natércia and I take turns holding her and try to make her laugh but to no avail. Another five minutes pass and Leo is at my side holding a bag. He reaches inside and pulls out a bottle, I jump for joy as tired as I am.

"Leo, how?"

He raises one eyebrow. "I know when I need to be charming."

"Charming? Seriously, that is how you get our granddaughter milk?"

"A man will do what he must to feed his granddaughter. I do not take no for an answer," he teases. "But seriously, one of the boat crew went to the kitchen and got me a bottle. I had to beg."

"Well, I am sure you were charming when you begged," I tease back.

Wasting no time, I grab the bottle from him and squirt a small amount onto the inside of my wrist to check the temperature. I need to make sure it is not too hot, it is perfect. Telma's eyes brighten and grow wide when she sees the bottle. She reaches out with her little hands, and her stomach continues to growl. "Okay sweetie, it is coming. I know how hungry you are."

I jam the bottle into her mouth, and the instant her tongue makes contact, she sucks hard and deep, as if this is the last bottle on earth, I fear one bottle will not be enough.

When I finish feeding Telma, I change her bum, but I am careful and wrap the soiled diaper, so its content does not spill out and soil the clean diapers. I place the soiled diaper back into the same bag as the clean diapers; I do not have an extra bag for garbage. Where are the washrooms? I need to get there to wash the soiled diapers, but first I wait for Telma to fall asleep. In less than five minutes she is asleep in my sore arms. She looks like an angel as I watch her sleep peacefully with a full belly. Her tiny chest rises and falls with every breath, and this small thing brings me much comfort.

Leo tries to take her from my arms. "Why don't you lay her on the floor? You can rest while she sleeps. You must be tired."

"I think I might."

"You can lay her on the blanket you brought."

"Yes, good idea, can you get the blanket for me?"

Natércia brings the blanket. She has been holding it this entire time and guarding it so no one steals it. This is the same blanket I grabbed from the house before we left, so the blanket is proving to be useful. I am glad I had the instinct to bring it along. Natércia lays the blanket on the cleanest part of the floor she finds, and I lay Telma down. I yawn a few times and cover my mouth. My head lies next to Telma's, and in less than ten seconds, my eyelids become heavy, and I shut my eyes. "A few minutes are all I need," I say to whoever is listening.

Less than an hour later, Leo wakes me up. "Rosa, darling, we are in Luanda."

I wipe the sleep from my eyes and look out the window, there is land where there was once nothing but ocean. Natércia holds the baby and sits on a chair a few feet from where I am. She is making funny noises, causing the baby to laugh, and I smile at them. I take the baby from her, pick up the blanket off the floor and fold it neatly. Each of us picks up our own bag, and João takes mine, Leo takes Telma's. We walk off the boat, not knowing what our future holds. We do not know where our next meal will come from, and we do not know where we will sleep tonight or the next night after.

CHAPTER 62

Luanda, Angola
1975

R ED CROSS STATIONS are setup around at the dock at the Portuguese army base, directing families when they disembark. Red Cross' priority is children, so they stop families with small kids before tending to others, this lifts my spirits. We are standing in one spot not knowing what to do or where to go when we are approached by a middle-aged woman wearing a Red Cross uniform. She gives me a warm smile.

"How old is your daughter?"

Daughter, she says, but I do not correct her. "Fifteen months."

"Come with me, all of you." She points in the direction she wants us to go.

I grab her sleeve and say, "Please, she is hungry, do you have milk?"

"What is her name?"

"Telma."

"Telma will have everything she needs soon enough."

She continues to lead us towards a soldier. Red Cross is matching families who have children, with soldiers or other residents willing to help displaced families. The woman tells us to relax as we will stay together and not be separated, so this sets my mind at ease. We will billet with a soldier and his wife, and their names are Daniel and Madelina. The couple has no children of their own and is willing to have us stay as long as necessary.

The couple's house is on the ocean, so this is familiar to me. The house is comfortable and inviting with many pictures of landscapes hanging on the walls, and lots of tiny soldier ornaments out for display. The sink and counters are as clean as a museum, and there is not one speck of visible dust anywhere. There is a refreshing breeze blowing in from the veranda. The front yard is all sand, so that is how close to the ocean the house is. In the yard, I kick off my shoes, so my feet can touch the hot sand, and the money I hid falls, so I bend to pick it up. Telma wiggles in my arms, wanting to be put down. She learned how to walk in the last two months, but often stumbles on her tiny feet.

"It is not much, but please make yourselves at home," says Daniel.

His wife, Madelina appears at the door and introduces herself. "Please come in, we have milk for the baby, I also have a roasted chicken ready, you must be hungry?"

The growling in my stomach must be loud enough for her to hear. We sit to eat even before we see our rooms. The roasted chicken is juicy and marinated with pimento, garlic, lemon, and salt. My mouth waters as the chicken is cut up. Madelina passes a bottle to Telma, and Telma grabs it a little too fast and drops it, but Madelina says not to worry, they are well stocked by Red Cross. They must have expected a family with small children to billet here.

We finish the meal, and the couple shows us to our rooms. They provide us with two, one for Leo, me, and Telma to share; this is the smaller of the rooms. The second room is for Natércia, João, and Armando. I remind the kids to take the money out that's hidden in their socks.

The rooms are small but big enough and better than sleeping on the street or on the beach where we would be more vulnerable and exposed.

In each room is a double bed, a small wood dresser, and a matching night table with a lamp. I draw the curtains open to get a glimpse of the familiar ocean, and it is a beautiful view. Standing in this house, on the ocean, with our stomachs full, I can almost pretend we are no longer in the middle of a war. If I close my eyes and focus hard enough, I can transport myself someplace else.

Tonight, we go to our rooms early and I fall asleep right away, but I do not sleep through the night. The dreams that plague my mind are too real and vivid and keep me awake.

We are on a sinking boat, and people are jumping off. It is loud as the crowd screams into the night. I stand on the ledge contemplating jumping into the dark, deep sea water. I am carrying Telma in my arms, and her hands are wrapped tight around my neck, I can barely breathe. The sirens sound, warning of a bomb, and soon death. The boat explodes, but I do not jump in time. I am too late.

"Rosa, wake up, you are dreaming."

Leo stands over me, and Telma is asleep between the two of us.

"We are not on the boat anymore?"

"No. We are in Luanda."

When I remember my reality, the dream fades.

The next morning we eat breakfast in the bright and cheery dining room. The sun is beaming and illuminates the entire room. The house faces east, so we get the sunrise through the windows.

When breakfast is over, I suggest Leo go to the port to speak to whoever oversees Red Cross, I want to know what the plan is.

Natércia and João help with cleanup in the kitchen, while I tend to Telma's needs. Many soiled diapers accumulated, and I only have two clean diapers left. I need to do some much-needed laundry. Madelina sits on the back porch with a book and as I approach, she greets me warmly.

"Would it be possible to use your sink to wash diapers? I only have two clean diapers left."

"Why certainly, I will show you to the laundry basin. Do you have enough diapers overall? I have extras if you need them."

I thank her for the extra diapers and get to work. Natércia and João entertain Telma on the beach while I keep busy. I scrub each of the diapers and hang them outside to dry, and after this, I am set for another day, one less thing to worry about.

There is a cinema nearby, but of course, we cannot go, so instead, I dream of the days when Leo and I would go, and I long for those days once again. I used to get dressed up, put on lipstick, and felt like a lady for a night, but this life feels like it was a long time ago. Now, we have nothing, no home, no vehicle, and no belongings other than what little clothes we packed. Everything stayed behind. New furniture, beds, the couch we sat on each evening, it's all gone now. The dishes I fed my family meals three times a day on remain in the cupboards collecting dust. The truck Leo drove to work now sits at the port in Lobito, abandoned, like the house. The rug my mother gifted me one year for my birthday is under the coffee table, never for me to see again. That was one item I brought with me from the other house because it was special.

My mother. What happened to Antonietta, I do not know. I have not seen her for months, not since last April. I pray she is all right and finds safety and comfort, wherever she is. Antonietta would have loved Telminhas, but she never had the opportunity to meet her. I imagine the piles of toys my mother brought over the years for my children when they were little. I wish Telma would have the chance to play with them now. The toys now remain on the floor of an empty house, collecting dust. I hope one day I find my mother, or she finds me.

Daniel and Madelina are more than accommodating and welcoming the few days we stay with them. They open their home, their hearts, and share their food with us and we are forever grateful. They even top up Telma's bag, gifting us with more outfits, including a pair of boots for her and another bag to carry the new items.

Red Cross says not to worry about food and milk for Telma. They assure me the aircraft is equipped with everything the baby needs. I am also advised that when we arrive in Lisbon, we will be protected as 'retornados' a Portuguese word used to describe the evacuees. The protection is under the care of the government, so food and housing will be provided to us, and this news gives me assurance and hope.

This will be our first time on an airplane, and I have no idea what to expect. Leo is originally from São Miguel, Azores, but he came to Angola by boat when he arrived years ago, so this is his first plane ride as well. He, however, is not as nervous, he does not lose sleep over it like me. The uncertainty of what to expect has me biting my nails, a habit I never had before, this is Natércia's habit, not mine. Over the course of the next day, we wait.

CHAPTER 63

October 14, 1975

O UR FLIGHT IS at eight o'clock in the morning. The airport is in Southern Luanda and a fifteen-minute drive from Daniel and Madelina's house. We do not have much to pack, but I do not want to take any chances and be late, so I get things prepared the night before. I stay up long after everyone else, washing diapers and hanging them out to dry. I hope it does not rain tonight, but if it does, I must pack wet diapers. Feeling restless, I allow myself a few hours of sleep, but as I lie in bed, I toss and turn, and before long, I am dreaming about boats blowing up again.

For the rest of the night, I lie in bed awake. The dream must be my insecurity resurfacing, so I remind myself how we made it here alive. I force back the image of Carlos taking refuge on a Russian ship, and I pretend he, too, is here with us now. My nerves are getting the best of me, but I will not allow myself to succumb to my dark fears. "Shake it off," I say out loud. Despite the sleepless night, we need to arrive at the airport two hours before the flight, so I wake up early to allow myself enough time.

I walk to the back porch, and upon opening the door I taste the salt water. I lick my lips, and it tastes familiar. The morning horizon is clear, no clouds in the sky, and the porch appears dry, and so it did not rain last night. I work fast to get the diapers into the bags. Once I have the diaper bag zipped, I wake the others. After a quick breakfast of coffee and warm bread, we walk to the port and board the bus to the airport.

At the airport, there are many women who remind me of myself, scared females with babies, and I can see the fear in their eyes. I recognize the worry. One woman locks eyes with me, looks at Telma, then back at me. Her smile is soft but contains hints of desperation. She nods her head and turns and walks away, carrying her own child. Women carry a full load, always, even when our arms are empty.

I have never passed through a security checkpoint before, and the process is daunting. There are people rushing, it is loud, unorganized, and I hesitate to put down Telma's bags for fear I will lose one again. Once we are through security, a guard directs us where to go. Once the boarding starts, we are first in line. Families with babies and small children have priority. We present our names to the service personnel. The woman confirms we are on the evacuee list, so she crosses our names off, one by one.

"Proceed, through the door," she says.

We walk out on the tarmac, the airplane towers over us and waits for its passengers. Its size is intimidating, so big, and scary looking. Its wings stretch out farther than I ever imaged they would up close. I have never been this close to an aircraft before. There are other airplanes here picking up evacuees to get them to safety, we are not the only family in need.

We climb the steep, temporary, staircase, and my legs shake, so I pass Telma to João, fearing I will drop her if I fall. At the top of the stairs, a woman with a warm smile and soft face greets us and shows us to our seats. There are three rows of seats, an aisle, and another three sets of seats on the other side. Leo, Natércia and I sit on one side, Telma on my lap. Across the corridor are Armando, João, and an empty seat. The boys argue over the window seat, but Armando gives up and allows his brother to win.

Sitting to my right, so I can have the window seat, Leo reaches to grab my hand and squeezes it in his.

"Rosa, we made it."

"We are still on the ground. Let's be airborne before rejoicing."

Within a few minutes, the pilot's voice breaks through the speakers, and he announces we are ready for takeoff. I lay my head back on the seat and steal a glance out of the window. Telma is asleep, so I move her to Leo's lap, she is not used to so much commotion, and the day wore her out. As the engines roar to life, the aircraft gains speed and adrenaline runs through me. My breathing is quick but uneven. I tap Leo on the shoulder and invite him to look out the window with me.

"We are flying, we are really flying," I say.

The diminishing horizon becomes smaller and disappears like my old life. I say goodbye to the land I was born and raised in, the colony I gave birth to my six children in, and to the life I lived. In private, I say a final goodbye to Tavina, this was the soil my family buried her in, and I do not know when I can touch that soil again. Thoughts of my old life flood my head and I compare them to now, worrying about what our future brings, now that we are homeless.

CHAPTER 64

Lisbon, Portugal
1975

L ISBON AIRPORT IS international and located seven kilometres from the city centre. We arrive seven hours and thirty minutes from departure. My legs are cramping. I am not used to sitting for so long, so I need to stretch. This airport is similar to the airport in Luanda, but less modern. A security guard escorts us to the arrival area and to the registration desk for the Angolan evacuees to register.

Black and white people litter the airport floors looking for an empty spot, a place to claim as theirs. There are men and women, but no children, sleeping on the dirty floor. Suitcases are open, and belongings spill out for everyone to see. It is clear these people have spent a few days here already. Others look for displaced family members. But where are the children? This strikes me as rather odd, so I cling onto Telma tighter than ever.

Leo takes in the scene before us. "Oh my God. It is a jungle."

He finds an unoccupied bench, sets Telma's bags on it and lays my blanket on the floor. The bench and seventy-five square feet of floor space is now our home. The blanket protects our space and keeps others from encroaching. We brought Telma's bags on the plane, but the rest are in check-in, so we do not have them. Before Leo leaves to go get our luggage, he tells the others to stay close. I feel lost and do not like the unknown, so I do not want Leo to leave. I try to process the confusion around me, but it is too much, and I am dizzy. A woman approaches, wearing a gray and white button front dress with three-quarter sleeves. Over her left breast is the well-known Red Cross symbol.

"Madame, I need to take your daughter," she says.

Again, I do not correct that word.

"Where are you taking her?"

I grip Telminhas even tighter. I need specific details and reassurance before I hand her over to anyone, even a Red Cross worker.

"We are gathering babies and children and keeping them safe, away from the chaos out here. She will be all right. We will bathe and feed her. She will sleep in the children's ward with the others."

"That is not going to happen."

"You are welcome to visit anytime you like."

"No way."

People look at us, so I must be louder than I intend to be, but I do not care. There is no way I will allow a stranger to take my granddaughter from me.

"Madame, what is her name?"

"Telma, but we call her Telminhas, that is how she recognizes her name," I say calmer.

The woman asks my name, and I tell her.

"You should come with me to see for yourself how well cared-for the babies and children are."

"Fine, but I doubt it will change my mind."

I instruct the others to stay here and hold hands while I am gone. The children's centre is a better environment for a baby than the one out in the open airport floor, and even I must admit this. The room is large and full of babies and children of different ages, from a few months old to about six. Part of the room resembles the maternity ward in Benguela where Natércia, Armando, and Telma were born. Along the back wall are the cribs for the babies, and next to the cribs are rows of cots for the older children. There are many workers here, some are doing paperwork behind desks, but most are interacting with the children, caring for them. My anxiety is more at ease now that I am here. The worker points to Telma's crib and takes her from my arms. She asks me to give them a few hours, so they can feed, bathe, and let her have a proper nap. She suggests I come back later in the evening to see her.

Telma does not want to let go. She yells, "Vovo," *Grandma*.

She says a few words and amongst her vocabulary is Vovo.

"Please take care of her."

I peel my screaming granddaughter from my neck, hand her to this stranger, and turn my back. I do not want my granddaughter to see me cry.

As I walk back, I step over people, baggage, and food. So many evacuees are here with no home, no place to go, and the realization that I am one of them punches me in the stomach. I am no better off, I am no exception. Oh my God, we have no home.

The others are eating when I arrive, they were provided food while I was gone. Leo is still not back, and I pace looking for him. After a while, I sit on the blanket with my children while we wait for Leo to return. Natércia asks where we will sleep tonight.

"Right here," I say.

"For how long?"

"I do not know."

"So, we are sleeping on the airport floor?"

"That is right."

She goes back to eating her apple with her head down. I face the other way, so she does not see my tears. Crying is something I prefer to do in private and not in front of my children. Using the sleeve of my blouse to wipe my tears, I try to pull myself together because I need to be strong for them, and I cannot afford to fall apart.

Leo returns an hour later with bags under his eyes, and hair a mess. We have not moved the entire time for fear of having Telma's bag's stolen again. Red Cross has everything she needs, and I do not have to give them anything, so her belongings remain with us.

Leo tries to smooth his hair while pacing. "Our bags are missing; they were not at the luggage return. I waited for hours."

"Are you sure you looked hard enough?"

"Of course. I searched everywhere."

"Where would they be?"

"I don't know, but I have someone looking into it."

"Who?"

"A man who works for the airline."

Leo's eyes narrow, as he scans the floor and the bench. "Where is Telminhas?"

"Oh yes, about that."

I do not know how to tell him, he will be unhappy, so instead, I say, "You better sit, you look tired."

Leo's reaction to my news is as expected. He places his hands on his head and asks me many questions, but I cannot answer them. He calms down when I tell him that I saw the room and that it is a better and safer environment. He cannot sit still, so he leaves to deal with the lost luggage again, and I take this opportunity to go to the children's centre to check on Telma.

She is sitting in her crib when I arrive, and a big smile appears when she sees me. She is wearing clean, pink and white cotton pants, and a pink T-shirt I have not seen before. Someone brushed her hair, pushed it back behind her ears, and secured it with a pink ribbon. She grabs the side of the crib, pulls herself up, and tries to climb out. Thank goodness it is too tall, so she cannot fall over. Pleased and more relaxed now, I kiss her forehead, and hold her in my arms for about an hour before heading back to the others.

CHAPTER 65

1975

I T TURNS OUT our luggage was directed to Porto, a three-hour drive from Lisbon. Leo decides to go to Porto and get our bags. He prefers to take care of it, rather than wait for the airline to deliver the misdirected luggage. The airline assists and arranges for Leo to take the first bus in the morning, expenses paid. He will be gone for most of the day tomorrow, so this will leave me alone to entertain everyone again. It is now late; the sun sets over the horizon as I admire the bright colours. The kids go for a walk around the airport to explore and stretch their legs. Leo and I stay behind to keep watch over our space and Telma's belongings. We are tired of sitting, so we stand often to stretch our legs.

Leo places his arm around me and pulls me into a side hug. "This is temporary, you do know that?"

"Yes, I know."

People watching is the only thing to do, and it helps to keep the worries away, knowing I am not alone. There are so many displaced families and so little space. Where will these people go? Where will we live?

—⁓—

The airport floor is hard, dirty and cold, but at least we have a roof and food, so I am grateful. Aid workers and security guards tell us not to worry about bomb threats, and enemies, but I still do, it is now ingrained in me to worry. I try to be the strong one and to make the most of the situation, but as much as I try to be positive, the reality is still grey, and we are still homeless.

The first night at the airport is the most difficult. There are too many people sleeping close by, loud noise, and lights that are too bright, so this makes it impossible to sleep. I go say goodnight to Telminhas one last time, and Leo comes with me. He still has not forgiven me for allowing them to take her away.

"You think this is a good idea?" He asks.

"We do not have a choice."

"We always have a choice."

"Leo, they assured me it is for the best. She is well cared for there."

"You believe these strangers?"

"They might be strangers, but they work for Red Cross, and they have the best intentions. Do you think I would let Telminhas out of my sight if I had the slightest doubt?"

It takes much effort to be away from my granddaughter, but I am putting her needs before mine. I am not comfortable with the situation, but I cannot admit this to Leo. I need to convince him and myself that she is better off there.

Night falls, and as I lie on my back staring at the airport ceiling, I cannot help but worry about Telma. I have never spent a night away from her, so this is a first. I have a sudden urge to go to her, to get her through the night, but I talk myself into staying where I am and convince myself I am acting foolish and being overprotective. I consider Leo's reaction earlier and wonder if he is right and if I should have kept her here. Once again, this is another sleepless night, consumed with worry.

Morning could not have come quick enough, and the second the early morning light seeps in through the large windows, I am up and running to the nursery to check on my granddaughter. Everyone is still asleep when I leave, and I do not even wake Leo to tell him I am leaving. He will know where I am when he wakes and finds me gone.

A big steel door secures the nursey walls, and as I turn the large handle to the right, I am shocked to find it locked, it was not locked yesterday. The night before, I was able to walk in when I wanted, even in late evening. Perhaps the guards lock the door through the night for security. I look around eager to find someone to talk to and who can unlock the door for me so I can be with my granddaughter, but it is too early, and there is nobody in sight. I go to the ladies' room as I am bursting to pee and realize it only now. I walk down the hallway until I come to the washroom signs and follow them. After what feels like forever, I come across the entrance to the women's washroom. Two women talk by the sink, and I do not want to disturb them, so I tiptoe. One is in her mid-forties, my age. The other is older, by about ten years judging by the grey hair. The younger woman washes her hands and the older woman stands beside her, rubbing her hands under the dryer, they are whispering.

"Such a tragedy, the child was barely two years old. A girl I believe," says the older woman.

"Do they know what happened?" asks the younger woman.

"No, but I heard they have security guards searching."

"Excuse me." I walk past them and open the door to the stall.

"The workers are upset and sick with worry."

My ears perk up and I listen.

"Can you blame them? You would worry too if a child in your care disappeared."

This is the last thing I hear before they close the door behind them, and silence fills the room.

My world comes to a stop at the realization that they are referring to the nursery. Dizziness sets in, and the room spins. I cannot see anything before me. I barely manage to finish my business before I stumble to open the lock on the door of my stall. My nerves make it difficult for me to focus, and it takes several tries before I get the lock unlatched. Each try is harder than the last. When I am finally able to unlock the latch, I run out without washing my hands, and I slip on the wet floor and crash into another woman walking in.

I do not make eye contact with her and run straight to the nursery.

CHAPTER 66
1975

AS I RACE through the hallway, I try to reason with myself saying over and over that I am mistaken about what I heard. But it is true, and as much as I do not want to believe it there is a missing child. It cannot be my granddaughter. It must not be Telminhas. My world will end if she is missing.

When I arrive, there is a security guard at the door, but it is still locked when I try to open it. I bang my fists on the door.

"I need to get in, my granddaughter is in there."

"Madame, step away from the door."

"I must get in."

"I am sorry, but you must wait." The guard holds up his arms to keep me from moving forward.

"Wait? You want me to wait? You do not tell a grandmother to wait when her grandchild is in a room where another child has disappeared from."

"Madame, if you do not calm down, I will remove you from the nursery floor and you will not be able to see your granddaughter anymore."

This man cannot be threatening me, can he? I am about to yell at him when the door opens, and one of the workers walks through. Using this as an opportunity, I sneak in while the door is open. I make it in before the door shuts. My plan does not go unnoticed, and the guard comes after me, but I do not care if I am arrested. My only priority is my granddaughter, so I will deal with repercussions after I know she is safe. I hurry over to Telma's crib, and there she lays, so I let the breath that sits in my throat escape.

There is a tight squeeze on my right arm, I turn and the security guard towers over me. "What is the meaning of this?"

His deep voice draws attention, and several workers now watch the spectacle I cause.

There is laughter behind me; it is from one of the children. I focus on the soft voice to try to centre myself before I fall apart in front of strangers.

"I only want my granddaughter."

The tears now escape, and there is no stopping them. Recognizing me from the night before, a worker tells the guard I am no threat and asks the guard to release me. I reach into the crib and pick up Telma as she holds her arms out, begging me with her eyes to hold her.

I whisper in her little ear. "Telminhas, Grandma promises to never leave you again."

Holding my granddaughter close to my heart, I walk away with my head held high, but I only get ten feet before another arm grabs my shoulder.

"Where do you think you are going with the child?"

"I am keeping her with me."

"You cannot take her from here. You are welcome to stay as long as you want, but out there is no place for a baby," says one of the workers.

A rage boils inside me and I can no longer contain my fury. In my mind, I imagine the guards arresting me for what I am about to do, what I want to do, but then Telma lays her head on my shoulder, and the touch of her soft cheek on my skin relaxes me.

"Yes, I understand you have good intentions, but I can't let my granddaughter out of my sight any longer."

"That is not possible."

"You will step away from the door, and let me leave with my grand-daughter, or I cannot control what I will do."

The worker hesitates, but steps aside and allows me to leave with Telma.

As I walk through the crowded airport, a woman calls me from behind. "Please wait."

Turning around, I face another worker. She pants from running to catch up to me.

"We only need to know what part of the airport you are at, so we can bring the baby food, and anything else she needs."

Relief washes over me.

We are at the airport a week now, but still do not have anywhere to go. The government is working hard to accommodate evacuees, but each day more boats dock and planes land, flooding the airport floors with more displaced families. On the seventh night, we run into my niece, Necas, my brother Julio's daughter, whom I have not seen in years. She is here with her husband. They have a hotel lined up, so they help us find a place to live close to them. Homeless families like mine, occupy most hotels in Portugal.

The day we leave the airport is bittersweet. I have butterflies in my stomach and I am filled with different emotions. There is sadness in leaving because it means parting with the safety and protection of the airport walls. Up until now, we have people helping, providing food, blankets, and anything we need. Once we leave this building, we are on our own and must make our own way. We will have to start over again.

The airport is no permanent home, and it is no place to raise a baby, so it is with a positive attitude and a strong will that I climb the stairs of the bus that takes me and my family to our next home, a hotel in Estoril.

CHAPTER 67

1975

WE MAKE THE hotel in Estoril a home as best we can, and within two weeks of moving in, Carlos' boat arrives from Luanda. My son made it to safety, and we celebrate with a special dinner the night he arrives. We indulge in a full course meal; including wine my brother Julio gives us. Only one of my children is missing now, and I pray every day for Bella's arrival. Julio, his wife Beatriz, and their younger children are living at a hotel nearby, so we see them often. There is a lush, colourful garden near the hotel, and we spend a lot of time there. There are big, full shrubs and yellow, white, and purple irises line many pathways. There is an ornamental statue made of three umbrellas: yellow, red, and green with white polka dots. A cement base holds them up. Telma loves to sit underneath and have us take her picture with a camera my brother gives us. She sits on the cement base wearing a pink long sleeve shirt, a blue and pink skirt, and grey socks, and she looks happy. She has not yet given up her soother, so that hangs from her neck in place of a necklace.

Natércia writes to Bella to let her know where we are. She addresses the letter to Bella's place of employment.

Dear Bella,

I hope you are well. We arrived safely in Estoril. We are staying at a hotel here and we have everything we need. Uncle Julio is here with Aunt Beatriz. It has been lovely to see them and spend time together.

Carlos arrived yesterday, and it was a nice reunion.

I am sure you are wondering about your daughter. She is well and has grown lots in the last few weeks. I expect she will be even bigger when you see her. Mother is taking great care of her. She loves to have her picture taken at a nearby park.

We hope you can leave soon. There are rumours that things are deteriorating day by day there, so do not delay things any longer my sister, it is not safe for you. Your daughter needs you.

Enclosed is a business card for the hotel, and it contains the name, address, and telephone number so you know how to find us. We hope to see you soon.

Mother and Father send their love.

Natércia.

We do not know if the letter will reach her, but we need to try. Leo still listens to the radio, and the news informs us that open fire and battles now happen more often and get worse each day. I pray Bella receives the letter and can escape to safety.

The following week, we go see my brother Eduardo. He moved to Lisbon years ago, back when Mina came to live with us. He has made a good life for himself here and invited us to his house for the day. We have an enjoyable time, and it is a treat to be away from the hotel and to see my eldest brother again.

We get back to the hotel late at night, and I am ready to put Telma to bed and retire for the night myself. As I climb out of Eduardo's car, I blink several times, sure my vision fails me. Bella is sitting outside the door on the step, waiting for us. At first, I am certain she is a ghost, and my heart sinks thinking something happened, and she did not make it. But Natércia runs to her open arms, and Leo gasps, so I know it is her, she is alive and here in Estoril.

After hugging her sister, Bella runs to us and we take turns embracing her. Telma avoids her mother at first and does not want to go to her when she tries to take her out of my arms. Telma needs time to get to know her mother again.

It is by chance that Bella received our letter because she had already made plans to leave on the next boat. If the letter arrived only one day later, she would have missed it, and she would be on route to Lisbon with no information on our whereabouts.

By the next afternoon, Telma warms up to Bella, and she is happy to see her mother again. Mother/daughter reunions are sweet, and tonight there is not one, but two.

Bella is not back for more than two weeks when she meets a young man who also lives at the hotel. Within days, the three of them spend most of their time together. His name is Francisco Guerra, an Angolan native from Benguela and an evacuee himself. Frank is sweet and kind to my granddaughter, spends time with her, and entertains her. It is evident he cares for both my girls.

Leo communicates often with his family in Canada, and they discuss sponsorship. It is easy to immigrate to Canada; the country opens its doors to refugees. The Canadian government introduces a new act that recognizes refugees as a special class of immigrants. Nonetheless, Leo's family sponsors us, and it takes five months to get passports for all, but Telma.

We need Telma's father's consent to get a passport for her, but of course he died back in Lobito, so this is a major problem as we do not have a death certificate. When I discover this, I do not eat for two days, and I cry day and night. I tell Leo I can't leave without her, Leo agrees for now. Leo works day and night on this problem, trying to find a loophole, anything that will help. He consults a lawyer paid for by my brothers. After a few days of no news, he comes up with an idea I am willing to entertain.

"We will adopt her if we have to. We will register her as our child."

"Will this work?"

"It must."

We present the idea to Bella, however, she dismisses this plan instantly. She does not want us to adopt her daughter, so we are back to finding another solution. Our flights leave in two weeks, but we have no plan for Telma so I die a little each day. We are running out of time. I cannot leave my granddaughter; I do not have it in me. I prefer to give up the prospect of Canadian life and remain here with her. I do nothing but cry for days and days on end. Tears become a part of my routine, greeting me first thing in the morning, and plaguing me at night as I try to fall asleep. After much discussion with lawyers, Leo tells me we do not have a choice in the matter, we must leave and Telma and Bella must remain behind.

If leaving my granddaughter is not bad enough, João announces he too is not moving to Canada. He found himself a job working as a mechanic and wants to stay and build his life here. My family is falling apart again, and there is nothing I can do to change it.

On November 11, 1975, MPLA celebrates the win in Luanda, so they are now recognized as the official government by the Soviet Union, Cuba and most of Africa. This is a sad day for Holden Roberto, the president, and leader of the FNLA group as well as Jonas Savimbi, the leader of the UNITA group.

Over 300,000 evacuees left Angola before Independence Day, including my family. TAP, the Portuguese airline we flew with, evacuated most of the refugees. Other countries helped, such as the British air force, to get evacuees out before it became too late.

CHAPTER 68

Ontario, Canada
June 1976

CARLOS IS THE first in our family to leave. He boards a plane for Canada in June, three weeks before the rest of us. We say good-bye to my son at the airport and hope we will be together soon.

The day the rest of us leave is one of the saddest days of my life; I must leave my granddaughter behind, and I still do not know if I can physically do this. This is a goodbye I tried to ignore, and hoped would not happen. But it has, the day is here, and it's one of the darkest days of my life.

When the time comes, and I must part with my granddaughter, she screams, clings to me and begs me not to let her go. This is a promise I am breaking, because back at the airport, at the children's nursey, I made a promise to never leave her again. I am now doing the thing I promised her I would never do. I am leaving her. The only thought that brings me comfort is that she does not know this is a promise broken. She is too young to understand what a promise means. I pry her little fingers off my neck, hand her to her mother, and hope she will one day forgive me for leaving her.

When it is time to board, I am not sure I can cross the path of no return and get on the plane. Leo takes my hand as I look back over my shoulder at her big, brown eyes, her high sculpted cheek bones, inherited from her mother, and her long, silky hair falling over her shoulders. Her hair has finally gained length, and Leo likes it long, so we never cut it. Frank stands next to Bella, holding her hand and trying to comfort Telma. João is here also, to see us off. Having Frank here brings me comfort knowing he will take care of my girls. We have come to know him well over these last few months and he is a good man. The image of my daughter, grandchild, and son standing on the other side of the terminal, waving goodbye as I walk through the door, is the image I paint in my memory. This image stays with me as I turn away for the last time and walk onto the airplane that is to take us to our new country, our new home.

As we take our seats on the plane for the second time, Leo reaches out his hand and takes mine in his. He leans in close and whispers in my ear. "Rosa darling, I am hurting too, they will be back with us in no time. I promise."

"Don't make promises you cannot keep."

With my eyes shut, I lean my head back in my seat, waiting for takeoff. I recline my chair back to try to sleep, but the flight attendant making her final rounds before takeoff asks me to sit up.

The eight-hour flight from Lisbon to Toronto International Airport is long and feels as if it never ends. I do not sleep much, and instead, I cry for most of the way. When I do manage to fall asleep for a few minutes at a time, I dream of my granddaughter. Even when I am awake, my eyes remain closed, and I do not want to see or talk to anyone.

Leo shakes me awake, he thinks I am sleeping. "Rosa, wake up, we are now in Toronto."

I open my eyes, hoping to see my granddaughter, but I only see the back of a stranger's head. The flight attendants make their final rounds and ask everyone to sit up to prepare for landing.

We are greeted at the airport in Toronto, Ontario by Leo's brothers. Leo has not seen his extended family in many years, not since in São Miguel as a young man. We do not have a home yet, so we stay with his younger brother for a short while until Leo finds employment, and we find a place we call home.

After a few months, Leo finds a job and a house to rent. Our first home in Canada is a house on River Street in Cambridge, Ontario, and the house sits on the bank of the Grand River. The view is not as spectacular as the view we had in Lobito, it is no ocean, but at least we have a body of water to look out on to. I miss the ocean back home, the salt water, the sea breeze, but I get used to the new house and our new routine within time.

A day does not go by that I do not think of my granddaughter, my daughter, and my son. I long for them daily, especially my granddaughter. My son and daughter are old enough to make their own choices, but Telma, she is only two, and it breaks my heart that she does not know why I left her. Is she wondering where I am, and why I have abandoned her? Does she call out for me in the middle of the night when she is hungry or scared?

CHAPTER 69
November 1976

I WRITE TO BELLA and João often, and each day I check the mailbox for new mail as I wait for a return letter. For a long time, no return letters come, but I continue writing letter after letter. After a month, a letter arrives, and I blink a few times to make sure I am seeing straight, afraid my vision is failing me. When the letter is still in the mailbox after I blink the last time, I reach in and retrieve it. I run to the house, leaving the mailbox door open. I bolt up the stairs eager to rip the envelope open and read it, but before I do, I read the return name and address. It is from Bella, as I had hoped.

Dear Mother and Father,

I hope this letter reaches you well and in good health. Telma and I are fine. We are still at the hotel while we plan to come to Canada. We have the help of a lawyer, paid for by the Portuguese government, and this lawyer has made significant progress. We should have everything settled within a month. It will not be long now before we see each other, I am sure.

In case you have not heard from him, João is well. He has a little apartment, and he makes enough money to live off. He is happy here and has no regrets about his decision. He sends his love and says he did write also, but I do not know whose letter will arrive first.

Mother, and Father, I also must tell you I am in love. Frank and I spend each day together and he too is now getting his paperwork to come to Canada. He asked me to marry him, and I accepted. We decided to wait until we are in Canada because I want my family with me on my special day. It does not appear as if Frank's paperwork will be ready at the same time as ours, so Telma and I will leave first. Frank will join us when he can. I will arrange a phone call to you once I receive confirmation of my departure date and flight schedule, so you can pick us up at the airport. I miss you all, and I cannot wait until we are together again. Please send my love to Natércia and my brothers and tell them we will be there soon.

Love always, your daughter,
Bella

After reading the letter I wipe my face, stained with tears. I smile for the first time since arriving in this beautiful country. Once my face is tear-free, I take the letter and search for Leo. I run through the house looking for him. "Leo, Leo, where are you? We need to buy a car. Leo, can you hear me?"

I find him in the kitchen getting a cup of coffee, and he looks at me startled. "What on Earth do we need a car for?"

"To pick up the girls from the Toronto airport, in about a month."

"You're kidding?"

"Here, read this."

I pass the letter to him, he looks at it and then back at me before he reads it.

⸎

This same week I receive another letter, and I am certain it is from João, but it is not. Instead, it is a letter from Antonietta. She found me after searching for a long time. She is still in Angola, she never left, but for now, she is safe. I write her back updating her on the last few years of my life, but I receive no response. This is the last time my mother and I have any communication.

Bella and Telma arrive in Toronto three months after I received Bella's letter. The morning of their arrival I walk through the house with a grin. I clean our new home, prepare soup my granddaughter enjoys, and I make an extra trip to the store to buy new blankets and two stuffed animals. One is a monkey with long arms she can wrap around her neck, and the other, a red and white bear. I bring both the monkey and the bear to the airport. We drive to Toronto International Airport in the new, green station wagon that Leo purchased, but Leo does not yet have a valid driver's license, so we bring along one of his brothers to drive. We wait for the girls' arrival in the designated area of the airport, where other family members also wait for their loved ones. There are many Portuguese families nearby, and this comforts me. The flight is delayed by an hour, and I am on the edge of my seat. My palms are sweaty, and my heart beats fast as I wait.

Telma turns the corner from the jet bridge, the hallway that connects the airplane to the airport. The moment her smile comes into view, I jump off my seat and run to the glass window. My heart skips a beat when she gets near. She is healthy-looking with pink cheeks and chubby legs. She wears a jean skirt, a pink flowery top, and black leather boots. She has grown so much in the last five months, I cannot believe my eyes. I take a moment to admire her, and I stare at her little face. She looks like an angel, running with arms flapping through the air. When she notices me, she looks up and her mouth opens right away and with eyes enlarged. My granddaughter mouths the word "Vovo," *Grandmother*. I cannot hear her, because she is still behind the glass window. She runs to the window, places her hands on it and presses her face up against the glass. I do the exact same from my side. Our hands would touch if not for the pane of glass separating us. Behind Telma is Bella, waving. Telma's little hand slips away off the glass and into her mother's. My girls fight their way through crowds as they make their way into my empty and waiting arms.

EPILOGUE

2018

THE DEVASTATING WAR lasted until 2002 with some small periods of peace throughout the years, but the majority of this long twenty-seven-year struggle resulted in over 500,000 casualties, both soldiers and civilians. When the war was declared to be over, Angola remained in turmoil, socially and economically. Many landmines are still left scattered through my precious land.

I have not visited Angola since I fled. Angola is still not the country it once was, even after all these years. The country has potential, but there is still a lot of corruption. Angola has come a long way since 2002, and the country is at peace, but there is now more poverty than when it was under Portuguese rule. The middle class no longer exists, so if you live in Angola today, you are either rich or poor.

War affects people in different ways. The war taught me many things, important life lessons. It shaped me into the woman I am today. It made me stronger emotionally. It provided me with the strength to cope with my husband Leo's death back in 1996, and it gave me the ability to bury my son Armando only three short years ago. I always thought it would be my children to bury me, but now at the age of ninety, I have already buried two. The war made me more capable to deal with life's difficult situations and has expanded my faith beyond belief.

I never did find my mother again, the last letter I received after moving to Canada was the last time we communicated, so she forever remains lost to me, like my country.

Everything I have endured in my life, each event, and each person I have crossed paths with gave me the power of accomplishing what I set out to do and has taught me to never take anything in life for granted. No person, place, or thing should ever be considered less, no matter how small and insignificant it may seem.

Every person we meet, every situation we encounter, and every circumstance we tolerate, has a specific purpose and message to share. We must look deep within to find the true meaning of things; for it is the earth-shattering moments that fill our soul with courage.

ACKNOWLEDGEMENTS

Many wonderful people helped bring this book to publication. First, I want to thank my grandmother, Rosa, for sharing your story and trusting me to write it.

To my critique partners/beta readers, Elsa Miranda, and Sarah Graham. You two girls are amazing, and I thank you from the bottom of my heart for reading all the chapters I threw at you during the drafting stage.

To Rhonda Forrest for helping polish the first part of my manuscript and for helping me in my writing journey.

To my copy editor and proof-reader, Catherine Muss, and Tara Mondou for your meticulous eye and for making my manuscript shine. To Chrissy from Indie Publishing Group for the interior design.

To my aunt, Rose Pontes, for your feedback, support, and for bringing authenticity to the book.

To my mother, Bella, my father, Frank, and Uncles Carlos and Joao, for sharing your stories that are in the book. To my sisters, Melissa and Tiffany, for your continued support, I love you both.

Finally, to my husband, Terry, and my two boys, Alex and Jenson; you three have been with me since this book was only a dream, and thank you to each of you for sticking with me and believing in me. Jenson, thank you for letting me ramble on about my book and showing so much excitement. Alex, thank you for being my biggest fan. You can now put a copy of my book on your bookshelf. Terry, thank you for all that you have done over the last few months. Your encouragement, support, cover design, logos, media kit, and my author website would not have been as beautiful without you. I feel as if this book is as much your baby as it is mine.

ABOUT THE AUTHOR

T ELMA ROCHA IS an avid reader, reviewer, and blogger. She documents and shares her reading and writing journey on Instagram and is an active member of various groups dedicated to promoting local talent.

Telma lives in southern Ontario with her husband and two sons. When she is not reading or writing, she can be found enjoying the outdoors with her family or sharing meals and laughter with good friends.

Born in Angola, Telma immigrated to Canada in 1976, avoiding the turbulent civil war that erupted there in 1974. These events are documented in her first novel,

The Angolan Girl, the story about her grandmother's life from childhood through the early stages of the war.

Telma is currently working on her second novel, a story that takes place on Manitoulin Island. Inspired by a motorcycle trip to the island with her husband, it is sure to capture the freedom and beauty of the great Canadian landscape.

Visit Telma at: telmarocha.com

CPSIA information can be obtained
at www.ICGtesting.com
Printed in the USA
LVHW041617170619
621482LV00003B/479/P